ABOUT THE AUTHOR
Sally Russell

Sally Russell has published local histories, stories and poems.
She raised six children on the rural Northern California coast.
She now lives in the high desert of Nevada.

Passion Walk

Sally Russell

High Desert Books

Passion Walk

Published in the United States
by High Desert Books, Reno NV
www.highdesertbooks.com

Russell, Sally
Passion Walk/Sally Russell

ISBN

978-0-615-15609-5

Layout and design by Jesse Russell

For my beloved:
Henry E. Bates
1932-2007

Passion Walk

1

"Good Lord, I am cold clear through." Elizabeth paced up and down the porch. "I don't understand. How could Old Chief let Pahto take Alexander? I can understand the whole tribe wanting to flee, but why take little Alex? And I don't understand why you won't go for help at the fort. You know Captain Hall would send the militia after them if they've stolen a child." She paced and fretted. "Pahto wouldn't let Alex be harmed, would he? We must go to the fort for help...Willie!" Elizabeth stopped her pacing and stood in front of Willie who sat staring wide-eyed into the darkness. "Willie, come inside. It is freezing out here. We can decide what to do inside and get warm too!"

Willie turned her gaze on Elizabeth. "You must hush now while I think. Go inside and wait for me. I need time to think. Make a fire and warm the house. I will be in straight away and we can talk." Elizabeth muttered under her breath and went into the house.

Willie continued her watch. Is he warm enough? she thought. Is he frightened? He does like to sleep outside, but the sound of the crickets frightens him. She rocked back and forth, wrapping the memory of her baby boy in her arms. She could feel the touch of his hand on her cheek. She could hear the echo of his voice, "We like each other, right, Mama?"

There was no moon yet. The black night would stop Willie from any attempt at pursuit until near dawn. Once the blanket of fog had lifted, the temperature dropped hard. The icy sparkle on the ground warned that this night would know the first frost of the season. An early frost. It was fall 1864.

No, the pompous Captain Hall could not help her. Nobody could; Marcus and Daniel were with Miles at the war; her family was far away. But she knew what Miles would do and what she must do. "You have passion enough for both of us," he had told her before he left for the battlefields of the East.

Passion. The wild card. All she held. She would have to go for Alexander herself. Fetch him home.

She went inside the house. Elizabeth had fallen asleep by the fire. Willie sat on the hearth that she had watched her father build years ago. He had kept her safe as a child. He made it seem so easy. She had never felt in danger. Now Alexander was stolen and she could not keep him safe.

Elizabeth slept in a chair, her cheeks pallid and her eyes lined red from crying. How much could Willie ask her to do? She has fallen asleep even now, and they have only one horse since Pahto took Rojo.

Willie was chilled with a sense of being completely alone. But there was a freedom in that. She need not waste any time looking around to see who was with her, where the help was coming from. She had just this one card. She would play it and continue to play it until she found her son and together they would wait for Miles. To that end she planned.

She took a lantern outside. Her feet slipped on the icy ground. She went into the stable and dug through the tack box to find the old canvas saddle bags. They were stiff from lack of use and needed repair. She hurried back inside and got out her sewing kit. She mended the torn seams with stout thread.

Her thoughts raced. Blood pounded in her temples. She could barely keep up with the lists that ran through her head. Don't forget this! and this! and this! Her hands fumbled the stitching, but the repair was adequate. As she was about to put the needle and thread back into the sewing kit she paused, reconsidered, and tossed them into the saddle bags instead.

The shotgun! She should take it. Where was it? Still outside? Had someone else found it, taken it? She ran back outside. There it was where she had left it behind the rose bush, by the fence. Was that yesterday?

Carefully she packed the things she felt were most important. A loaf and a half of bread were left from the baking two days ago. She had only a few cartridges for the gun. She rinsed out an old canteen. It could hang off the saddle horn and would not take space in the bags. She wrapped her phosphorus-tipped wooden matches in a double layer of oil cloth and packed them. She would cover the saddle bags and a rolled-up blanket with her rubber parka once she had all her gear secured. A pan. A good knife. What else? A small amount of flour would not take up much space and she could make good use of it. She put a measure of flour in a small basket that Blue Feather had made for her. Blue Feather! My wounded friend, watch over my boy!

She dragged out the trunk of clothing Miles had left behind. A wool serge shirt worn over a cotton undershirt would serve her well. Woolen long johns under a pair of coarse denim pants rolled at the cuff and cinched at the waist would work better than her skirts. She was still wearing the dress she had put on two days ago when she, Elizabeth and Blue Feather had taken Alexander into town on a lark. Now she changed into Miles' clothes. They were musty from long storage. She packed another shirt and a heavy sweater into the saddle bags.

Finally she could think of nothing more to pack. Elizabeth still slept. Willie sat down at her writing desk and wrote a letter to Miles. She tried to tell him the whole story, simply. She told him her plan to rescue their son. Since the siege at Vicksburg had begun, mail delivery between them had been sporadic. She could not know when or where he would receive the letter. But she must try to reach him. It was stretched so thin, the bond between them. She needed him to know of their situation. But was she making herself clear? She had trouble controlling the pen. Was it legible? She did not have time to reread or rewrite. For two nights now she had not slept. Determination moved her forward. The spirit's will against the body's fatigue. She sealed the letter and went outside to saddle Glory.

Pahto had taken the strong sorrel Rojo. She would have to make do with slow but steady Glory. Her fingers were numb with the cold. She struggled with the tack. The leather straps of the old bridle were frozen and unyielding. Now she felt like crying. Her confidence cracked. Nothing worked. Pahto had also taken the good saddle. The one she had was barely functional. She could not remember it being used for years. Nothing was adjusted evenly. One stirrup hung six inches longer than the other.

By the time she finished tacking up, she was no longer cold. Inside her shirt, sweat ran from under her arm down the side of her breast. Anxiety teased every muscle into readiness. Fear lay quietly in the shadows. She would be all right once she was on her way, she reassured herself.

The moon rose. Glints of moonlight lustered the nickel conchos of the bridle. She finished securing all the gear to the saddle and went inside to wake Elizabeth.

"Lizzie." She shook her friend's shoulder.

"Aa-a-a!" Elizabeth cried out, startled by the apparition before her. Willie's hair was wild, flying in all directions about her head. The look in her eyes was intense. The house was too warm for all the oversized clothing she wore; beads of sweat formed on her forehead.

"Willie! Goodness! Look at you! Where did you get those clothes? What are you doing?"

"I am going after Alexander."

"But, Willie..."

"Listen to me Elizabeth. I haven't much time. You will have to cover up my absence. Don't let anyone know what has happened for as long as you can. The further away I can get, the greater my chances are of not being overtaken. We can't go to the fort for help, Lizzie. The militia would put Alexander in danger. Their main concern would be capturing Pahto, not saving Alexander. Do you understand?"

Elizabeth nodded her agreement. "Your plan makes more sense than your appearance."

"Go to town to call on Reverend Justus before he comes here to check on us. Tell him everything is all right. Stay with the Justus family when you are afraid to be here alone, but I think you will be safe now. It should be some time before I am discovered missing if you are clever."

"I can do that."

"Yes. Please post my letter to Miles. I left it there. I walked around the rancheria with the lantern. Everything is gone. It's as though no one ever lived there."

Willie turned toward the door. She paused by the crockery yeast jar and lifted the lid, releasing a waft of fresh bread yeast.

"Would you feed my yeast? It needs using. I don't know how long I'll be gone." She pulled on a broad-brimmed wool felt hat.

"I'll take care of everything, honey."

They walked outside to where Glory was hitched.

"You won't have a horse for the buggy. That might look odd. Perhaps you can borrow one. Claim Glory is lame."

"I'll manage." Elizabeth examined the well-packed horse. "You've been busy. And I slept through it all. You should have waked me."

"I needed to work it out." Willie threw her leg over the saddle and settled herself in among the gear. "I'm scared."

Elizabeth put her hand on Willie's leg and looked up at her. "I know you are, honey. And brave."

"I don't feel brave."

"You are as brave as you are scared."

Willie smiled at the familiar words, but wet eyes and quivering chin threatened her composure. "Then I must be very brave indeed."

"Yes." Elizabeth stepped back and Willie put Glory in an easy lope in the direction of the flushed horizon. Dawn was breaking.

As Willie rode away from the house, a memory flooded her grief: a memory of an evening three-and-a-half years ago, returning home from work, walking through this same yard, this same rosy light. It had been the spring of 1861, before she met Miles. Before any of this happened.

2

With the return of spring Willie's hope returned. She seldom noticed losing it, but she always felt its return. It seemed an especially promising spring as she stepped out into the sharp bite of foggy air that morning. It was a long walking distance from her family's farm to the schoolhouse where she taught, but she liked it best when the weather allowed her to walk it. Otherwise she tacked up one of the horses; or if the weather was severe she rode into town with her father in the light buggy.

Surrounding her family's home was a cluster of small outbuildings and little yards. There was a vegetable garden and a chicken coop. The two horses had a stable that opened onto a corral. An adjoining structure provided a roof for the buggy.

This morning even the thrush's song sounded urgent, expectant. Not like his melancholic air last night. The thrush always sat in the same spot high in the cypress outside her house. Whenever she tried to spot him, as soon as she got near he stopped his singing. She knew he was a small gray brown bird, not so splendid in his color as in his song. Last night at sunset as she worked in the kitchen with her mother she heard him, reaching for his highest plaintive notes. It sounded as though he were mourning the passing of the day as he watched the sun go down over the ocean—even though Willie knew he was actually declaring his territorial rights to the Jackson gardens.

She slipped out of the house while the family all still lay sleeping and hurried along the path toward town. She wanted time to meet with Elizabeth before school began.

On the other side of the farmyard she passed through the rancheria, the simple buildings where the Bokaima tribe lived. Two small houses and one large house were built in the Bokaima traditional style, conical structures made with large slabs of redwood bark. The Bokaima used these for their primary living needs; but Old Chief especially had grown accustomed to the wood-frame cabin her father had helped him build. Reverend Cornelius Jackson believed in giving the Indians opportunities to learn how to live in the white man's world, learning carpentry and farming. Willie questioned the effectiveness of his plan though, since the plight of the local Indians—in town, on the reservation and in the surrounding countryside—grew more desperate every passing year, skills or not.

Round Face Woman and Blue Feather had already built fires and were boiling great pans of water for wash day. They greeted her as she passed. Sweet Round Face Woman had a smooth warm-toned skin that belied her age. Blue Feather was young and beautiful and cheerful. Old Chief was headman, but Round Face Woman was in charge of most activities. Old Chief preferred congeniality and comfort to strife and struggle. He reserved his participation for benevolent edicts and gambling games. He and the other men folk still lay abed this morning. Except for Pahto, of course. She had seen him at first light, moving with noiseless speed into the woods, his bow and a quiver of arrows slung over his shoulder.

Her trail climbed up along the edge of the bluffs high above the surf. The ocean, frenzied by spring, was resplendent in sea green and cap white.

The five years her father had committed to serve at the Mendocino Indian Reservation had stretched to six. Willie understood that now he needed to relocate his family to his new parish assignment in San Francisco, but she did not want to return to the city herself. Willie was comfortable and safe with her family, but it was a confining comfort. She wanted to risk freedom now.

She had waited until the last minute to tell her parents of her decision to stay behind. She knew once they had finished their fretting they would not stand in her way, but still the image of her mother's drawn face and hurt tears, her knuckles white from their grip on the edge of the kitchen sink, rested heavy in Willie's thoughts.

"I won't be going with you to San Francisco," Willie had told them last night. She was drying the dishes after the evening meal and stacking them on a counter, ready for the packing boxes.

"Why, what nonsense!" Viola Jackson had said. "What would you do? Who would look after you?"

Willie looked back at the reflection of her gray eyes in a wet plate before she wiped it dry with embroidered flour sacking. Viola would never use flour sacking for towels or curtains without first adding some embroidery or lace to them. Willie had been a young girl when she tried with awkward fingers to stitch the flowers on this towel. Her work was loose and uneven, not precise and tidy like her mother's.

"Mama, Round Face Woman and Old Chief and Blue Feather and Sun Ray and all of them live right here with us.

They will help me and I'll be able to help them. And you know I have very good friends in town and at the fort. They will be near if I need them."

"Goodness, Wilhemina! If you would control your sharp tongue and stop being so nervous you would have a husband by now! You are getting too old to be alone! It's not proper. You will end up living like an Indian and talking like a logger."

This morning, as Willie broke through the trees at the top of the south ridge overlooking the Noyo River, she could see the wide river flats along both sides of the river. A teeming town had grown up around a lumber mill there. Even at this early hour it was a bustle of activity.

Since the Jackson family came here in 1855, when the reservation was first established, Willie had seen settlements appear all along this stretch of California's north coast. There was a mill built at the mouth of every creek and river where it was remotely feasible for the doghole schooners to approach and take on their loads. Each schooner that delivered the lumber down below to San Francisco returned with supplies and yet more men to fall the trees, bring the logs in, work the mills, build the new towns, farm the land. They came for the work, and although many eventually returned to their homes far away—Italy, Finland, Maine—most stayed, sent for their families and started new lives. And few ever understood the devastation their arrival had on the people who had been living on this land since the mythic beginning of time.

Willie walked down the ridge slope and rode the hand-pulled ferry to the other side of the river. The mill at the river mouth had been built in the spring of 1858. Willie's father had protested when he first learned of the proposed mill.

"Stay in the buggy, Daughter," he had told her when

he went into the reservation headquarters to confront Indian Agent Henley. But she had grown bored and her curiosity led her to the porch where she stood out of sight and listened at the open door. Her father was using his hellfire sermon voice to yell at Henley.

"This will attract more settlers who will want more land. This site was chosen for a reservation because it was remote and unsettled. And now you import profiteers. You gave Indian land to these men to build a mill on. The Indians will be exploited by this venture!"

"Come now, Reverend Jackson. You know I am always looking after the welfare of the Indians. This will be a means of providing them jobs. Even though they are a primitive race, they are capable of learning simple tasks. They must be shown how to be industrious and useful. The mill will provide a very good opportunity for those who wish to work. Those who don't, well... The white settlers need protection."

"It's the Indians who need protection! And this horrible practice of stealing Indian children is carried on under your very nose."

"Lieutenant Gibson and I are doing everything we can to put a stop to that, you know that."

"Lieutenant Gibson?" he repeated the name with a snort of disdain. "That rooster! He is also in cahoots with these men. How cleverly his head has been turned. Or did you just pay the scoundrel off?"

"I may have had my differences with officers at the fort in the past..."

"That was perhaps when Gibson reported you for starving the Indians you are supposed to be feeding! As you well know, it is actually the Indians who need protection from the heavy hand of white vindication. They are punished for every mishap to the ranchers' livestock, every missing kernel of grain."

"They are chastised."

"They are murdered!"

"Mr. Jackson! I resent your implications. I shall exercise the duties of my office as I see fit. You should tend to your own affairs of seeing to the salvation of these heathens' souls."

Jackson burst through the door and stomped across the porch. He scowled when he saw Willie.

"Get into the buggy, Daughter!" he snapped. She did. And she sat silently all the way home while he lectured her on the seductive evils of power and capitalism. Her father was a devoted reader of European political essays that she could make little sense of when she tried to read them. The translations were choppy and the ideas obscure. But when he warmed to the subject and launched into extensive explanations and lectures, she loved listening to him.

Nevertheless, her father's modern words did not translate to the real world. He had made little headway in his plans for social revolution for the Indians.

Neither Lieutenant Gibson nor his artillery company stationed at Fort Bragg made it through that summer of 1858. The infantry garrison that replaced them was small, never more than twenty men, but these soldiers at least made an effort to curb both the profitable kidnapping and the vigilante punishment of the Indians who remained on the reservation. They could do little to protect the Indians off the reservation from harassment, but bringing them onto the reservation was a catastrophe too. That year when a thousand Indians were gathered up and herded onto the reservation at one time, the available resources were overwhelmed and hundreds died.

Willie's hope was that the situation at the reservation would stabilize now, give everyone a chance to grow healthy. Even though malnutrition and disease still took their toll daily, the Indians who got work at the mill were paid now—half of what white workers were paid, but paid nonetheless. There were few free Indians left in the hills nearby. The white tide would not be turned. This was California, the land of the golden dream.

Willie stepped off the ferry onto the north bank of the Noyo River. She tried to keep her skirts gathered in her hands and lifted free of the wet sandy ground. Her head was down as she concentrated on her footing, but she looked up when she heard her name called out.

Aloysious Brown, who was called Pink for the peculiar coloring of his skin, greeted her from the porch of his hotel. Willie played cards with her friends in the back room of Pink's saloon, the room where ladies were allowed. The saloon was a popular meeting place for the townspeople. It was rowdy at times but well run by the stern hand of Pink.

Yes, this spring morning felt bright and hopeful. She waved to Pink. Maybe she would be lucky at cards tonight.

She made the stiff climb up the hill to the top of the north ridge of the river. She was greeted often as she walked. There was a good supply of unattached men here. Why did she no longer even look for a beau among them? She yearned to be touched but resigned herself to dream touches only. Perhaps her mother had been right last night. Perhaps there was no man for her now. Perhaps this ocean breeze lifting the hair off the back of her neck was all the touch she would know.

At top of the ridge, she paused and surveyed the sprawl of dilapidated buildings that were the reservation headquarters. She skirted the edge of the complex and headed toward the fort and the small cabin where her friend Elizabeth lived with her soldier husband Sergeant Cletis Carter. Willie hoped they would not be fighting, but even more she hoped they were not still in bed. She hated it when she came for Elizabeth and found the couple still in bed. Elizabeth would come out of the bedroom laughing, wrapping a shawl around her, offering Willie coffee, apologizing. Cletis would come into the kitchen in his undershirt and pass very close to Willie as he greeted her, so close she could smell him.

3

The Mendocino Indian Reservation lay on a coastal strip from south of the Noyo River ten miles north to the Ten Mile River and east to the coastal mountain range. It was a vaguely stated boundary lending itself to encroachment from settlers. Willie walked along the fence line of a settler's farmyard. White smoke from the chimney of a small house mingled with the low morning fog. Fields planted in potatoes stretched out behind the house. Willie knew the Miller family who farmed this place. They were unassuming and industrious. They had brought their dream west to make a better life for their family. Willie taught their bright and lively children how to read. Like others here, the Millers were squatters on prime reservation land.

As she followed the trail to the edge of the pine woods east of the parade grounds and rough buildings of the post, Willie recalled Lieutenant Horatio Gibson, the artillery officer who had built the fort with his small company of men. He had named it after his hero, Colonel Braxton Bragg, who had been his commanding officer during the war with Mexico.

She remembered Horatio Gibson's dreams of glory for his Fort Bragg, and her own dreams for the young man with his wild ways and easy hands.

But time proved his style to have more substance than his heart. After the first winter he had become sullen, then discouraged and ill. He fell into bad stead with his superiors. The army found a more appropriate assignment for him and Willie never saw Horatio Gibson again.

These days she thought she only wanted to be rid of yearning. To be independent. To be no longer daunted by the deep twinges of her body that seized her thoughts and made her heart race. How could she live her life with any dignity if she were forever intimidated by this ache? It was bewildering and disgraceful whenever she found herself tempted to give her heart to any rake who offered the balm for her ailment.

She stepped onto the porch of the small cabin and knocked softly. "Come on in," Elizabeth answered from inside, and Willie let herself in. Elizabeth sat alone at the kitchen table staring into her coffee. Her red hair shone coppery in the morning light; she had pulled her chair close to the window to catch a warm spot of sun. Although the fire she had built this morning in the cook stove was hot enough to make the coffee the air in the room was still cold.

"Lizzie! Such a long face." Willie greeted her with a kiss.

"Oh, Willie. I am so glad you're here," Elizabeth spoke in a whisper. She left her sunny spot to pour Willie a cup of coffee. A worried scowl pinched her eyebrows together. "Listen! We must hurry. That government investigation team finally arrived late yesterday, and, Willie..." Elizabeth paused to emphasize her next statement, "five hundred Indian prisoners are expected at the reservation today. They've been force-marched for three weeks to get here."

"What? They promised not to do that anymore.

Why haven't we heard about this before? And why are we whispering?"

Elizabeth averted her eyes. "I don't want to wake Cletis. He's not...he didn't come home until almost dawn. He met up with that investigation bunch, and they investigated Pink's all night, I guess," she whispered. Her eyes were puffy and red-rimmed.

"However," Elizabeth drew herself up and forgoing her whisper said, "What do I care? Just means I don't have to fix his damn breakfast! Drink your coffee, Willie, and let's get out of here."

"I don't need any coffee; let's just go." Willie stood to return her coffee cup to the sink when a sudden stirring from the bedroom interrupted her. The two women turned to look at Cletis who stood in the bedroom doorway. His hair was rumpled, his eyes half-closed. He raised one arm above his head and supported himself against the lintel above the doorway. The other hand scratched at the curly black hair at the open neck of his gray woolen undershirt. The only sound in the room was the slight clatter of the cup in Elizabeth's saucer.

Willie was unsure of where one should stand in a room whose air cracked with marital tension. She took a step back. Should she leave? Cletis' breath heaved in a guttural rumble. The air around him carried the tart smell of stale alcohol. He kept his gaze on Willie until her hand flew to her throat and she retreated another step. He turned veiled cold eyes to his wife then stepped back into the bedroom.

The two women did not move. They heard the metallic rattle of the chamber pot as he relieved himself and then the groan of the bed springs as he fell back into bed.

Elizabeth grabbed a piece of wood to stoke the fire in the cook stove. Her eyes flashed with the reflected flames. She choked down the damper and shoved the tin coffee pot to the back of the stove.

Elizabeth pulled on a sweater. She slipped her arm through Willie's and they walked outside together. She tossed her head back to survey the weather.

"Yes! We'll have sun now," Elizabeth declared, eager to leave her problems with Cletis behind. She launched into their plans for the day and filled Willie in on the latest pressing reservation developments. Only her tight grip on Willie's arm betrayed her.

"I don't understand: they have brought more captives to the reservation? Tell me," Willie said.

"From some place way up north, I don't know, where there has been some fighting. Five hundred men, women and children; although Cletis said there won't be many men since most of them have been killed. He says the Army thinks if tribes are exiled far from their home territory they will not be able to escape and find their way back and resume fighting with the settlers."

"But it just makes it hopeless for the reservation to turn into a cooperative farm project if they persist in turning it into a prison camp. It's ghastly!"

"Took them three weeks to get here. Cletis said they are a different people yet from any of the other tribes already here. Once again they they'll speak yet another language. And a lot of them are sick and wounded."

"Maybe you should go ahead and help at the hospital today and I'll hold school by myself."

"Good idea. Damn. Am I a ghoul? Here I am actually looking forward to a hard day's work trying to patch together broken and diseased people. When your home life is miserable, other people's misery can be a welcome distraction." Elizabeth laughed at herself, her heavy mood lifting. "At least that investigation bunch is finally here. I met them last night before they went out to Pink's."

"I'll bet they take their work seriously enough that they wouldn't like to be referred to as an investigation bunch."

"I know that's true! They take themselves quite seriously. We have been clamoring for the government to do something about these miserable conditions, then when these Jacks finally get here they act as though we are the ignorant-Nellies and..."

"They must have ruffled your feathers! Are they really so awful?"

"Oh, Willie, I am glad they are here. I'm just mad at Cletis. No point in my taking it out on them. And Cletis probably has plenty of his own misery this morning, God willing." With a movement of her head she shook off her peevishness again and changed the subject.

"Anyway, they are an officer from the Presidio in San Francisco and two state legislators from Sacramento. One is too old, one is married and one has a fiancee back home waiting for him, so I can't even find a good marriage prospect for you there."

"A good marriage prospect? Marriage?" Willie smiled ironically at Elizabeth who dropped her eyes and shrugged defeat.

"Still," Elizabeth said, defending her notion, "I think it is possible to have a good marriage."

They had stopped at a crossroads and were standing there quietly. Elizabeth kicked at a clump of damp earth. She looked back up at Willie. "Will you be all right alone then?"

"You mean...today?"

"Yes. Today."

"You mean will I get flustered and stutter and break out in a sweat if I happen to meet these strangers and have to talk to them?" Willie sighed. "Other than old friends, when it comes to talking to men I am socially inept."

"Inept?"

"My conversations with men always seems to have a danger that I can never escape. It's like walking alongside a creek that's threatening to overflow its banks. It's always right there, at the edge of my vision. I try to think neutral, like, I'm a person, he's a person. But the water spills over the banks and laps at my feet and distracts me. Pretty soon the water is over my head and I start stuttering and can't breathe."

"Land sakes, Willie. Such silly talk."

"I don't know how not to be nervous, Lizzie."

"I know, honey. It's part of your charm. I just don't want you to fret about it."

"I woke up this morning feeling hopeful. I like that feeling."

"So I guess that means your conversation with your parents went well last night, telling them you're not moving to Frisco with them?"

"It went well. I'll tell you about it later. If I don't hurry I'll be late for school."

They parted, each to her own day. Before they were out of earshot of each other Willie called back to Elizabeth, "I'll see you at Pink's later. I do feel lucky."

Willie moved along at a brisk pace now, the children would be arriving at school soon. She and Elizabeth were not allowed to have both Indian and white children at the school at the same time. They held class for the white children in the morning and Indian children in the afternoon. A few times when she was working late in the afternoon Indian and white children lingered in the play yard. They played together then, color-blind as young children can be. And now there was a Chinese boy in town whose father was a cook in a logging camp up river. Willie hoped the boy would be able to come to school.

Which school would I have to put him in? she wondered.

The deep ruts made by wagon wheels during the long wet winter still held puddles of spring rain. By the time she reached the schoolhouse the hem of her skirt was muddied, her cheeks were flushed red and her hair clung in damp disarray to her neck and brow.

When she saw the unfamiliar horses tethered in front of the unpainted redwood building a race of panic sped her heartbeat. A man she did not know with a bright display of ribbons and officer's insignia on his blue uniform stood in the shadows on the porch observing her approach. Her step paused; she wanted a moment to calm the fluster that rushed to her throat. The man stepped forward into the sun and watched her. Willie's breath tightened. Her hesitation made her feel even more awkward and self-conscious. A tingle of perspiration broke under her arms.

Speak slowly and you won't stutter. Speak slowly and you won't stutter. Take breaths from time to time. Don't forget to swallow.

4

Nine men rode hard out of the cool shelter of the trees into the exposed heat of the inland ridge overlooking the Eel River valley. Immediately below them a dozen brush houses lay in an orderly scatter along the high ground of the valley floor. The riders halted their horses at the edge of the bluff.

One of the men rested his arm on his saddle pommel. The heat made his head feel light and dull. He removed his hat and fanned his sweat-drenched face. His damp hair was the color of dust .

"Goddammit Nate, put that hat back on your head. You trying to warn them we're here? Whoever heard of a goddamn grown man wearing a goddamn red hat anyways. Waving a red hat at a bunch of Digger Injuns. I don't know why I let you ride with me."

Nate gestured with the hat still in his hand toward the village below. "Look there, Jarboe, them squaws is fixin' to carve up that horse right now. See 'em there? They must be some hungry Diggers. Eat a white man's horse. Don't seem worth dying for." He yanked his hat on tight and turned to face Jarboe.

"The reason you ast me to ride with you is I'm the best Injun hunter you got. And don't get high-falutin' with me, Captain Jarboe. Just cause we got commissioned by the Governor don't mean nothin's changed. We're still just paid to kill thieving grub-eating savages. Only thing different is we're legal now. Official. When this is all over we'll still just be cattle punchers."

Jarboe gave orders to his men as they prepared to ride down on the village. Nate sat contented watching the villagers below. The women were working preparing food. A group of men lay about in the shade smoking and playing gambling games. The laughter of children splashing in the river drifted up to the ridge. A few bare-breasted girls gathered berries along the bank of the river.

Nate whistled low and shook his head. "Look at the tits on them women. Look at them black tits."

"Nate! Are you ready to ride?"

A cheery grin broke bright across Nate's face. He drew his shotgun out of its saddle holster.

"I'm always ready Jarboe. You know that." His spurs dug into his horse's ribs. The raiders drove their mounts down the steep ridge and burst with a fury into the midst of the village.

Jarboe took four of his raiders and chased down the women who ran to the children playing in the river. Their screams were silenced by the thunder of gun fire. The river ran in a red eddy around the dead and dying bodies.

Nate and the other three raiders pursued the men who were reaching for bows and arrows and running for cover. The raiders, skillfully reloading as they rode, ran circles around the frightened men and shot them down one by one.

Two of the girls who had been on the riverbank gathering berries ran across a field toward the trees. Nate holstered his shotgun and took after them. He freed his coiled lariat from the saddle and flailed his horse with it. He spurred the frantic animal in a rhythm with its labored breathing. Blood flecked the lather on its flanks.

Nate whooped and yelled as he did when chasing an errant calf at branding time. When he drew close to the girls, he twirled his lariat above his head and caught them both in one throw. He quickly dallied the rope around the saddle pommel and vaulted gracefully to the ground. The well-trained cow horse leaned back on his haunches and kept the rope taut.

"Good afternoon ladies! Nathan Pickett at your service." He grabbed the dusty red felt hat from his head with a flourish, clutched it to his chest and bowed to the girls who lay on the ground, struggling to free themselves.

"Now, now! Let's not get all in a dither," he said as he reached down to help them to their feet. One girl was hysterical and did not respond. The other accepted his hand, yanked him to her and bit down hard on his arm, not letting loose until he drew his revolver and shot her through the head. Her sister screamed helplessly, but when Nate slapped her with the gun and told her to shut up her screams choked to sobs. He put her on his horse in front of him and rode back to the others who were finishing their search for survivors.

"Listen up, men! Let's torch these shacks," Jarboe was saying just as one of the raiders came out of a small brush house dangling a cradle basket. A baby, who had slept through the whole thing, was wrapped snug in the fine woven basket decorated with strings of colored beads.

"Cute little bastard, ain't he? What d'ya want to do with him, Captain. We can't just leave him here in the sun."

The men all stopped and looked at Jarboe. Excited horses threw their heads and fought against their bits. Dust clouds hovered around their prancing hooves.

"You want to take him home to the missus, Clinton?" Jarboe chided.

"I just said he was cute, that's all."

The baby woke and blinked into the sunlight just before the gunshot tore through him and shattered the basket, which swung from the raider's callused hand in the hot windless air.

All eyes turned to Nate. He held the captured girl on the horse in front of him with one hand and the smoking revolver in the other.

"No one's left to tend him and he's too young to sell," Nate said. "He's better off dead." The girl fainted and almost fell from the horse. Nate slipped the gun into his belt. He secured his grip on the girl and pulled her back by her hair. Her head fell back against his shoulder.

"Look at them tits," he marveled.

5

In two long strides the officer met Willie at the bottom of the schoolhouse steps. He put his hand to his hat with casual ceremony and introduced himself.

"Major Miles Randall Early, ma'am. I hope we are not inconveniencing you by calling at this hour."

He watched her boldly, though his tone was formal and discreet. She did not speak but gathered her skirts and stepped quickly up to the porch. His two associates came out of the schoolhouse onto the porch.

"Miss Jackson, may I introduce Assemblyman Andrew Phillips and Senator Thayer Dickins from the State Legislature."

How did he know her name already? She resented her own vulnerability and shored herself with a gruff attitude, like sandbags against a flood. She stood scowling, her clenched fists still clutching her skirts.

"These gentlemen have been investigating Indian conditions around the state," Early said. "They are winding up their tour at this reservation. They were hoping you might be of some assistance to them."

"The conditions are abominable. As you can see."

"Miss Jackson, I am pleased to meet you," Senator Dickins stepped forward and greeted her with a slight bow from the waist. When he took off his hat he uncovered a shock of white hair that framed a full face with eyes almost hidden in a lugubrious droop. The flash of a good-humored twinkle was not hidden though, and Willie was grateful. His diffidence calmed her.

"Agent Reasoner at reservation headquarters has told us you work closely with many of the Indian families and there are some you can communicate with comfortably. We could use an interpreter," Dickins said.

"Mr. Reasoner's big problem is they cut his budget for the reservation. Reasoner's budget is cut because Henley was squandering it. Rather like closing the barn door after the horse gets loose." She could not keep the quiver out of her voice, but she did not stutter.

"Once it was revealed that Agent Henley was embezzling supplies, food and cattle, he was removed from office quickly," Phillips said.

"Not quickly enough! Henley experimented with how little he could feed the Indians and still get them to work. And only those who worked ate. He still has too much power. Now he's running cattle on his ranch inland at Round Valley. When he was still Agent he established the Nome Cult reservation there. Now he wants the land for his own ranch and he's trying to eliminate the reservation and the Indians. He should be shot."

"Our committee is planning to recommend that Congress buy out the settlers in Round Valley," Phillips said, "and leave the entire valley for the inland reservation. Then the Indians on this coastal reservation could be moved there and we could provide them all with productivity and dignity."

"With Henley and his cronies in high places, I have trouble believing that will ever happen." She began to stutter. "It was they who demanded that your governor commission Jarboe and his gang to chastise the Indians around Round Valley—which meant to hunt them down and murder them! Walter Jarboe's raiders plunder and kill with the blessing of the State of California. He too should be shot"

Embarrassed now by her angry outburst, Willie struggled to quiet down. She ran her sleeve across her damp forehead. She swallowed. Breathed.

"Well," she said quietly. "I don't actually want these or any men shot, but I do want to see them brought to justice. I want these children to be told we will not tolerate this killing." She gestured then to the children who had quietly gathered at the foot of the steps.

"I must tend to my students now, gentlemen. I am very glad you are here. Just your presence here is promising." She reached her hand toward the students, "Now, children. Inside." They clamored into the classroom.

"Thank you for receiving us at this early hour," Dickins said. "May we meet with you later today at a better time for you?"

They were interrupted by the sound of pounding hooves and the calls of two soldiers approaching rapidly on horseback.

"Willie!" they yelled to her as they galloped their horses to the front of the schoolhouse. "We'll pick you up tonight, Willie! You be ready for us!"

Belatedly the young men noticed Willie's visitors standing in the shadows on the porch. They stilled their horses, drew to attention and saluted Major Early.

Early stepped to the edge of the porch and returned their salute. "Good morning Corporals. Do you men have business here?"

"No, sir. Delivering a message to Miss Jackson. Apologies for the interruption. We'll be on our way now, sir." They saluted Early again, tipped their hats to Willie, and withdrew at a speedy lope.

Willie's cheeks burned as she hurried in after her young students. She called back over her shoulder, "I'll be here all afternoon, if you wish to see me."

"Thank you, ma'am," Early replied. "We are on our way to see your father now. We hope to arrange a sit-down with both of you."

The three men left. Willie turned to her class and began her lesson. As the children quieted down she could hear the fading sounds of voices, creaking leather and hooves on damp ground. She was distracted and her thoughts tumbled.

I wonder which one he is, she thought, too old, married or engaged?

She would be prepared next time they met. The proximity of a stranger making her heart beat fast—it was undignified. Stumbling and stuttering. Someone she doesn't even know. When they next met she would tend to business. No more ranting about people needing to be shot. Damn! How could I be so easily rattled. Her thoughts were interrupted by a young student tugging on her sleeve.

"Can I, Miss Jackson. Can I? Miss Jackson! Can I? Can I?"

"Can you what, Orvin?"

"Can I write the answers on the blackboard?"

"You may, Orvin."

That afternoon, after the students had all gone home, Reverend Jackson arrived at the schoolhouse in his buggy to meet with the investigators. Willie cleared off a large wooden table. It was rather a low table, but it would do. The two legislators and Major Early joined them, and the five of them settled formally and quietly into the business at hand. They worked out a list of major needs the reservation Indians had right now and recommendations for the future.

Their talk turned to the kidnappings, rapes and killing of the Indians who were still living outside the reservations. Early repeated what other army officers had told them before: "It is extremely difficult if not impossible for the Army to offer protection to the tribes who will not come in."

"But they cannot trust the same promises they've heard before and seen broken," Jackson said. "They've seen Indians on the reservations die of disease and starvation They know the reservations aren't safe. Why should they come in?"

"They are dying of disease and hunger out there too," Dickins said. "Their women and children are stolen and sold into servitude. At times they have been traded for horses to stock the new ranches in the inland valleys. And the men, young and old, are hunted down like trophy game animals.

"We know all that, but we don't know why more is not being done to stop it," Willie pleaded.

"We are trying, Miss Jackson," Dickins said. "These inland ranchers and their hired vigilantes call their punitive actions war, but we know it is not war.

Early had been leaning back in his chair, hands in his pockets, eyes tense, listening to the discussion. Now he shifted forward and spoke directly to Willie.

"When the ranchers requested that Governor Weller commission Jarboe's Rangers, they claimed—in a letter we have—that the Army is of no help to them because we are friends with the Indians. Many of the Indians are finding that out too. Jarboe and the other vigilantes will soon lose their sanctions; their raids will no longer be legal. We cannot stop settlement of this territory. That is the way it is. We have served notice that no brutality against the Indians will be tolerated, but we are given no authority to discipline civilians for their actions against Indians outside the reservations."

"Some tribes and bands know that and are coming in, asking for protection," Jackson said. "How can any of us have any understanding of the desperation they face?"

"In war I have seen men capable of villainy and abuse. It is not necessary for me to be an Indian to understand what they are up against," Early said. "I probably understand the bleakness of their prospects more than they do. They think they can still go back to their old ways. They cannot. It is not necessary for me to be starved into submission to be able to recognize defeat."

The room was silent until finally Phillips spoke up in frustration, "I don't understand why these tribes are as passive as they are. They seem so backward."

"Forever they've had an ample food supply to hunt and gather," Jackson said. "They developed no agriculture, they had no great grain stores, they had no wealth to fight over, they had no standing armies."

The group fell silent again, each of them staring at the specter of the future and its inevitable loss of old ways. Dickins attempted to shrug off the hovering pall. He cleared his throat and began the plans and arrangements necessary to conduct their investigations and interviews. It was decided he would meet with Willie the next morning and they would visit some leaders in the camps on the reservation.

They parted ways, Willie closed up school and headed off to walk the three miles home. Her father offered to take her home with the buggy if she were willing to wait until he finished his afternoon calls, but she chose the time alone.

Earlier in the day the fog had burned off and the sun had warmed the ground. Willie could still feel the warmth beneath her feet. But late afternoon had cooled and the fog hung close again, lying heavy on the gray ocean. Weather-twisted cypress at the bluff's edge made ragged silhouettes against the sky. The tide was low and the surf quiet. Lanky water birds fished in the exposed kelp beds.

Willie crossed the river on the ferry without having to speak to anyone and followed the steep trail up the ridge.

At a spot where the bluffs angled south at the mouth of the river the trail climbed out of the fog. Willie stood for a while in the late sun watching the mist pour into the river canyon below. The day's talks about harsh circumstances—how they came to be, who should have done this, who should not have done that—at first made her angry, but now threatened her with a despair she knew could leave her depressed and immobilized. It was better for her when everyone could settle on a plan of action and get to work. Helping plan solutions is good; she wanted to stay focused on that.

Her trail dropped back into the fog. A family of deer scattered before her, losing themselves in the mist and the trees. She liked this solitude, still and severe. Her step became light and her head cleared. A thrush sang his salute to the dusk, claiming his turf.

Where the trail made the last turn to her home, she was startled by a figure crouching on a small hillside above her. It was Pahto, keeping watch. Eternal watch. For what, Willie was never sure. Pahto kept to the edges, seldom participating in any work on the farm. He watched. It was clear life here did not taste good to him, but he was devoted to his people. In the early mornings he would slip past the outskirts of the white settlements, hunting and trapping, then smuggling his catch back to the evening campfire.

He did like to help her father with the horses. Willie hoped maybe that was a kind of work he would like to do, handling horses. She was sorry now that he had seen her startle because she did not want him to think she was afraid of him. He was not afraid of her. She acknowledged him with a nod of her head. He watched her impassively as she finished her walk home.

The yard was a jumble of activity as crates packed with the family's belongings were arranged and rearranged, stacked and re-stacked, awaiting transport to the dock, there to be loaded to the schooner that would take them to San Francisco.

Willie went inside. The large central room of the house was the kitchen where they cooked and ate their meals. In the large brick fireplace two pot cranes held kettles over the hot coals. The bricks held the heat well, keeping the house warm long after the fire went out.

Willie went to the small cabinet built into the bricks where they kept the sourdough bread starter that they used for their leavening. It gave a biting, rich flavor to the bread. The starter needed to be cared for, used and renewed regularly to stay fresh. Willie liked to tend the yeast. It was much like tending any other barnyard critter; it responded to care.

She removed the yeast crock from the cabinet and mixed a large scoop with flour and milk to start the bread rising for the next day. Then she added some of the fresh dough back to the crock to replenish the yeast.

Willie's young sister burst into the house from outdoors. "Willie, Willie! Look what Round Face Women gave me!" The girl held a small basket with feathers woven into the fine pattern. The feathers radiated a brilliance of color. "I must use it to pack my best hair ribbons in."

"Round Face Woman must love you very much," Willie said and touched her sister's pink cheeks and fair hair—the blond ringlets that somehow gave this child chances their Bokaima neighbors would never know. Willie could not shake the fear that there was a terrible price to pay; the differences were slight and the privileges great. The child ran off to gather her ribbons.

Dinner with the family was quick and chatty. Viola's resignation to Willie's staying behind came easy finally. As they cleared away the dishes Viola chattered, her words falling like flower petals, pleasant, without pattern. Willie appreciated her mother's struggle to maintain a security of gentility to keep her children safe.

Willie mused: Gens, clan; gentilitis, clanship—she recalled an old Latin lesson. Belonging to a tribe. Membership in the correct tribe confers gentility.

Cornelius Jackson knew the two young men well who called for her this evening. He saw they were good friends to her. He was concerned that their assignment might change and they could be quickly transferred. But if her situation grew less secure she could always rejoin the family at San Francisco.

He watched with only a little sadness as the three of them rode out, the men on horses riding alongside as she drove the buggy.

6

Daniel, Marcus, and Willie rode out easy together. The friendship of the three was well made. Their horses' movement was smooth on the familiar road. The buggy's creak, the rasp of the wheels, the horses' breath, the clatter of hooves, the calls of the riders—all sounds were suspended in the muffle of fog, isolating the friends in their adventure. They too were on familiar ground.

Marcus Buckner and Daniel Finn had been stationed at Fort Bragg for two years. Marcus came from a military family and had followed the tradition of his father and brothers by his army service. It was unclear to him why he was in this strange place so far from his Maryland home but he accepted it with equanimity. Sometimes he brooded and pined, but those moods passed. He saw himself as a soldier who would probably always be far from home. He gave little thought to the possibility of returning to Baltimore. He had no problem with the soldier's life. He had more trouble adjusting to the foreign attitudes and raw manners of the settlers of this new land than he did to soldiering. Dark and large-framed, he was bear-like with slow easy movements yet capable of moving his big body quickly into an agile rowdiness. He was a good balance for his friend Daniel.

Daniel knew that. The fair-haired slightly-built Daniel Finn was energetic and volatile and apt to let his mouth get himself into situations it could not get him out of. His parents had come to America to escape the desperation of the potato famine in Ireland but had improved their circumstances little. He had joined the army to escape the squalor and poverty of his New York City neighborhood.

They were on their way to Pink's saloon. The back room of Pink's was the only place in town the soldiers and lumber men could bring their wives and girls for an evening out. There were few white women in the area, but the town was beginning to boom with a influx of settlers and families. In the back room they could eat Pink's simple fare, play cards, even dance if they could enlist a piano or fiddle player.

The back room at Pink's had a different atmosphere than the main saloon. The clientele in the front saloon was a rough mix of high-stakes gamblers, hired women, single men far from home and drifters passing through keeping just beyond the reach of legitimacy.

There was no ferryman on duty that night; Marcus and Daniel pulled the ferry across the river. As they reached the opposite shore and were securing the ferry to the moorings, they could see a ruckus in front of Pink's. A group of men were shouting at two blanket-clad Indians. They began beating on the Indians until they fell to the ground. Pink ran out onto the porch with his long Brown Bess musket.

Willie could see the smoke from Pink's gun before she heard the report. He had fired into the air. Marcus and Daniel mounted their horses and took off toward Pink's. Willie was left to lead the horse and buggy onto land.

"You stay here, Willie," Daniel yelled to her. "You just

make them madder."

"I will not," she yelled back, but by the time she got the buggy under way and pulled up to Pink's the ruffians had been chased off. Pink was trying to do the same with the two Indian men using hand gestures to send them on their way. They begged for alcohol and would not go.

Willie got out of the buggy and approached the Indian men. She could see by the lamplight from the saloon porch where mud clung to the blood on their faces. She tried to talk to them, but she knew no language they understood. They ignored her and held their hands out to Pink for a bottle. They pulled their blankets around their shoulders. They wore no shirts. Pink went back inside and brought them out a half-empty bottle. They stole away. Marcus and Daniel watched until the two native men reached the safety of the woods.

"Who were those guys beating on them?" Daniel asked Pink. Pink's saloon was on reservation land in army jurisdiction.

"Just some of them boys that come out of the woods and got nothing better to do than make sport with those poor savages," Pink replied. "Y'all have got to do something with them Indians. They are a nuisance to people around here. You know I don't let them get hurt at my place, but they are a disgrace, living in the mud, begging on the streets. Move them some place else where they're not in the middle of a town of white folks."

"Pink!" Willie's tone was hurt and angry. "This land is supposed to be theirs. You move."

"It's too late for that now, Willie love," Pink said. "Come inside now where it's warm. Nothing you can do out here."

"Yeah, come on, Willie," Daniel said.

Marcus and Daniel walked toward the side entrance that opened onto the back room. Willie followed the men inside.

In the back room, Marcus and Daniel looked for players for their poker game. Willie walked over and stood by the doorway that led to the front saloon. Behind the door was a window that overlooked the river. Outside where the fighting had just been, still pools of dark rain water shone red from the porch lamp.

"Is Cletis coming?" Daniel asked Marcus.

"He'll be here," Marcus said. Daniel got a draught of beer and played at the tinny piano that had been removed from the main saloon in favor of a newly-arrived player piano. Marcus settled at a table and dealt a hand of solitaire.

"It's over now, Willie. Nothing you can do," Marcus said.

"It's not over."

"Come play cards now. I'll buy you a beer." Marcus went to the bar. "Pink, draw me a beer for Willie."

"Yeah! Pink!" Daniel called out. "Go out front and fetch the major and them big shots in here for a little poker. I heard them coming in. Go invite them. Let's have some fresh blood in here. You can explain the meaning of life to Phillips, who could use some straightening out, and we can play cards with the other two. How about it?"

"Be hospitable, Pink," Marcus added. "I'm tired of shuffling these cards. Besides, Willie needs some cheering up."

"I don't need cheering up."

On his errand to round up players, Pink passed where Willie stood at the window. He paused with his hand on the door and started to speak to her. She cut him short.

"Don't talk to me Pink."

He shook his head and opened the door to the noisy saloon.

"Just the thing," Dickins answered to Pink's invitation. He was standing at the bar with Early and Phillips. "Just the thing, eh, Phillips?"

Pink put his arm around Phillips' shoulder and led him toward the back room. "What about that new governor?" Pink asked Phillips. "He gonna work out?" Dickins paid the bar tab and moved to follow them. Major Early hung back.

"Miles, come along," Dickins said. "Let's play cards. That Jackson woman will be there. I think you've caught her interest. You don't want Phillips to move in on you, now do you?"

Early got up and walked toward the back room. "Let him move. She'd be too much trouble."

"She doesn't appear to be here anyway," Dickins said as they stood in the doorway and surveyed the room. "Too bad."

"No matter, Dickins. I'm telling you. She's too dry. Shut up about it now and let's just play cards."

It was not until the door closed behind them that Early noticed her standing there, staring out the window. She looked somber. He could not sense if she had overheard them.

"Good evening, Miss Jackson," he said.

"Major Early," she replied.

"Why, good evening, Miss Jackson," Dickins laughed his big laugh and kissed her hand with a flourish. "How good to see you. I didn't notice you standing behind that door."

"I've drawn you fresh beers, gentlemen," Pink announced as he set the drinks on the gaming table.

Early and Dickins sat down and Daniel came away from the piano.

Marcus arranged himself ceremoniously with his cigar and his playing chips. Daniel complained at length about the scuffed cards, the uneven table, the flat beer. Cletis and Elizabeth arrived and Cletis joined the men at the table. Elizabeth walked over to where Willie stood by the window and spoke quietly, her hand on Willie's shoulder.

"Willie, get over here," Daniel said. "How many chips do you want to buy?"

"Miss Jackson is going to play poker with us?" Early asked.

"Hell, yes," Daniel answered. "Hang on to your money."

Willie left the window and settled herself at the table. Elizabeth joined Phillips and Pink at the bar.

"Pink, where's Willie's beer?" Marcus asked.

"No, Pink, bring me a whiskey."

"Whiskey?" Marcus asked.

"Whiskey!" Daniel said. "Good idea. Bring me one too, Pink. Yessir! Hang on to your money."

Marcus dealt the cards. "My older brother served under Jubal Early in the war with Mexico. Any relation to you, sir?"

"Yes, he is my cousin, from Franklin County, Virginia. My family is in Pennsylvania," Major Early replied. The table talk warmed around him, but he remained formal still trying to get a sense of the house culture. Military formality was often relaxed in situations like this, Early was used to that, but the casual familiarity the men showed toward the women present was unusual. Early had seen this type of behavior before in California. Marcus smoked and Daniel peppered his speech with colorful expletives. And they addressed everyone with first names. Except the newcomers of course. It would be interesting to see how that played out. Dickins handled the situation graciously, not the least unsettled by the lack of formality.

After a while Pink left them to tend his main bar. He touched Willie's shoulder as he passed from the room and spoke to her quietly, "It pleases me to hear you have decided to stay."

"Yes, sir. Yes!" Cletis drawled. "Whatever would I do without you to listen to my wife! I would have to do it myself."

"Do I understand correctly that you will not go with your family when they return to San Francisco?" Dickins asked.

"No, Senator, I won't."

"An unusual choice for a young woman in so remote an outpost, isn't it?"

"I have my school of course and my work at the clinic," A slight quiver in her voice.

"I do wish you'd reconsider moving in closer to the fort, though. I don't think you'll be safe enough out there," Marcus blurted out before Willie's glare cut him short.

"You plan to live alone, miles out of town?" Early asked.

"I will not be alone. A band of Bokaima lives with us. They will still be here, of course. Only my family is leaving. And I have run the place on my own before when my father has taken a leave and the family traveled down below."

Daniel shook his head in disapproval. "Yeah, I can't see anybody is going to get past that big buck Pahto. I've seen him guarding. He barely tolerates me and Marcus coming out there. How safe is that Willie?"

"You have an Indian guarding your home?" Early asked.

Willie met his eyes now. "He is not guarding my home. His people work the farm with us. It is his tribe he is guarding. In view of the treatment of the Indians hereabouts I am sure I can't blame him." She inhaled slowly. "Whose bet is it anyway?"

"I'd still like it if you'd move in closer, Marcus

repeated.

"Would you hush, Marcus."

"We never saw Pahto's motives quite the same as Willie does," Daniel added, "but we've been forced to abandon the argument many times before."

"Daniel," Willie snapped at him. "Hush!"

"You have no one to protect you," Early stated rather than asked.

Elizabeth was on the other side of the room listening to Assemblyman Phillips, but her attention was on the conversation at the poker table. She strolled over and stood close behind Willie.

"Major Early, does your fiancee also live in Pennsylvania?" Elizabeth asked.

A flush colored Early's suddenly tight jaw.

Phillips was a politician not a military man and did not share the soldier's sense of closed-rank loyalty. He had no reluctance to harass Early. He too came across the room to join this conversation.

"Why, he has no actual real-life fiancee, Mrs. Carter," Phillips answered Elizabeth.

The players hardly noticed as Dickins took the small pot with three of a kind. "Watch out now, Andrew. You'll be getting Miles in hot water here," he said.

Cletis chortled as he dealt the cards for the next hand. Now he could not contain himself from joining the fray. "He has no fiancee back home, Lizzie," Cletis said.

"No," Phillips said, "He just tells people that because he gets tired of being pursued by every young woman's mother as a likely marriage prospect for her daughter."

Marcus and Daniel hooted and cackled. Willie tried to join in the laughter, but her smile was thin. Daniel made a strong bet on the new hand.

"Why Major Early, you poor thing," Elizabeth said

with feigned sympathy.

"I have made no such false claim to this or any other company. My friends like to try to embarrass me with the spread of sly stories. Whether they should be called friends is another matter," he said, with a stern look in Phillips direction.

Phillips laughed as though that were best joke of all and returned to the bar for a fresh drink.

Elizabeth followed him laughing. "Why Mr. Phillips what a gossip you are. You should be ashamed of yourself."

While the card players were still caught up in this distraction, Early saw Daniel's bet on the hand and raised it another dollar, forcing everyone to fold except Willie. He had her attention now. He was betting that she would not yield this hand no matter what cards she held. She met his raise and called him.

He laid his cards on the table. "Jacks over queens, Miss Jackson." He drew the pot in without waiting to see her cards.

"Ah, ha!" cried Daniel. He could not disguise his glee.

"Willie has met her match for mean poker playing," said Marcus, chomping on his cigar.

"Deal another one like that, Sergeant Carter," Early asked.

Early had shifted the focus of revelry back onto her, and he kept it there. Laughter, another round of whiskey and friendly chatter kept the table conversation easy and open, but Willie avoided ever speaking directly to Major Early. Every hand she showed an interest in he bet up, causing her either to fold or stay in and lose more money. He forced her hand every time, unconcerned about his own losses or wins.

"Willie! You've lost ten dollars," Daniel pointed out. "I didn't even know you had ten dollars."

"I don't now, do I Daniel?"

Elizabeth and Cletis were the first to leave at the end of the evening. Phillips and Dickins followed them and returned to their quarters at the fort; but Early lingered. He offered to accompany Marcus and Daniel when they escorted Willie home. He was their senior officer; there was little they could do to discourage him even if they had wanted to.

The ride home was pleasant. A full moon making a blue halo through the fog gave them some light on the road, but the horses picked their way at a slow pace. Daniel shepherded the foursome through songs they all knew. As they approached the drive to the Jackson place, he sang alone—a song that left them silent for the rest of the ride.

> ...She was walking o'er the fields
> She heard the death bell knellin'
> And every stroke did seem to say
> Unworthy Barbara Allen.
>
> When he was dead and laid in grave
> Her heart was struck with sorrow
> "Oh Mother, Mother, make my bed
> For I shall die tomorrow... "

It was only Early who saw Pahto in the shadow, a gleam of moonlight on his bare back.

7

Since the war with Mexico had ended, Miles Randall Early had been detailed to western outposts as a troubleshooter. He reported directly to General Albert Sidney Johnston, commanding officer for the Department of the Pacific, headquartered at the Presidio in San Francisco.

Early had broad authority to make needed changes without waiting for further advice or orders. The difficulties of travel between San Francisco and the remote forts and camps made communications with headquarters slow and inefficient. He was supposed to determine the problem and craft the solution.

He had been observing and inspecting the operations at Fort Bragg and its outpost at Camp Wright in Round Valley seventy-five miles inland. It was clear now what the next step had to be. This morning he would relieve Captain Naughthen of command of the fort and send him with orders back to the Presidio. No longer should these reservation Indians have to endure their tormentors with the tacit support of the commanding officer of this post.

Although Naughthen received this news with anger he actually was relieved. He had never been happy with his assignment here. He had never been able to understand the country, the men or the desperate redskins he despised. His predecessor had been the well-respected Major Johnson; the men never accepted Naughthen.

Johnson's ally, Lieutenant Dillon, would now be recalled from Camp Wright to take over this command. Major Early would remain as acting commanding officer until Dillon's arrival.

"Dillon can have it," Naughthen snarled. "I don't care where the Army sends me next. Any place but this gray God-forsaken place. But I might never forgive them for sending a cold-blooded imperious sonofabitch like you to cut my throat. Anyways, I smell war in the air. I want to be back home in South Carolina before it starts."

Early waited until Naughthen regained composure, "Shall we address the men now, Captain?"

They stepped out of the headquarters office. The thud of their boots on the wooden-plank porch carried across the parade grounds where the troops stood in formation. The morning was clear. The fog had completely lifted and the sun was breaking through the trees shining dappled on the groomed grounds. Naughthen and Early announced the change of command. Before dismissing the men to the day's duties, Major Early asked to meet with Sergeant Cletis Carter and Corporals Marcus Buckner and Daniel Finn.

The three men were still stunned about the sudden change in command when they met with Early in Naughthen's office. Early gave his orders briefly knowing these men knew best what the day entailed. He left it to them to discharge their regular duties.

"Sergeant Carter, I expect you to see to any needs Captain Naughthen might have to make his removal without delay. Without any delay." Major Early spoke with cool authority but his manner was reassuring. "We want to make this command transition smooth. You all have much to do. I will not be back on the post until later today; I will meet with you again then. Phillips and Dickins have gone to observe the encampment of that northern tribe that was brought in two days ago, so I will go to interview the Pon-kow people Miss Jackson has communication with."

"But sir," Daniel blurted. "I thought Willie, uh, Miss Jackson, would be accompanied by Senator Dickins." Daniel's eyes twittered fearfully at the transgression of his mouth.

Early let silence settle over his men. "Since Senator Dickins is otherwise occupied I shall go." With a tone that left no room for further discussion he dismissed them and walked alone across the green field to the stable to collect his horse. Corporal Finn's voice giving orders to a crew working on a fence on the other side of the post carried sharply on the clear air.

The fort was a simple collection of utilitarian buildings, not a fortress. It was located in a clearing in the pines about half a mile from the ocean and a mile north of the Noyo River.

Early knew it was sometimes difficult for the men in this isolated outpost to understand why they were here. Who were they protecting from whom? The influx of newcomers to California searching for gold had created a great need for lumber in the boom towns, especially the sprawling San Francisco. The newly powerful lumber companies wanted the safety of their mills to be insured. Governmental authorities wanted to establish control over the wildly growing state.

The many small local tribes were overrun by the vast numbers of white miners, settlers, ranchers, lumberjacks, hustlers and outlaws who were by and large oblivious to the imminent destruction of the Indian culture.

Major Early's job was to establish stability to the Army's presence here. At his various assignments around the county, circumstances changed for Early rapidly. Unique problems challenged him every day. He dealt with them with creative efficiency. Once the situations were straightened out and he had placed men in charge who he thought could keep matters under control, he left.

He had been young when he fought in the war with Mexico in 1846 and 47. The end of the war left him unsettled and rootless. He stayed in the Army with some vague notion of overseeing the orderly settlement of this new country. For fourteen years he has traveled widely for the Army, usually alone, and has called no place home.

But he caught himself hesitating now, clinging to the idea of staying, perhaps helping young Lieutenant Dillon build up the post. Was it the bloodhounds of time dogging his steps that slowed him now? Or was it this place that held him? The drama of the coast enraptured him. He was in no hurry to leave. He wanted to see the Jackson woman again. She lingered in his thoughts. Her image was not dry. He was troubled to think she had overheard his comment to Dickins. He'd have to figure a way past that.

When he arrived at the stable he made inquires concerning the care and feeding given his mount. He liked to groom and saddle him himself whenever he could. Early depended on his horse in volatile situations and always wanted to be sure he was tacked up properly. Slats was a dark bay, almost a black, taller and more lean than most of the mounts men rode in the west. He was also of a more fiery temperament. This morning he was pacing nervous circles in his box stall.

Once they were on the road it was difficult for Early to keep Slats at a quiet pace. A family of quail scurrying across his path spooked the horse. He took a sudden sideways jump and broke into a mincing sidestepping lope. Early's steady seat and strong leg held the horse in check. Early eased Slats back into his hands, and then when he felt the big horse respond to his commands—shifts of his weight, movements of his fingers on the reins, pressure from his thighs—Early gradually drove him to lengthen his stride and move out into a full gallop.

As they came closer to the Jackson homestead Early avoided giving full thought to the problems his interest in the woman presented. His habit was to stride into the fray at hand relying on his wits. The nagging thought that perhaps this time he was in over his head was buried in a flurry of forward motion in which he felt more passenger than driver.

8

Willie lay in bed longer than usual, burying her head deep in her pillow, trying to avoid the morning. She was only driven to rise when the persistent sunshine filled her small room and finally convinced her to loose her hold on the night. She was up and dressed quickly then and left the house before anyone was awake. She had plans to be at Elizabeth's for coffee and then to meet Senator Dickins; she would return home later to help with the moving.

She avoided the muddy road through the farmyard by cutting across the woods to the main wagon road. She held her skirts up around her knees so that she could scurry along the rough path.

They did not see each other until it was too late. The same moment she stepped from the trail onto the road Early was approaching at a gallop. Her sudden appearance startled Slats, and before Early could put him under control he reared up, his hooves striking the air in front of him. Willie was thrown back and fell hard. Early leapt to the ground. Slats bolted down the trail. Early was immediately at Willie's side.

His hands were on her, gathering her off the wet ground, holding her.

She rubbed the back of her head where it had struck the same tree root she had tripped over when she fell.

"Are you all right, Miss Jackson?"

She could not answer right away. She lay against his arm. Fine wool fibers of his jacket caught the early sunlight and shone radiant blue. His smell was sharp and warm and made her drowsy. She could not understand his words that drifted muffled at the cotton edges of the moment that enveloped them, a moment not so much stolen as lost. He brushed back a lock of her brown hair that had broken free from its clasp and lay across her cheek.

"Willie," he spoke softly. "Willie, are you all right? You took a fall." He watched her closely. She raised her eyes and looked at him.

They had been thrown past barriers of decorum and social reserve. For a moment they were still. The connection was brief but complete—until her head cleared and she pulled away suddenly. They rose. She took a step back.

"I startled your horse! I am sorry." Her hand fluttered to her face, brushing the still errant hair back into its clasp.

"A horse poorly ridden evidently. He should have been better in hand. Are you hurt?"

The distance of propriety was reestablished between them. Terse formality lay thinly over their nervous movements. It was difficult for her to feel secure behind those hastily resurrected and modest barricades.

"No, I've only bumped my head." Her hand went to the back of her head again and felt the goose egg raised there. "I tripped," she said.

A snorting commotion distracted them as Slats came along the road in a stiff prance, throwing his head, resisting his capture by Pahto. Wordlessly Pahto handed the reins to

Major Early. The two men regarded each other, wary. Early thanked Pahto and offered a handshake. Pahto did not acknowledge the gesture and retreated back into the woods. Early watched him until he was out of sight and then turned back to Willie.

They both spoke at the same time, stopped, deferred to each other, tried to decide who would speak first.

"I have come in Senator Dickins' stead," Early said, explaining his presence on the road to her home. "He has other affairs to attend to this morning, but we do need these interviews and your assistance would be greatly appreciated."

"I have so little time, so little time today...I don't know..." stuttering stole her words. She paused and looked away from him. "Sometimes I stutter when I'm nervous."

"I know."

She took one slow deep breath. She turned back to him and spoke clearly, "I can go with you for the morning only. My family will be leaving on the schooner late this afternoon. I will be helping them and seeing them off. They are expecting me back after noon. I am free this morning."

"So, shall we begin?" Early suggested. They turned and walked up the road, Slats following on a lead.

"We must first go to Elizabeth's house because she is waiting for me. I have school papers for her; she'll be teaching today."

"Was that the big Indian you spoke of last night, that man who brought Slats back?"

"Yes. Pahto. He likes handling the horses. He has the knack for it I think, a finesse. Many of the Bokaima go by English names that have similar meaning to their Bokaima names. It is a way they try to assimilate. Pahto, of course, is one who will not do that."

"Do they work for you, or rather for your family?"

"The homestead and farm my father established here is theirs. He set it up as a trust for them. He wants them to be able to maintain it themselves communally now. It lies just outside of the reservation proper. I'll still live in the house my father built on the compound so I will be able to speak for them if that becomes necessary, even though I am like Moses—inadequate of speech. Still, I'm all they've got right now." Her chatter was nervous. He listened.

"We can get a horse for you at the post, or I can arrange a carriage; I believe a carriage was what Senator Dickins had in mind."

"A horse will do." She waited at Elizabeth's while Major Early secured her a mount from the post stable. Elizabeth sat on the edge of her bed while Willie found clothes to borrow more suited to riding than the long heavy skirts she wore.

"You will be spending the day with Major Early, Willie?" Elizabeth asked.

"Yes...well...the morning anyway. He needs help talking with the Pon Kow leaders. I guess I can help him. We're going up to their camp."

"Do you need help? That's what I want to know. I don't know about this alliance. The man never stays in one place more than a month. And what about that fiancee story?"

"What are you talking about, Lizzie?"

"Are you becoming fond of him?" Elizabeth challenged.

"Fond? Well, no, of course not. He's much too hard. Fond? No, that's not what I feel. No, not fondness." She fidgeted through the changing and was ready to ride when Miles arrived with the horses.

9

They rode to the north end of the reservation and then turned inland along a grassy river valley at the edge of the redwood forest.

"They are a Pon-kow group from the Feather River valley in the northern Sierra. They were brought here last year. Twenty-five years ago a cholera epidemic wiped out hundreds and hundreds of Indians in that area. Then came the gold rush and they were forced from their villages and began to starve. But here their people are still dying of hunger and disease. So, Pon-ya-nom has requested Agent Reasoner to allow them to move into the Nome Cult reservation. He thinks they will be better off there."

"They won't," Early said.

"I know. But he thinks there is a headman somewhere who will help him."

They rode past several small encampments along a narrow river valley. Residents of each camp were usually of the same extended clan or survivors of related groups. Unblinking eyes in weathered faces watched them ride by. No one greeted them or acknowledged their passing.

The farther from headquarters, the more varied was the people's clothing. Native internees of the reservation were discouraged from coming into town with their bodies uncovered, but their clothing provisions were paltry and shoddy. Often one intact dress or one presentable shirt and jacket was shared communally for whoever might be making a trip to town. But in these outlying camps the children were seldom dressed in white man's fashion, and the adults were layered with as many garments as they could glean from handouts and hand-me-downs. Each woman wore a dress that covered her breasts regardless of its being dirty, tattered and threadbare.

When they reached the Pon-kow camp Pon-ya-nom was sitting in front of a conical house built with lumber mill slash. Two women sat on either side of him, one holding a baby. Other men gathered and stood nearby. Agent Reasoner had gotten word to Pon-ya-nom that he would be called on by an important visitor this morning.

Major Early tied the horses to a manzanita shrub and he and Willie sat on the ground facing Pon-ya-nom. Strong Water, one of Willie's best pupils, a boy of about twelve, joined them.

Pon-ya-nom made a speech in broken English that was predominantly a mix of conciliatory phrases. He had been diligent in his efforts to learn English so that he could negotiate concessions and assistance for his tribe, but his command of the language was limited to diplomatic overtures. Word had traveled to him of Major Early's arrival at the post and he was counting on Early being the headman who would save them. Once he had voiced his statesmanlike preamble, it was left to Strong Water to translate his story while he spoke freely in his own language.

"We did not always live like this," Strong Water

repeated for him. "These young ones do not remember the old ways." Pon-ya-nom gestured to the young woman sitting beside him. "Before Toe-a-ne was born many many of our people died from the white man poison fever. Now, our women who lie down with the white man for food to bring back to our children and old ones have this new poison." He grabbed Toe-a-ne's chin and lifted her head to show the syphilitic sores on her mouth and rash across her throat. He ran his fingers over her head and showed them the wisps of thick dark hair that easily pulled loose from her scalp. "Your medicine doctor tells us this poison comes from lying down with men and that she cannot do it anymore. But then we will starve. He gives medicine for this to white man but not for Indian."

The baby Toe-a-ne was holding began to whimper with a thin monotone cry. The woman rocked back and forth and sang quietly. Willie leaned toward Early and told him, "She has syphilis. Her baby was born with it and is deaf and blind."

Pon-ya-nom heard her and recognized the word. "Yes, syphilis," he said through Strong Water. "Doctor calls this poison syphilis. White man poison. White man has all the power in this place. We cannot heal our people. White men came for gold in our home place. We could not collect medicine from our power places. We could not go to the river to fish. White men shoot us. We walked around. We hid. Cold and hungry. The people of the village of my cousin were shot and killed when white men thought they stole their food. I don't know if they took it. They were hungry. Maybe somebody else took it. All Indian people are hungry.

"Government man said to me, come to reservation. Food and blankets. We walked here long way. Not enough food. Our people were weak. More died. My daughters. Now we are still cold and hungry and poisoned with the syphilis poison our women got from lying down with white men so that we can eat. We need headman to help us leave this place. We can go to Nome Cult. Better there. Closer to old place there."

Early replied carefully, waiting for Strong Water to translate. "We can move your people to Nome Cult but it will be very hard on them, and the conditions there are no better than here."

"We do not want to stay here. This is poison place."

"I will see what we can do. We are trying to get more supplies to this reservation for your people as well as all the others."

"I would like whiskey. If Toe-a-ne's sister goes to lie down with the white men, would she also get the syphilis poison?"

Early looked quizzically at Pon-ya-nom, unsure of what Pon-ya-nom's question implied.

"Toe-a-ne used to bring me whiskey. No more," Pon-ya-nom said.

Willie leaned forward and spoke sharply, "No! you must not send Toe-a-ne's sister! She will get the syphilis poison. Do not send her to them!" Strong Water hesitated a moment, then repeated the angry words.

Pon-ya-nom bristled at Willie's reproach. His face stiffened; Willie slumped.

She knew she had overstepped. She left the circle and joined the women gathered at the cook fire. They had gleaned discarded parts of butchered cattle and were making a soup. She visited with the women with broken bits of language and asked after the children.

Through Strong Water, Early conferred with the chief and questioned him about how many of his people would make the trek to the Nome Cult reservation. Willie hoped Pon-ya-nom would not be too stiff with him because of her outburst.

Miles Early took his leave from Pon-ya-nom and got up from the circle. "Let's go Willie," he said. He touched her arm as they walked to where their horses were tied. "Don't worry about it," he said. "The old man says he has always thought you were odd."

As Willie and Miles rode back down the valley, Miles told her of his recent visit to Camp Wright in Round Valley.

"Your friend Major Johnson told the cattle baron George White that he would arrest him if he killed any more Indians. But George White has powerful friends. He finances Jarboe's raiders."

"Why don't politicians do something about it? Why don't the people of California protest?"

"They don't know about it, Willie. There are some journalists who champion the Indians' cause, but they have trouble getting work. My friend Rune Kalevala—he's a writer. Do you know his work?"

"Yes. I've read his stories about the logging camps; they're wonderful. You really know him?"

"My oldest friend. He took a job on a newspaper up near Eureka. When he wrote an editorial denouncing some of the local men for their part in an Indian massacre, some of the townspeople were up in arms and forced him to leave town. But—the editorial got a lot of attention all the way to Sacramento. It's one of the reasons I'm here."

"Where is he now?"

"Back in San Francisco where I first met him years ago. I'd bet he was ready to move on anyway. He never stays in those backwoods burgs any longer than necessary to 'observe the local humanity' as he calls it. Then he's back to civilization."

"You find us uncivilized, but it is the government

you work for, your civilization, who allows this inhumanity to continue."

Miles did not respond and they rode in silence. Their pace was slow. Willie was unused to the strange mount that was responding more to her tension than the commands of her hand or heel. Miles kept Slats quiet and even, trying to give the stocky, stubborn dun Willie rode less reason to argue with her.

Willie was disturbed, her thoughts jumbled—visiting the camps was always depressing; she had mixed feelings about her family leaving; losing her temper with Pon-ya-nom was a mistake—but these were familiar concerns she had fretted through many times. They were not the source of her discomfort today.

"Have you ever been to Round Valley? Do you know anybody from there besides Johnson and Dillon?" Miles asked.

"No, I haven't been there, but some of the ranch hands come over for the horse races."

"I've seen your race course. How are the races? Fast?"

"Wonderful! The best horses and riders in the county come around."

"Do you wager?"

"I might," she answered evasively. It was this man, she thought. He makes me uncomfortable. He's so cock-sure of himself.

They were riding along together with an intimate tension. His easy familiarities caught her unawares and shook her composure.

"Does anyone from the George White ranch come over?" Miles asked.

"George White himself has come. He likes the horses and from here he can catch the schooner when he goes down below to Frisco to consult with his seer to have his stars read."

"No."

"Yes."

"A seer?"

"The spiritualist Mrs. J. J. Whitney."

He laughed at this unlikely picture of the tough and brutal man he knew. Willie smiled at her small storytelling success until Miles shifted the conversation suddenly.

"What do you think the source of the syphilis epidemic is?" he asked.

"White men," she answered flatly.

"Many of those men claim they got it from the Indian women."

"Well, naturally it's passed back and forth now, but until they had contact with whites none of these tribes knew this disease. Reservation agents, mill hands, loggers, merchant sailors who pass through here think nothing of taking advantage of these women who will be lucky if they are paid enough to buy food to take back to the tribe and feed their hungry children. These men keep them until they tire of them. Even the women who seem willing are actually forced into the liaison by their circumstance. The women become infected with syphilis and carry the infection back to their own men. Then to add the offense, these men blaming their victims for the disease..."

"Sailors, perhaps, but not soldiers," Miles interrupted her.

"What?"

"Soldiers are very cautious where these matters are concerned," he grinned.

She looked at him, startled. She was caught off guard again. "Well, apparently not if they are still catching it." She felt the warmth of embarrassment spread to her face and turn to the heat of anger.

He's doing this on purpose, she thought, trifling with me. He thinks it's funny.

"You know you're being high-handed," she said low and quiet. "I don't want to ride with you anymore." Willie wanted to pull away quickly, and she put her heel hard into her horse; but instead of moving out he dropped his head, rolled his back, took a couple of stiff-legged hops and threatened to buck. His twisting resistance crashed him into Slats. Miles reached down and grabbed the animal's bridle, steadying him. He halted Slats and brought Willie's mount close by.

"We can take it easy, Willie."

"I don't know how to take it easy."

He loosed his hand from her bridle and put Slats into a easy canter; the dun followed freely.

10

They rode the rest of the way to the Jackson homestead without speaking. When they arrived they found carts and buckboards packed and loaded. The yard was a din of shouted orders and exasperated responses. Many earnest but inexperienced hands had worked on the packing and some of the loads were coming undone already. Reverend Jackson was trying to rearrange the loads. Viola Jackson was wringing her hands.

Major Early stepped in and helped Jackson settle and tie the wagons. When the work was done Early and Jackson stood back with their hands in their pockets to examine their job and discuss horses.

"You've done quite enough Major Early," Willie said to him. "You can leave now."

"Thank you, Miss Jackson," Early responded.

"Willie, my word," her father said. "I don't think we want to be rude to our guest on our last day here."

"It's all right, sir. It's time I rejoined my men. I believe we have these loads secure now."

"Major Early!" Viola Jackson said. "Our friends are having a bon voyage dinner for us later this afternoon. We wish you would join us." Cornelius Jackson also pressed the invitation until Early accepted and promised he would see them that afternoon.

"Papa, please, let's not trouble Major Early any further."

Early checked one more wobbling cart load and then turned to Willie.

"This is not your worry, Willie."

"No? You'll be on your way then Major?"

"Now, now!" Viola interrupted her daughter. "I'm terribly sorry Major Early. Our Willie has a short temper and a sharp tongue I'm afraid."

"Mama, do not apologize for me. It is his arrogance that shortens my temper."

"Willie! Good Gracious!"

Early fetched Slats and the dun from the hitching post. "Don't worry, Mrs. Jackson. I'm not afraid of her." Early laughed easily as he swung himself into the saddle with one fluid movement; but in his last look at Willie, his eyes were sharp with anger too.

"Until this afternoon then," Viola said as he led the dun out of the yard.

The harbor at the mouth of the river was small and shallow, affording just enough room for the doghole schooners to turn around. Today they would load their belongings on the Golden Rule and sail before sunset. The sea was calm now and Captain Iversen expected it to stay that way. They would be in San Francisco tomorrow. When the ocean was rough it could take much longer to complete the trip.

As soon as they were dismissed from their duties at the fort, Daniel and Marcus showed up to deliver the goods to the harbor. Elizabeth had organized friends and neighbors into preparing the farewell meal. Tables were set up in the churchyard. The Jacksons had many friends in the area and they all showed up for this last gathering. The afternoon grew festive.

Willie sat next to her father who talked of politics and plans to the men who gathered around him. Occasionally he turned from the conversation, smiled at Willie and patted her hand.

"I like this," she leaned forward and said to her father. "I like to see you and Mama laugh and be celebrated."

"I like it too," he replied. "Seeing the goodness of this circle of friends makes me think you will be well looked after."

Major Early had joined the group of men, and now the talk centered on the changes at the reservation and fort—new leadership, new directions, new hope. Willie slipped away from her parents' table and joined Marcus and Daniel who were passing through the food line once again.

"I don't know, Willie. Things are changing around here pretty fast," Daniel said. "The Major is cracking the whip. Until Lieutenant Dillon gets back here, the Major's not going to let us go off fort limits as much as Captain Naughthen did. He keeps his eye on us."

"Major Early won't be leaving anytime soon, I take it?" Willie asked.

"No, and he's not going to let us leave the post anytime we want, Willie. We won't be able to check on you all the time," Marcus said. "It would make a lot more sense if you would move closer in."

"You know I can't do that. I'm not going to leave the Bokaima alone."

"You can't guarantee their safety, Willie," Marcus said. "Those bigwigs over there are deciding on the future of your

Indians. It is not in the Indians' hands."

"They did just fine before we got here. They must be given time to adjust and rebuild." Willie was weary of this same argument they had many times before.

"How did your morning go with the major?" Daniel asked.

"It went well enough, I guess. Your Major Early is difficult. We did not talk to the Bokaima yet. Senator Dickins might come to the farm to visit them tomorrow. He and Phillips are leaving Sunday."

"You can't do it tomorrow! Tomorrow is Saturday. There will be races all day," Daniel reminded her. "Those boys from Round Valley will be coming in with mounts and with money to put on them. Big races tomorrow."

Marcus and Daniel, with their plates full of chicken and corn bread, fell into an animated discussion of horses, betting and racing. Willie leaned against a tree and watched her father talking to the men at his table. His gentle and intelligent manner always made the conversation around him seem so civilized, Willie thought, that one could almost think there was a chance for solutions that actually worked.

But her gaze was drawn to Major Early. She could tell when he was unsure of or in disagreement with some point being discussed, because he would tip his head back and narrow his eyes as he listened. She had noticed his doing that at the card game last week. His focus was unwavering. Unforgiving, Willie thought.

Willie stood mesmerized watching him move and gesture, only half listening to Daniel and Marcus chatter next to her. She watched him as the warm rose light of the setting sun bathed the remnant-laden tables and the sated diners. She watched him as again he tipped his head back and squinted, and then suddenly turned his head toward her, meeting her gaze, catching her staring at him. Motionless but for a tremble she stood frozen, unable to retreat or recover, unable to avert her eyes. Only the sudden clamor of Cletis' warning that the Golden Rule's departure time was upon them gave her opportunity for flight.

She rode down to the harbor in the buggy with Elizabeth and Cletis; Marcus and Daniel came on horseback; the Jacksons rode in the buckboard; and the rest of the company of friends remained behind, calling out their farewells.

The travelers were hurried off to the loading craft once they arrived at the harbor, and there was little time for emotional leave-taking. Embraces and assurances of many visits were exchanged. Willie and her mother stood quietly together, the two women peaceful with the sure knowledge of their bond being greater than the distance between them.

Willie waved good-bye to her beloved family. She stood in the chilly evening with her friends, crying for losses she did not know yet.

11

No one was stirring the next morning when Pahto rose to tend Glory and Rojo and found the two extra horses in the corral. He would not feed these unwelcome ones. He caught them and was leading them out of the corral when they threw their heads and whinnied to the sound of approaching horses. Three riders were coming at a trot down the wagon drive. Pahto continued on his tasks, ignoring the new visitors. The commotion in the yard woke the occupants of the Jackson house.

"Oh, shit!" Daniel shouted as he looked out the window. "Marcus! Godammit, it's the Major."

"What's he doing here? What time is it?"

There were footsteps on the porch and a knock on the door just as Daniel pulled his boots on.

"Shit, shit, shit," he ranted under his breath as he opened the door. It was Senator Dickins who stood at the door; Major Early stayed mounted on his horse at the foot of the steps. Daniel stepped out onto the porch, joined now by Marcus who had put on his coat and was trying to smooth down his hair.

Slats pranced, fighting the tight grip Early held him in. Major Early had clearly not expected to find Corporals Buckner and Finn awakening in this house.

"This is not where you men belong. Report back to the fort immediately." Cold, cold was his voice, and the men moved quickly.

"Yes sir. Major Early, sir, Sergeant Carter was aware of our quarters for the night...we told him...Miss Jackson was alone...we have no duty today..." Daniel's disjointed explanation fell on un-hearing ears. He gave up trying to explain himself and followed Marcus to the corral where Pahto stood holding their horses.

Willie stood just inside the house, in the shadows, wrapped in a shawl. She had not asked them to stay, of course. Along with Elizabeth and Cletis they had come back to Willie's house after they saw the Golden Rule put to sea. They drank wine and talked late into the night. When Elizabeth and Cletis left, Marcus and Daniel were unwilling to leave Willie alone the first night she would spend without her family. She had been happy enough to have them camp on the floor.

Pahto watched the way Daniel and Marcus adjusted their McClellan saddles, gear that was new to him. Early kept his eye on his men and did not speak to anyone. He had come to accompany Willie and the Senator on the tour of the Jackson rancheria, but now once his men were mounted he rode back to the fort with them. Senator Dickins remained.

"Good morning, Senator Dickins," Willie greeted him. Her attempt to remain poised throughout the awkward situation only increased Dickins' amusement. He laughed aloud.

"Oh, you're no help. Come on in, I'll make you a cup of coffee." Willie invited the Senator inside and gave him a chair in a warm spot by the fire, which still smoldered from the late night before. She stoked the fire, put coffee on to brew and excused herself to get ready for their outing. As she dressed she could hear this good-humored man break into laughter periodically.

When she rejoined him she was smiling as she shook her head, trying to protest his teasing, "I suppose I must resign myself to a certain lack of dignity this morning if you are going to have such sport at my expense." After they had their coffee, they stepped out into the bright morning to begin their walk around the rancheria. He offered his arm and patted her hand comfortingly when she took it.

"You must not take offense, my dear. Actually it is Major Early's plight that amuses me." This time when he laughed she felt safe and the threat to her dignity waned.

Willie introduced Senator Dickins to Old Chief and Round Face Woman, explaining they were patriarch and matriarch of the extended Bokaima family. The senator's amiability was a good match for Old Chief, but they were limited by language to nods and smiles.

Blue Feather joined Dickins and Willie in their walk. Blue Feather was Willie's friend. They each spoke the other's language equally poorly, but they were learning and were teachers to one another. Their friendship struggled to bridge the rift of their different cultures. Both lived in worlds vastly different from what their parents had known as young people. It was a new world for both of them. Blue Feather was slipping past marrying age. There were few eligible men who could ask for her hand. Willie had thought Pahto would be a good match for her, but with his grasping onto old ways and Blue Feather's turning from them, it seemed unlikely now.

Blue Feather had become a devoted Christian, learning to read her Bible and teaching the younger children. Most of the Bokaima did not understand and many distrusted this inclination, but as in many ways they yielded to compromise with this new culture. They hoped there was safety in learning white ways.

She had a gracious manner and adapted well to the style of white conversation. Today she had her lustrous dark hair pulled back into a clasp Willie had given her, and her face glowed with her pleasure at chatting in her broken English with this white visitor.

Willie and Elizabeth escorted Senator Dickins around the rancheria, explaining the operation to him and then headed back to Willie's house for more coffee.

"My main fear is that this rancheria is located too close to the enterprise of the coast," Dickins said. "Mills are being built or being planned at an astounding rate. In Mendocino City, seven miles south, they are milling eighty thousand board feet of lumber a day. Here at Noyo they are doing almost as much. These trees are red gold, and the Indians are merely in the way."

"My people must become like white people," Blue Feather offered. "Learn and speak and work."

"I do not think that will solve the problem, my dear, even with so an exemplary model as yourself. The differences and distances are too great. And I think it better that all people, whites or Indians or Arabs or yellow Chinamen, be allowed their own ways, do you agree?" Dickins put another sugar in his coffee. Willie could see that Blue Feather grasped the concept—even though she did not know who the Arabs were—but she did not agree with him.

"With old ways Indians die," she said.

"That must be stopped," the senator replied firmly.

Willie felt a foreboding chill. "I am glad that Lieutenant Dillon will be returning," she said.

"I agree, Willie," Dickins said. "But Early will be here until Dillon returns. I think you'll find him effective as well."

"All right then, if your friend the Major will release my friends Marcus and Daniel, we can all go to the races. Won't you join us? And I want to see if I can get Pahto to go with us. He likes the horses. I know he would like to see the races. Blue Feather, help me tell him about it, would you? He can travel with us."

She knew Pahto would be reluctant to go near a crowd of white men. Indeed, it was not a safe place for him to be alone. He was not civilized to their ways. But if he stayed with their party, with Marcus and Daniel and Cletis, she felt he would be all right. Blue Feather chose to remain behind; the races did not interest her.

Pahto listened to Blue Feather's relayed invitation, but he did not look up from his task of grooming Rojo. Willie told him she needed the sorrel for the buggy; he helped her set the harness. Once Dickins was mounted on his horse and Willie was on board the buggy, she offered the reins to Pahto.

His hesitation was brief. He took the offer and after some bumbling trial and error drove them to the race track. Dickins was tactful enough to keep his amusement to himself.

Once at the track Willie found Daniel and Marcus where they had staked out a spot on the grassy hillside with a good view. Daniel was excited by all the race day commotion and jabbered constantly. Marcus was brooding about the morning's undignified rout and was not yet able to enjoy the proceedings. Willie asked him to tell her what had happened after they got back to the fort, but he would not.

"Willie, Major Early expects us to maintain discipline even if we are on this obscure outpost. Relaying his conversations with us back to you is out of line," Marcus said. "He expects us to behave like soldiers. There could be war soon."

Willie was taken aback. She looked quizzically at

Daniel, who shrugged.

"Marcus is in love with the major, Willie."

Daniel's remark made Willie laugh and Marcus lose his patience. He rose to his feet and stomped off toward the track. "I'm going to get a better look at the horses," he grumbled, then paused and gestured to Pahto, "Come with me, Pahto?" Again Pahto's hesitation was brief. He strode off with Marcus.

Willie sat silently then, basking in the sunshine. The crisp colors of the spring day, the festive air, the warmth of the sun on her skin washed over Willie, leaving her with a disarming contentment. Her foreboding faded like the wisps of cloud in the clear sky. Everything seemed to be as it should. Where had her turmoil gone? She heard Daniel announce he was going to fetch bread and sausages from the Chinese vendor. She basked, her arms wrapped around her knees. She could almost drift into sleep, sitting on the blanket on the hillside, watching the people, the colors, the horses anxiously pawing the starting line.

Then Early was there at her side, casually greeting Senator Dickins who was engrossed in the race.

"Afternoon, Thayer."

"Afternoon, Miles," Dickins answered without taking his attention from the track.

He did not speak, but sat beside her. Even though her heart drove red to her cheeks, she could not rouse herself from her sleepy reverie. The sun, the colors, the air gave her peace. There is a place where there is no resistance.

He pulled at the grass, absorbed, silent. He gathered a few small wild daisies—their tiny white petals tinged with violet—tied them together with a spear of grass and handed them to her. Slowly slowly, as though through dream time, with her life in her hand she reached for the flowers and looked up at him.

It was overwhelming, this thing that was happening to her. But she only wondered at the sky and his eyes being the same color.

From the track, shrieks and sudden fierce shouting shattered the moment. Early sprang to his feet. The dull crack of a gunshot quickened his pace to a run. Without breaking stride he vaulted the top rail of the track barricade and was immediately out of Willie's sight.

12

Tempers were high when Early approached the group of men. Their attention was focused on a cowboy wearing a red felt hat and waving a revolver. He was standing over Pahto who lay on the ground. Pahto was struggling to get up, but he was being restrained by three friends of the man with the gun. Marcus was there trying to extricate Pahto. The men were holding Pahto so that the man in the red hat could shoot him. They were all shouting drunkenly at Marcus that he was standing in the way of the shot.

Early moved to the center of the group. He addressed Marcus, but looked only at the cowboy brandishing the gun. "Corporal Buckner, what is going on here?"

"Pahto has been beaten, but he is all right, sir. He is not shot, but I'll feel a lot better when that jackass puts his gun away," Marcus answered.

Pahto struggled again and the men holding him delivered several more kicks to subdue him. There was more shouting between Marcus and the men.

The crowd eased back as Early stepped closer to the

staggering cowboy, never turning his eyes from him as spoke to the three who held Pahto, "You men turn loose of that Indian."

Daniel and three other troops from the fort stood with Marcus and Early now. Marcus backed the men off who had been restraining Pahto. Daniel helped him to his feet.

Early still confronted the gunman. "Put your gun away, man," Early demanded.

"That black Digger Injun touched my horse. Probably trying to poison him. They're always trying to poison something." Drunken spittle turned to froth at the corners of the cowboy's mouth.

"The horse had gotten loose, Major," Marcus said. "Pahto caught him and was leading him back when these yahoos jumped him."

"Let a white man catch him then. We don't let no Diggers touch our horses where we come from. They either want to poison 'em or eat 'em," the cowboy gained confidence as his friends gathered around him. Alcohol and hatred twisted their faces.

"Whose buck is he anyway? You let your Diggers out alone, stealing white men's property?" one of them asked.

"He was with me," Willie said and stepped from the crowd so the cowboys could see her. She had followed Daniel down to the track to see what the excitement was. She had stood in quiet horror to see what was happening to Pahto, but now she spoke up.

"He was not here alone, he came with me," Willie repeated.

Early winced visibly to hear her. The cowboys hooted as they turned their attention to her.

"Corporal, get her out of here, now!" he shouted to Marcus.

Marcus moved quickly and drew her away from the

action. Willie resisted angrily.

"Turn loose of me Marcus."

The man in the red hat yelled at her, "With you? Where we come from we don't allow white women to take up with black Diggers. We shoot 'em both." He made a move to follow her. Early moved in very close now and with a quiet hard voice said, "She's with me, he's her friend, you shut up and put your gun away."

"You don't have no authority with me."

"I have all the authority I need to deal with you. Put your gun away and take care of your horse." Early stood so close the man was forced to lean back or else lose ground. He glanced anxiously around at the number of soldiers who had gathered. He returned his gun to its holster and spat curses to cover his wobbling retreat.

The crowd dispersed. Major Early conferred with his men about the explosive situation. The day was young yet and there was much drinking ahead. If they were prepared and alert, there would be no further trouble. He wanted none of the troops visiting the drinking establishments tonight, and the watches would be doubled.

Pahto looked beat up, but moved easily and shrugged off all attentions to his well-being. Daniel and Marcus tried to walk with him back their hillside spot. He would not allow himself to be escorted, but instead walked a distance behind them. When they reached the rest of their party on the hillside Pahto did not stay near them, but sat at the top of the hill, away from everybody.

Elizabeth and Cletis had only just arrived and were eager to hear the story, which was recounted and argued. Cletis, Senator Dickins and Major Early discussed the legal and political problem of administering justice in remote settlements like this. Elizabeth was listening to Willie's angry account when Marcus interrupted her.

"But you shouldn't have gone down there, Willie. Look what you exposed yourself to. It was dangerous and you only made matters worse."

"What are you saying, Marcus? I shouldn't go there? It was the thugs who should not have been there." Her words began to stutter in her mouth. "Next you're going to tell me Pahto is responsible for getting beaten." She struck her fist against her knee in frustration. "What's wrong with you, Marcus?"

Marcus only shook his head in annoyance and moved over to join the conversation with Early and Dickins.

Willie turned puzzled to Daniel. "What was that all about?"

"I told you so," Daniel responded.

Willie's anger was not to be turned away from, however, and she raised her voice to Marcus, talking over the top of the men's conversation, clearly, without a stutter, "you are more concerned because I got yelled at by that drunk than you are because Pahto was assaulted. If it is the presence of women on the frontier that forces the removal of these abusers of the powerless, then here we are."

Marcus would not look up at her, but Early turned toward her, his manner serious. "He is right, Willie. You should be more cautious."

"If I am not safe in the same public area with those men, they should be removed, not I."

"What will happen when I am gone, Willie? When Marcus and Daniel are gone?"

Silence fell on the group. Willie's breathing was still heavy after her outburst. She was afraid she might cry. Mercifully, Elizabeth calmed into the awkward breach.

"See what I've brought! A succulent selection of leftovers from last night's going-away dinner!" Daniel brought out the sausages and bread he had bought before the melee erupted and helped Elizabeth prepare the spread. The men resumed their conversation. Willie remained tense and angry. Her right hand was clenched in a tight fist and her left hand held her arms close across her chest.

She looked to the top of the hill, but Pahto had left. Daniel put his arm around her. "He'll be all right. Come eat now. I placed a bet on this next race. Help me get my horse in." Elizabeth continued to lay out the picnic. Willie did not eat, but neither did she argue any more.

She tried to will herself to relax, not to cry. When she finally released her fist she looked down to see clutched inside a small crushed bundle of wild daisies.

13

That night she was alone in her home for the first time. In seasons past she had occasionally stayed by herself when the family had gone down below on vacation or business trips, but the tokens of their lives surrounded her then and presumed their imminent return. Now the house lay in disorder from the wrenching loose of occupants whose smells and fingerprints were all that remained.

She had so far only made this front room tidy and sat there now by the warm brick hearth. She still did not feel like eating and she worried about the raspy tightness in her throat. Was she getting sick? No, she just needed to make herself comfortable with her tea and her book. She was almost content. When her thoughts wanted to drift to Miles Early she resisted.

It hardly seems fair, she thought, to be distracted by this man I am not even sure I like and I hardly know. Is passion God's way of driving men and women from their comforting walls? Otherwise, perhaps, we would all choose solitude. I choose solitude now. Peace and contemplation. Passion has not been my friend.

In the distance she could occasionally hear the sharp reports of gunfire. Today's races had attracted men from far reaches; they were having their night in town. Troops from the fort were patrolling the camps of the reservation tonight to protect the Indians from the revelers. Marcus and Daniel would be on duty all night. Willie felt safe; the raucous activity seemed far from her haven.

But then— a stirring at the back of the house! A crash and the sound of glass breaking. The rumble of a chair overturned.

Her hand shook as she grabbed the kindling hatchet from the hearth and walked cautiously toward the noise. A dark form skittered past her and scrambled onto the sill of an open window. Her surprised scream startled the masked raccoon that looked back at her from his perch on the sill before easing back out into the night. A dish of cookie remnants lay broken on the floor, overturned by the thief.

"Good gracious!" she yelled out the window. "I like you guys fine when I see you skittering around out in the woods but not in my house." She muttered to herself, "Maybe I'll have to get myself a dog."

As she reached to close the window she saw the silhouette of a man darting out of the darkness and approaching the house. Oh, no no no, she thought. She held the hatchet in front of her and moved to the front door. The house shook with heavy boot steps on the porch. Silence. Then a knock. She opened the door.

"Miles!"

"Willie...I've startled you...I heard you yelling...I've come by to make sure you are safe."

She stood before him wild-eyed, the hatchet trembling in her hand.

"Am I?"

He stepped inside and slipped the hatchet from her hand. "You won't need this anymore." She took only one step back from him before his hand caught her waist.

The woman's sheltering veil of propriety falls with fluttering abandon when her lover's hand draws her fast to him, pulling her beneath the surface of fearful passion; she surrenders and cannot return.

In the dark hour before dawn they watched the moon drop behind the trees. While the first light of morning was still a suggestion on the horizon, she watched him dress by candlelight, draw on his boots and arrange his uniform. As she burrowed deep into her blankets and sleep, her skin still could feel the cold buttons and rough fabric of his jacket where he had held her once more before he left.

14

"Willie, honey. Willie! Wake up now." A hand was gently shaking her shoulder, bringing her out of a deep sleep.

"Elizabeth!" she said groggily. "What are you doing here?"

"Why, it's ten o'clock, honey. If you don't get moving, we'll be late for church. What is wrong with you? Are you ill?"

"No, I just overslept."

"Well, when you didn't show up for breakfast, I got worried. I thought maybe some of those good ol' boys found you down here last night, had their way and left you for dead! Turns out you are only lazy," Elizabeth laughed. "Now are you going to get ready and come with us?" She was wandering about Willie's bedroom, fiddling and straightening.

"Is Cletis with you?"

"Yes, he's waiting outside on the buckboard. I can call him in. It's just that I didn't know..." Elizabeth did not finish her sentence. She retrieved a casually discarded skirt from the floor and draped it neatly over the back of a chair.

"No, no, no," Willie said. "I'll be right out. It will just take me one minute to get ready." What is Elizabeth looking for? she thought.

Hurriedly she dressed and pinned her disheveled hair into a tight bun. She stepped out onto the porch. She hesitated for a moment, unsure of herself. The scenery had shifted somehow. Tilted.

"Come on, honey," Elizabeth called to her. Willie climbed onto the buckboard. "Are you sure you're not ill? Your cheeks are so red they almost look bruised."

"I'll be all right. I am all right, actually." She needed to get the focus of attention off of herself.

"Good morning, Cletis. Thank you for coming out for me. I'm sorry for troubling you."

"Oh, it's no trouble, Willie. I've been up since dawn." He looked at her with a one-sided smile that seemed to Willie more like a smirk. The trees tilted again. Her stomach turned.

"Yep," Cletis continued, "an Army courier arrived very early this morning. There has been fighting up north. Armed bands of Indians have been attacking settlers, they say. The troops at Fort Humboldt need reinforcement. Major Early was ordered to march north with twenty men. Marcus went with him, Daniel stayed back with my detachment. I am in charge until Lieutenant Dillon arrives, which should be later today or tomorrow."

Willie had difficulty processing this information. Her lips moved silently as she repeated the words to herself.

Elizabeth patted Willie's knee reassuringly. "He'll be back before long."

"Who will?" Willie tried not to sound desperate.

"Marcus, of course! All the men from Company D will return to Fort Bragg soon. Cletis says that since Major

Early will not be returning, Marcus will be in charge of bringing the troops back."

They arrived at the white wood-frame church. Willie sat staring at the tops of the trees waving in the spring breeze. Friends greeted them. Cletis climbed down and came around to where Willie was seated.

"Want me to help you down, Willie?" he asked.

"No." Although the day was uncommonly warm she shivered with a chill.

"I do think she is ill," Elizabeth said to Cletis. "Maybe we should take her back home."

"No, no. I'll be all right." She needed time to think. If only her head would stop spinning she could figure this out. She walked with Elizabeth into the church. Blue Feather was standing behind the pews. Why was she standing there? Neither woman smiled when their eyes met. Blue Feather must know, Willie thought.

Willie cast herself into the service, praying, trying to strike a bargain, pleading for support. So quickly she had convinced herself that Miles Early had been meant for her. A gift. She had received him. She had allowed him. But now he is gone.

The room was close and warm. Sounds clattered like shards of glass against the painted wooden walls. It was yesterday morning since she had eaten and no sleep last night. She rose with the congregation to sing, but her throat yielded no song. The singing swelled around her. It was joy to think of him. The room swirled. She thought she was slipping through the music when she fell.

She woke up in the back of the buckboard where she had been carried. Blue Feather and Elizabeth were with her. Elizabeth kept saying, "I knew she was sick." Blue Feather tried to make her comfortable and piled coats around her. The two women sat in the back with her while Cletis drove her home.

Willie lay back and closed her eyes to the blue sky and to the kind attentions of her friends.

For days she lay in her bed ill with fever and listened astonished to news of the world in upheaval. Every day the doctor brought her an elixir that he promised would make her well. He told her the same flu she had was sweeping the reservation. And every day the mail carried word of war. Fort Sumter, in the harbor of Charleston, North Carolina, had been fired on and had surrendered to forces of the newly declared Confederate States of America. Eleven states had seceded from the United States.

It was unclear to Willie what exactly the political and sectional issues were that brought the country to this impasse. It seemed to her once the high-blown phrases blew by that the issues were about commerce and money, as usual. For months the saber-rattling had been dramatic. Each side thought bravado would cause the other to back down; but now, both sides were arming themselves and mobilizing for war.

Willie had read Uncle Tom's Cabin like everybody else, but she had never seen a slave. She feared for the lives of the Negro slaves, war or no war. They're like the Indians, she thought. Powerless.

Everything made her cry.

On the evening of the sixth day of her confinement Willie was sitting up in bed, her arms wrapped around her raised knees. Blue Feather sat behind her with comb and brush, slowly working out the tangles in her hair. Elizabeth had brought a pot of soup and was heating it on the cook stove. She clanked and rattled the pots and pans as she worked and swore under her breath when she burned her finger. Whenever she spoke to Willie though, she used her cheerful sing-song voice.

"Elizabeth! Tell me!" Willie said. "What is it you are troubled about. I am quite well now. You needn't baby me."

Elizabeth needed little encouragement. "Oh, Willie! Lieutenant Dillon told us yesterday that he won't be staying here at all. He's going to San Francisco to join Major Johnson who has already resigned his commission in the United States Army in order to enlist in the Confederate Army. Have mercy on us!" Now it was Elizabeth's turn to lie sobbing on the bed while Willie soothed her.

"Dillon leaves tomorrow," Elizabeth cried. "I know Cletis will join them. What will I ever do?" Willie started crying too.

Blue Feather laughed, distracting Willie and Elizabeth.

"We are each woman with no man and no home," Blue Feather said. She giggled as though that were a fine joke. "We live in houses with no roots in land we do not belong. Our men are taken away, called away, gone away. We are alone. Indian way is—old maids starve. Now we have only each other. Some day maybe a man will come for us, but now we have only each other. We have mercy on us. We are strong woman." Blue Feather laughed some more. Elizabeth and Willie smiled at her through sniffling tears. Chuckles replaced sobs. Soon a sense of amusing absurdity infected each of them and they rolled about in helpless laughter.

Willie rose from her bed and served supper to her silly guests who knew no limit to the things they found hysterically funny.

"At least the old maids won't starve tonight," she reminded them.

By the end of their evening the muscles of their tear-streaked cheeks ached from laughing. Eventually Blue Feather returned to her own home; a sullen Cletis came for Elizabeth; and Willie climbed back into bed.

Strong woman, indeed, she thought.

Willie got well. She busied herself and filled her days.

The school session was nearing an end. The men returned from Fort Humboldt without having engaged any fighting, and without Major Early. Lieutenant Dillon left on a steamer before Willie ever got a chance to see him. Cletis prepared to leave. Marcus and Daniel argued tirelessly with him trying to convince him not to join the new Confederate Army, but to no end. Although everyone hoped the fighting would be over before Cletis even reached the battleground, a gloomy pall of war's inevitability loomed over the hopes of even the staunchest hearts.

Willie's heart ached. She knew Marcus and Daniel also would be called back east if the fighting was not over soon. Cletis insisted that Elizabeth move to San Francisco while he was gone. She had people there. Would Willie stay on here alone if they all left? Old friends, old alliances—even the threat of her losing them all paled before her secret grief over a man she had only recently met and lost.

She was both sad and relieved when her monthly time came. She washed the soft cotton cloth rags she used to tend her flow and hung them in a sunny spot behind the house, wondering at her hunger.

15

She leaned into her tasks. She made bread daily. The Bokaima women no longer had access to the type of acorns they needed to gather, store and grind for the meal, mush and acorn flour bread that had long been their staple food. However, they all took a liking to wheat flour bread. It was Willie's pride to meticulously maintain her sharp-flavored sourdough starter and contribute her bread to the Bokaima food stores. In turn the Bokaima brought in fish and abalone and shellfish that they shared with her.

Willie was diligent with her vegetable garden this spring. She spent long hours with her hands in the soil. It was a small but promising garden even though she had to share it with the deer and gophers.

She took long walks hoping to leave her emotional turmoil out there on the shore for the brusque ocean breeze to sweep away. Often she was gone for hours, returning tongue-tied and avoiding conversation with others.

This morning she walked along the bluffs above of the sea, watching for the arrival of the Golden Rule into the harbor. Captain Iversen would be bringing the vegetable seeds she had ordered. He had promised that he personally was going to pick them up for her.

She did not spot the Golden Rule in the harbor yet so she continued her walk north along the coastline for miles, fording small creeks and climbing ridges. It was the first hot day of the year, unseasonably warm for May.

When she returned midday she saw that the schooner had arrived. She headed to Elizabeth's house. Perhaps Elizabeth would want to go down to the harbor with her to pick up the mail.

Willie knocked at the door and let herself in. She thought for a moment she had entered the wrong home when she saw a stranger smiling at her from the kitchen table; but then she heard Elizabeth talking from the other room, and there was Cletis at the table too. The stranger stood and bowed in an elaborate welcome and greeted Willie as though she were his guest. Cletis didn't look up. Willie thought he was supposed to have left by now. She was definitely not prepared to talk to Cletis, let alone this stranger. She hung back, still gripping the door handle. She felt foolish but could think of nothing to say.

The man stood grinning at her. Sunlight from the window set a glow to a cap of blond curls. Elizabeth came in and introduced them. He was Rune Kalevala. He was delighted to meet her. Delighted. His enthusiasm did not put Willie at ease. The fullness of his white sleeve fluttered in another grand sweep as he kissed the back of her hand. Willie withdrew her hand and tried to hide it in the folds of her skirts.

Elizabeth watched the man adoringly. Cletis looked bored with the company. He was engrossed packing his gear and cleaning his guns.

"Rune is an old friend of Major Early's," Elizabeth told

Willie. "He saw Major Early last month in Eureka and has come down from there thinking he'd find Miles here. I told him we don't expect the Major to return."

"Mr. Kalevala. I...I've enjoyed your stories," Willie tried to swallow her stutter. "And Major Early spoke well of you."

"And of you," he laughed.

Willie retreated further into the shadows of the doorway and turned the door handle ready to flee.

"Willie!" Elizabeth's voice scolded her awkwardness. Elizabeth turned to Rune with an apologetic explanation. "I'm afraid there is no love lost between Miss Jackson and Major Early."

Rune put his hands on his hips, white sleeves billowing. "Unbelievable!" he declared.

At the table sitting alone, Cletis shook his head cynically and downed his glass of ale. Elizabeth tried to bring Willie in to join them, but she declined.

"No, no. I am on my way to the schooner. It has just arrived. I'm awaiting a packet of seeds. I've been walking. It is very warm in here." Sweat glistened on her brow. She ducked her head and muttered, "Good to have met you, Mr...." Wait, breathe, "Mr. Kalevala," and rushed out of the house.

Elizabeth ran out right behind her and walked with her to the harbor.

"Oh oh oh. Now. Now I see it," Elizabeth was saying half to herself half to Willie. "Unbelievable, indeed. Right under my nose and I was ignorant of the whole thing. No wonder you were so miserable. Have mercy on us. How could you let yourself be taken in by him, honey?"

"I thought we were...he would...oh, I don't know. I don't know." Willie shook her head. She could not find the sense to it and resisted any further conversation. When they got to the schooner, Elizabeth picked up her mail, embraced

Willie and returned home to her guest.

Captain Iversen had brought Willie the seeds. There was also a letter from her mother in the mail. She read it as she walked home, happy to hear the news. Even her mother's advice on how Willie should dress when she came to the city to visit made Willie smile.

… therefore, Wilhemina, you see there are no young ladies of good standing here who live alone and run around freely with Indians and play cards in saloons. In the City you must always wear a hat and not let your hair escape. We live in a fine neighborhood where good families have settled. Oh, I must tell you that Major Early came to call on us twice. He seemed ill at ease, but there were other guests here both times so we couldn't really visit with him alone. I know you don't like him much, but he seems a good man. I can't think why he called on us. He sat silently for the most part and only talked when the conversation turned to the war. He is very concerned about the fighting back east, as is your father. Such a terrible thing, that war. If you need anything, please call on Pastor Justus and Annalee. They will take care of you. You are in our prayers. With love, Mother.

Oh, my heart, why do you betray me? She finished the letter under the welcoming shade of her porch. Her dress was wet through with sweat from her vigorous walk. Escaped hair fell loose in damp ringlets. She grabbed the lower back hem of her skirt and pulled it through between her legs, drew it all the way up and tucked it into her belt, fashioning a rude functional pair of gardening trousers. She opened the small boxes of seeds and lost herself in the planting, the afternoon sun and the soft sounds of her garden.

She did not look up when she heard a horse and rider arrive out of her vision at the front of the house. She knew who it would be, but what was she to do? She kept her hands in the warm earth. She did not even look up when he stood next to her or when he lowered himself to sit on the heels of his black polished boots, the knees of his ever-so-clean uniform hovering just above the freshly cultivated soil.

Her breath gasped. Tears fell on the ground and stayed in little powdery droplets a moment before they broke and soaked into the earth. She erased their traces with her dirt-caked fingertips.

"It's good soil, just a little dry," she explained.

"You knew I was coming back."

Had she known that? Perhaps she had. But she'd had no comfort of certainty.

"I was afraid," she said. She was frightened now and could not look up or stop planting.

"I know Willie, but I'm here now. I had to go to the Presidio to arrange a personal extended leave. Don't be afraid anymore, Willie."

The time spent waiting for him when the yearning was not sweet left her without protection.

"I have no skin anymore," she told him.

"I'll be your skin," he answered.

Her box of seeds tipped and spilled. His knees sank into the soft earth as he gathered her into his arms. Her tears were sweet and his arms were grand. Their passion rattled the sky.

Spring rains fell on the freshly turned soil. Moisture soaked through the hard dry walls of the waiting seeds and seeped into the dormant grooves of thirsty proteins that needed only to bind water to themselves to become life.

The next day the Reverend Justus officiated, Rune and Elizabeth stood beside them, surprised but happy friends celebrated, and Miles Randall Early and Wilhemina Jackson were married.

16

With June came the summer fog. Often the sun broke through midday, but usually a low cool fog began and ended the day.

Lieutenant Orlando Moore came to assume command of the fort. He consulted frequently with Major Early at first, but the summer was quiet and few demands were made on the soldiers. In the immediate area there were no major hostilities between the whites and Indians. The native people confined to the camps were allowed more freedom to tend their own needs as they could. Some small family bands quietly left the reservation to try to return to their homelands. Two tribes were transferred inland to the Nome Cult reservation. The shortage of blankets and warm clothing was less critical during the summer months.

Elizabeth and Cletis left for San Francisco. Elizabeth was bitter and unhappy about the move and about Cletis leaving her for the war.

"I don't think his joining the Confederate Army and going off to war has much to do with his love for the

South. He's just tired of being cooped up with me," Elizabeth confided to Willie. "I do not want to be left alone in San Francisco. But he won't listen to me."

"He might have had to go even if he hadn't decided to join the Confederates right away. Miles still might have to go if they don't settle this thing soon. I can't think of it."

"Things change pretty fast around here! You have to keep on your toes. They say that soon a telegraph line will be finished from the east coast all the way to California."

"I think that's just so they can run their war better." Willie was cynical about the motives behind the war preparations. "I am still hoping the country's leaders will come to their senses and settle the conflicts. Miles says the southern states are foolhardy to declare war on the United States, which has more men, more money, more industry, more railroads. People are going to be hurt and the southern states can't possibly win. It is irresponsible of them to start a war!"

"Cletis says the states have the right to run their own affairs, and it is only because of the superior strength of the northern states that the disputes haven't been settled peacefully. The Northerners think they don't have to. But they don't know how determined the people of the South are. If it comes to all-out war, it will be the fault of the North!" Elizabeth became indignant explaining the southern position. A chilling silence fell between the women.

They were sitting on packed moving crates in Elizabeth's house, waiting for the men to help with the loading. Dismayed by the specter of enmity between them, both women stared at the sunlight filtering through the swirling dust they had stirred up in the upheaval of packing.

"I love you, Lizzie," Willie said quietly.

"I love you too, honey."

And so it came that Willie stood once more on the landing, bidding farewell to a loved one.

Miles and Willie stayed close to home. Except for day-to-day interchanges around the homestead with their Bokaima neighbors, and except for regular visits from Daniel, Marcus and Rune—when the five friends grappled with the problems left to them by a changing world or else laughed and played cards late into the night—Miles and Willie kept to themselves for the most part that June. They knew their time together was short.

School was on summer recess. Rune left for San Francisco at the end of June. Marcus and Daniel played cards at Pink's more now. Willie and Miles were content alone.

Summer poured honey-like over days they spent in pastimes of planting and pruning, cooking and dreaming; and they were never far from their curtained bedroom. Summer was their backdrop, the canvas for the colors their passion used to paint each moment. They studied one another—every smell, gesture, resonance. They memorized the curves and lines of their bodies lying together.

"I no longer have any substance," Willie said.

"You feel substantial to me," Miles responded as he let his hand trace her body.

"Only because you envelope me." Her lips touched his as she spoke. She breathed his sweet warm breath. "Your breath is my breath."

But when his hands became demanding, and in the deepest reaches of her being his fingers and lips sought the source of her passion—even substance, skin, and breath surrendered.

"I'm falling," she gasped.

"I'll catch you," he murmured as he drew her further. In the fierce intensity of the moment she could still feel him, she could still feel herself, but then her breath suspended, substance was molten, her body trembled in his hands and flew away.

Finally Willie lay motionless, small sounds escaping her throat as her voice strained to return across the vast distance. Miles held her and softly kissed her ear, her neck.

"I flew away."

"Yes."

"Does my heart still beat?"

"I think so."

"You are my heart."

He stroked her belly, her hips. His kisses turned urgent once more and covered her mouth, her throat, her breasts. And then he was inside her. They flowed together as one flesh. From time to time he drew away to watch her, and then he entered her again and again every place her body could receive him. She was drunk with him and there were no limits.

17

As the weeks passed, Willie grew fragile. She cried at any mention of the news of the great irrevocable war machine moving into place. She asked Miles over and over why he must go if they called him.

"I'm a soldier, Willie. This is war. Soldiers haven't many options in time of war." He never talked to her about the horror of war, but she could see the heaviness of his face whenever they came close to the subject. It was true that he could not see his duty with the same clarity as he had in the past. How could she get on up here alone, without him? he wondered. She shifted swiftly between joy and sorrow. He could not be sure she would not shatter when he left her.

Abruptly truth was born out. They were at a Fourth of July picnic at the church grounds when Willie lost everything she had eaten, vomiting unceremoniously. Miles was shuffled aside as the ladies gathered around and led Willie inside the church where it was cool.

When Annalee Justus stepped back out she announced proudly as though it were her doing, "Congratulations, Major, the good Lord has surely blessed you."

It was not that it was difficult for him to regain his composure as he moved through the women's faces, but he could not remember ever being so nervous. He found Willie lying on a pew hovered over by the women. They retreated when he approached.

He held her as she wept, laughed, wept again.

"Oh, dear. Oh, dear. How can anyone be so happy and so scared at the same time?" Willie asked.

Annalee's words echoed in his ear. The irony of the good Lord's timing stunned him. Willie is with child, he thought. How can I leave her now.

More gentle and sweeter yet their days together became. Willie slept late and Miles tried to prepare food her stomach could tolerate. One morning early before she rose he slipped away to pick up a special shipment he was expecting on the schooner.

The August sun filled the kitchen when he returned to fix her a small breakfast. He brought her honeyed tea and peeled segments of the juicy orange fruit she had only heard rumors of.

"A few years ago when I was stationed near the Pueblo of Los Angeles I spent some time with an interesting man, German fellow, William Wolfskill, who was planting acres of orchards of sweet Valencia oranges. I heard they can now be found in the markets of San Francisco, so I sent for some." He pulled the crinkly packing tissue off another piece of golden fruit and peeled it for her.

"Ah, look at the beautiful picture on the crate! Does it really look like that where these came from."

"It probably does now. It was mostly sheep ranches when I was there. Wolfskill only had twenty acres in. I understand now there are thousands and thousands of acres of orange groves, tended by rosy-cheeked girls just like the girl in the picture who pick the fruit and pack them in tissue just for you."

Miles watched Willie eat four oranges. "Those seem to suit you, my love, but I only got one crate. It will never last the week at that rate!"

Willie laughed and reached her arm around him to thank him with orange-flavored kisses when her hand felt the edges of an envelope crammed in his back pocket.

"Oh! You picked up mail? Let's see." She reached around him for the envelope. Miles grabbed her hand and prevented her from taking the letter. When she tried to protest he quieted her.

They made love with desperation and abandon, the taste of oranges mingling with the taste of their love. Later as they lay still in one another's arms she did not ask to see the letter. She turned her head from him and stared with hopeless eyes at the wallpaper she had helped her mother hang years before. Miles brushed the hair back from her face. Her skin was ashen and blotchy. He knew that now she wanted nothing to do with the letter. Wanted it not to be.

Miles spoke softly. He told of events so far away and so grim he felt like a bully tormenting a child with a cruel story, a parable of evil. Curtained sunlight flickered in her eyes.

"There has been a battle near a creek called Bull Run, in Manassas, Virginia. The federal forces were overrun and retreated, apparently in disarray, to Washington. The troops are green and untrained. There were three or four thousand men killed. I think it is clear now the war will not be over so soon as many hoped. The Confederacy will be even more determined now and won't be easily discouraged. I am ordered back immediately and must leave tomorrow.

"Marcus and Daniel will probably be called back east

soon. They are on active duty and there is little need for regular army here. No doubt the fort can be manned by state militia. I do wish you would reconsider and move down to Frisco to be with your folks. You could even stay with Elizabeth."

He felt helpless, unable to offer her either solace or protection. Never before had his training as a soldier been so dangerously eroded; nonetheless these orders especially could not be disregarded. He would leave in the morning. All he could do now was hold her, his lips salty with her tears, and watch the light dull in her eyes.

Willie sat rocking on the front porch in the afternoon sun while Miles packed to leave. His activity was distant and dreamlike to Willie. She felt too weak to understand what was happening. Her prayers were pleas for strength.

Is there some message here? she thought. Some lesson I am to learn?

In the night she lay sleepless. The room was stuffy and she could not catch a clear breath. The more she tried not to thrash about, the more her muscles twitched. With every movement she made he muttered small sounds in his sleep and drew her closer to him.

Eventually she slipped from under his arm and walked outside in the moonlight. The warm still air was tense with crackling starlight. The dust of the roadway glowed with an eerie phosphorescence. Her heart's desire to hold heavy to him so that he could not possibly leave was muted and humbled out here. Fate and will at cross purposes was only tiring. Not all the cards were played yet. Something more was at stake.

I give him into your charge, God. But then return him to me.

She went back inside and lay easily with him until the morning. She studied his breathing and smelled his warmth and did not move.

Neither of them saw Pahto watching from the dawn shadows as Miles mounted Slats and rode south, taking the overland route to San Francisco.

18

The first few months passed well enough. It was not until November that orders were received that the infantry company at Fort Bragg should embark on the steamer Columbia and report to the Presidio. From there they would be sent to the escalating war in the east. Until now Willie had harbored hope that Miles would return soon. This removal of all regular army units on the west coast dashed those hopes.

Marcus and Daniel tried to see to her winter stores before they left and they laid in a supply of dry firewood for her. The three friends spent their last evenings together. Late night poker games in Pink's back room had been abandoned. Marcus and Daniel were too distracted by their orders; and Willie's condition left her feeling too awkward and sleepy for such adventures.

But soon these two old friends were gone too. Letters were her only connection with them all. Mail from Miles came regularly at first. Throughout the winter her family and Elizabeth continued to implore her to come to them in San Francisco. By spring they gave it up. There was a new staff of reservation employees who oversaw the hospital clinic; she was not needed they made clear. She taught school until her baby boy was born and she was replaced by Annalee Justus.

Willie went with Blue Feather to church each Sunday, but Willie's visits with her friends in town grew less and less frequent. She immersed herself in the care of her son. Round Face Woman wove a baby carrier for him. Willie often kept him in the basket snugly wrapped and propped up close to her while she worked around the house and garden or carried on her back when she took her walks.

Willie named the boy Alexander, but Old Chief called him Little Coyote.

Willie was becoming fluent enough in the Bokaima language to gossip along with the women as they attended their domestic chores. She achieved the invisibility of acceptance.

She loved to listen to the old stories about the sun and the moon, the fish and the animals, the rocks and the plants. They told stories to explain beginnings and endings, celebrations and taboos. They told her of the man who left the circle of his people and was turned into a bear. Only because he made a passion walk of great distance and danger and solitude could he be redeemed and turned back into a man and rejoin the people.

Their stories wove in and out of their conversation while the roots and reeds and fibers wove in and out of the patterns of their baskets.

"I think women's art thrives in peacetime," Willie theorized to Blue Feather one day. "Men's art does not seem greatly hindered by war. They write and paint dramatic works about war. They can even write war music. But women's art, like these baskets, relies on the stability and peacefulness of the family and the tribe."

"I do not know," Blue Feather responded. "I do not know about war, but I see we have fewer young girls helping with the weaving now." Sometimes Willie carried on about things for which Blue Feather had little concern. Things that were too abstract to worry about.

They were in the sun working together with the other women. Old Chief played with Alexander. Willie and Blue Feather were speaking in English, giving their conversation privacy even in the midst of the talkative group.

"You see how Old Chief takes care of the baby. We have had no baby here in a long time. Sun Ray carries a child now but has no husband. On the reservation there is much disease of the babies."

Willie found the matter depressing. Venereal disease had taken a toll among the reservation people. Influenza and small pox had killed more of them, but venereal disease sickened and crippled them and their babies were born dead or marked. The situation at the reservation had turned grievous once again. Agent Reasoner had been replaced. The entire operation fell into disrepair. The state militia that manned the fort consorted with the worst elements of the town and were sympathetic to their animosity towards the Indians.

Suddenly Pahto broke into her somber thoughts. He had approached unseen and said to Willie in Bokaima, "Headman is gone."

"Miles? Yes, you know Miles is gone."

"Forever?"

"No, not forever."

"Yes, forever. It is not good that he is gone."

"Not forever, Pahto. He will come home."

Pahto's eyes were hard, angry. "The soldiers here now are not good." His next words were spoken so fast they were unintelligible to Willie. She shook her head to express puzzlement, but Pahto walked away rapidly. He paused next to Old Chief and lowered himself to sit on his haunches. He dangled a trinket in front of Alexander and talked to him in the cooing language all babies understand. A smile softened the hard lines of Pahto's face. As he rose to leave he looked back at Willie. His look accused her. She lost sight of him in the shadows of the corral.

Fear sent a chill over her skin to hear his anger toward Miles and see his fondness for Alexander. "What did he say, I couldn't understand," she asked Blue Feather in English.

"He said headman has dishonored us. Major Early abandoned us here even though his soldiers made promises of our safety. The white men take Indian girls for their wives and then throw them out. Children are being stolen. Pahto thinks these things would not happen if Major Early had not left. He wants Old Chief to forbid me to go to church any longer. I try to tell him of the peace my faith has given me, but he thinks it is a bad spirit that draws me away."

The next spring Willie read newspaper accounts of two men who were arrested for stealing and selling Indian children. The men were fined one hundred dollars each and turned loose. The children had been taken to work in the new fields and orchards of southern California. Packing orange crates? Willie wondered.

Alexander grew and thrived but only knew of his father from the stiffly-posed photographs Willie kept close at hand. When his hair grew and fell in blond tumbles into his eyes she trimmed it and sent a lock to Miles.

It seemed the months flowed in a turbid current into years. Willie was pulled along by circumstances that she had little control over. Death, war, cruelty, hunger and sickness surrounded her.

She clutched the remnants of clarity that time left her. She could rock Alexander on the front porch in the bent rosy light of sunset or listen to him talk to himself self-absorbed in play near her while she worked in her garden. She could write to Miles in the late evening when Alexander slept and read her letters from him until the pages wore thin and tattered. During these moments she knew their love wove a connection that overcame time and distance between them. At those times her melancholia tasted more romantic than tragic.

Other times she was paralyzed by fears that she and Alexander were too isolated for her to keep them safe from easily supposed dangers or that Miles would be wounded or killed. News from the east horrified her with its accounts of thousands killed in battle.

19

Pahto fell into the company of young men at the reservation who refused to work for the white men. Many of their brothers and cousins had settled into jobs at one of the mills or the local farms, but Pahto and his new friends would not.

Pahto assumed a patronizing role with Willie and would not acknowledge either requests or offers from her. When she felt Pahto was endangering Alexander by putting him on a horse when he was too young, Pahto ignored her protests. In frustration she appealed to Old Chief to whose authority Pahto reluctantly deferred. Pahto backed off on interfering with Alexander but still kept close contact with him. In all other areas he never yielded, though he was protective of Willie and the boy and made certain they were provided with an ample share of the catch of his hunting and fishing.

In July of 1863, Willie read newspaper accounts of forty-thousand men killed during the battle of Gettysburg and twenty-thousand during the Siege of Vicksburg in Mississippi.

She knew Miles was not with the Army of the Potomac at Gettysburg but was serving in the Union's Army of the West. She had not heard from him since early spring. There had been fighting at Vicksburg since December and the town had been under siege from May to July Fourth. Even though the letter she finally received from him in late July was written from the outskirts of Vicksburg where he was camped with his regiment, he made no mention of the brutal fighting.

Seventh July, 1863
My Darling Willie,
It has been some time since I have been able to get mail out. I know you must have worried. I want you to know that the men who serve under me are good and brave men and I have much confidence in them. I tell you this so that you can be assured to know I am in a strong situation.

We are under the command now of Tecumseh Sherman. I have spoken to you of him before. I visited him and his family often when he was a banker in San Francisco and I was stationed at the Presidio. I like him, Willie. He hates the war as much as I do. He is deeply resentful of the men whose "trivial gallantry," as he calls it, brought us to it. His objective is constantly to avoid the loss of the lives of his men, and would rather outmaneuver the enemy than engage in battle. He is good at this. He is also very good in battle. He has grown hard and bitter though as the war drags on. The Rebs should by all means give it up now. The defeats they have suffered this summer have left them badly beaten without resources or manpower sufficient to give them any hope of victory. The capture of Vicksburg has split the Confederate territory in two. But still they resist and fight on. It seems every man, woman and child of the South wishes this thing to continue. I fear General Sherman's men harbor a bitterness that will visit great grief on the South.

I am sorry to read in your letters that the militia at the fort do so little to alleviate the problems there. I can understand Pahto's frustration. The federal armies are here freeing slaves of one race while his people are abused or sold into slavery themselves. I don't know what you can do for them at this point. Write to the governor or to Senator Dickins. Can your father help? Implore Pahto not to antagonize the men in power at the reservation or the fort. He does not understand the power of the forces they can throw against him. I don't think there are any real winners in war. Once unleashed, the warrior in men is not always honorable and has already convinced himself the enemy is not his brother. You must work for peaceful resolutions, Willie.

I see the plight of the women and children here left behind by their men folk who have gone off to fight. They are at the mercy of merciless men who tromp unhindered through their countryside. You must keep safe, my loves. I am counting on it.

I carry the silvery blond lock of hair of our son under the cover of my pocket watch. You say he has eyes the color of mine, but his hair must be fine like yours. I dream of kissing his rosy cheeks. I think I might go mad if I cannot come to you. I may never be able to make it up to you for this loneliness, but I promise you once I touch you again I will never leave. If I could lie with you, fill my head with the smell of you, put my hands on you, I could start to mend the broken places in our hearts. Do not be lost in despair, my love.

I send along a book I purchased in Vicksburg for Alexander and a photograph of me taken by a newspaper photographer traveling with Sherman's army. I hear that Rune also is traveling as a correspondent with the Army of the West, but I have not been able to meet up with him yet.

Kiss the boy for me. With love, Miles

She read the letter by light from the fire in the hearth. Miles had written it by the light of a campfire nearly three thousand miles away.

General Grant's army had scattered the Confederate forces who stood between him and Vicksburg. The countryside lay wasted. The people were without food or resources. Colonel Early's regiment kept the supply lines open to the Union forces, but they also had to see that no supplies reached the people of the South.

Early saw impoverished farmers whose families wore clothing made of rugs and curtains and ate their mules. He could do nothing to help them. Even with their economy shattered, the people passionately supported the Southern war effort. Their yielding was unlikely. Surrender unthinkable. Early saw the faces of his loved ones in the gaunt features of these sturdy people. He wanted to force them to give up so that he could return home to his own family. Could the situation Willie and Alex face be as grim as what these people suffer? Could Willie keep Alex warm? Did they have food? Were they threatened with armed oppressors? He knew Willie would not tell him if their trouble was grave. He was too far away to help them. He was left with crippling worry.

Union forces had besieged Vicksburg for six weeks. The city had been under constant artillery bombardment while many civilians hid in caves. The beleaguered Confederate garrison finally surrendered on the Fourth of July, the day after the South's defeat at Gettysburg. Within a week, the North controlled the Mississippi River. The South was indeed split in two.

Colonel Early's men, weary of camping in the soggy marshland north of Vicksburg, cheered what they hoped were the final victories of the war. But the South dug in. The

Union troops grew bitter with hatred against Confederate supporters—warmongers who kept them in this desolate place, separated from their loved ones and the green fields of home.

During this time of regrouping and recovery after Vicksburg fell Early sought out Marcus and Daniel. It took little maneuvering to have them transferred to his regiment. General Sherman relied heavily on the security of his supply routes in his tactical planning. Colonel Early became an important member of Sherman's staff. Sergeants Buckner and Finn were happy to join Sherman and Early.

As they sat outside Early's command tent, he asked if either Marcus or Daniel had any word of Cletis' whereabouts in the Confederate armies.

"No," Marcus said, "and we've asked anyone we've come into contact with, Reb or Yank, who might know. But we've heard nothing."

"Elizabeth wrote me a letter from San Francisco," Daniel said, "but she didn't mention which unit he was in, even if she did know. I got the feeling he hadn't been writing to her, to tell the truth."

Both of them had received letters from Willie and shared Miles' concern for her situation. "It doesn't seem right we're down here trying to get these southern folks to treat their Negro people right and we've left Indians to be mistreated worse back home," Daniel mused.

"I don't see the coloreds being treated real fine up north either, Daniel." Marcus was a Virginian by birth.

"Yeah, I know of very few abolitionists in the Union Army," Miles said. "A lot of these generals have got to claim they're for freeing the slaves, but they don't care. Lot of the boys fighting in the front lines don't even know what they're doing here. They just want to bring Johnny Reb to his knees so they can go home. They're real mad about having to be here, and the people of the South are who they're mad at. It's not good. Someday this war will be over and it will be difficult to go forward with brothers we were just shooting at."

"When we get back home..." Daniel could not finish. The rest of his thought drifted with the smoke of the campfire. He called the West "back home" and that is how each thought of it now. They too dreamed the American dream of a better life in the golden West. If only they could return. They talked by the fire late into the night telling each other the names of the many men they had known who were already fallen in this bloody war. Voices from surrounding campfires grew quiet. Marcus discarded the chewed remnant of his cigar to sizzle on the embers of the fire. The three men sat in silence, content in their friendship bonded by the memory of a distant place and the woman they all loved.

20

Alexander was walking now and had free run of the rancheria. As he became too heavy for Willie to carry along on her long walks or when she walked into town for supplies, he was looked after by Blue Feather and Round Face Woman. Sun Ray's new baby was nearly old enough to play with him.

Poverty gripped the reservation during the winter of 1863. More tribes were transferred inland to the Nome Cult reservation. Only those remaining families who had someone with a job were able to hang on. Others were driven to begging, prostitution or starvation.

Many of the staff who were left in charge of the remains of the reservation had settled on reservation land and were farming for themselves. They took Indian women as their wives, two or three at a time—women who had no place to go, women who were grateful to be taken in by a white man. They could not know the land they worked for him had been placed in trust by the federal government expressly for Indians like them. They did not know the source of money used to finance the planting of his crops had been siphoned from federal funds allocated for agricultural development for displaced native tribes.

The lumber mills thrived and Fort Bragg was becoming a wide-open boom town. Many families profited from the boom—farmers, retailers, ranchers—but swindlers and outlaws were also attracted to the area. Saloons flourished. None of this activity was of any help to the Indians whose numbers grew fewer and fewer. Townspeople found the pathetic condition of the Indians distressing and petitioned government officials to have them removed somewhere else. There was no longer any useful purpose to the reservation. Willie heard rumors that the fort would be permanently abandoned by next fall.

At the Jackson rancheria, the winter stores were slim but adequate. It was a long lean winter. Willie received an allotment check from the government as support for the family of an officer. She saved as much as she could for the seed money the farm would need in the spring.

As soon as spring tempted the air, Willie and the Bokaima fell to their planting with enthusiasm. Willie could lose her fears in the work of the day, in the comfort of the tribe, in the promise of the dry seed in the cold ground, in a letter from Miles. Generous sunsets over the ocean glowed warm on the garden. But their hope and planting was premature. The weather would not be so easily ignored. A menacing storm drove the pink from the sky. Thick clouds poured rain for days.

Willie and Alex stayed inside. Blue Feather would pick her way across the muddy yard to check in on them and take Alex to play with Sun Ray's children, but otherwise Willie saw no one. She read to Alex until he fell asleep at night. And then she was alone with her letters, her thoughts.

Late one night during the worst of the storm she stared out the window at the deep night and startled herself when her own reflection stared back at her. She laughed at herself. When there was a break in the rain she stepped out onto the porch. The clouds had pulled back their cover and stars clamored through making up for lost time with their brilliance. It made Willie smile. In the deep night under a stormy sky, the electric air a warm breath on her skin, it was easy to feel close to Miles. The simplicity of his love comforted her. The troubles of the world seemed as thin as the layer of light cast on the rain puddles from the lamp at her writing desk. She turned back inside to her desk where his letters lay and sought his touch in the ink strokes penned in his precise hand.

The Jackson rancheria was battered by the storm. Their supplies, already scant, were now decimated. They relied on the poached game and fishing catches of the young men who lived on the edges of the rancheria. These were Pahto's new companions, men whose tribes were scattered, lost, killed off. Men who stayed out of reach of the whites.

Young Jack was from a Pomo tribe south and east of Bokaima territory that spoke a language related to Bokaima. Long Tree was from an unrelated tribe from the north. His language made no sense to any of them. He was taller and thinner than Young Jack's people or the Bokaima. He was strong and owned a gun and a horse. Young Jack and Long Tree had been rounded up with other single Indian men to be moved to a ranch near Benicia where they would serve as laborers. The two young men escaped and found refuge at the Jackson rancheria and a comrade in Pahto. They stayed in the earth-covered dance house that they had built out of sight of the main compound of the rancheria or any passersby.

Willie only saw glimpses of these men from time to time. They had nothing to do with her. But she knew they were there. She also knew when others came to the dance house and stayed through the night. She could hear them singing until day broke. During daylight hours when they were not hunting, their time was spent gambling or repairing weapons.

Willie had learned many of the games of chance the Bokaima played. Round Face Woman was deft at throwing the dice-stones. She and Willie played often during breaks in the day's chores. Blue Feather sometimes joined them, but her heart was not in it. Old Chief was sorry when he played with them because he usually lost to his wife.

Except for Alexander who anchored her world and the Bokaima who accepted her as a beloved outsider, Willie was alone these days. She retreated to an isolation that came to encompass her life. She avoided leaving the house to go into town. Her conversations with the townspeople seemed garbled to her. Words she grasped to express herself escaped and tumbled into some meaning of their own, leaving her with a pounding pulse and a desire to flee. She could see confused looks of concern and perhaps pity on the faces of old friends, but she only wanted to escape back home and stay put. She had projects to keep her busy and to keep her mind occupied. And Alex, of course. She maintained for his sake. One is only as brave as one is afraid. Her love for the boy and her passion for his welfare were greater even than her fears. She could always be strong for him.

And so she was brave. When Alexander became sick during a late hard frost that set in after the rains, she stayed awake by his bedside day and night. When she went outside to fetch wood, the frozen mud puddles were brittle under her feet, but a fresh stash of dry firewood lay in the shed where Pahto and his friends had stacked it without a word to her.

Alex rested peacefully as long as he knew she was there, though sometimes when he was half-awake he talked fever gibberish and thought crickets were in his bed. She fixed him tea made from dandelion roots. Blue Feather burned

angelica in his room. His little body looked frail when she
removed his night shirt to bathe his skin with cool water and
a tincture of lobelia.

On the third night the fever passed. Blue Feather, who
had been hovering about fixing meals and offering in vain to
watch Alex while Willie slept, went home. Willie took the boy
into her bed so she could be sure to hear him if he needed her
in the night. He lay in her arms. As she crossed heavily into
sleep, a dream wrapped around the knocking at the door,
trying to answer it without turning loose of the dreamer.
Finally the pounding pulled Willie back into consciousness.
She rose hurriedly, struggling to clear her head as she opened
the door.

"Elizabeth!"

21

Willie slept through until noon the next day. She woke to the sound of Alexander chatting amiably with Elizabeth. He was sitting on the hearth in the kitchen where Elizabeth was preparing his lunch.

"I threw up on my mother."

"You look like you are feeling much better now."

"I was very sick. I threw up on my mother."

"You are hungry now."

"I always wanted a sandwich like this. My mother would like to have a sandwich like this."

"She was up for a long time when she was taking care of you. I am glad she is sleeping now."

"Sometimes my mother doesn't talk."

"Ah-ha. Well, sometimes you talk a lot, don't you."

"My mother lets me."

After Willie and Elizabeth's tearful reunion last night, Willie went right back to bed and slept soundly. She joined Elizabeth and Alexander now in the kitchen.

"Goodness, Alex, listen to you! You must be feeling

better," Willie said.

"I ate all my sandwich. Now I'm tired."

"A little nap for you and you can talk to Aunt Lizzie when you wake up." Willie carried him to his bed.

The two women sat together over coffee. As Elizabeth began to relax, Willie could see how upset she was. Her face was drawn and colorless. She had been a week trying to get here from San Francisco. The winds and rough seas had hindered her passage. Trying to make safe harbor was difficult. The schooner grounded outside the harbor near the mouth of Big River at Mendocino.

"We were horribly frightened being tossed around like so much flotsam and jetsam. It was very loud. When we finally crashed onto a sand bar in the bay, we were relieved at first. But then of course we thought we would sink and drown. It was dreadful! Some very brave men came out for us on fishing boats and ferried us to shore. That was scary, but we all got ashore safely thanks to those men. Lord have mercy!"

"Was anyone hurt? What happened to the schooner?"

"No one was hurt, though their stomachs might take some time to recover. The schooner is probably lost. It was taking a beating." Elizabeth threw her head back and covered her face with her hands. "Oh! I will never, never again go out into that dreadful ocean."

"Overland is no picnic," Willie reminded her.

"Oh, no! You're right about that. Then they brought us overland from Mendocino to here. That was harrowing too. Mercy! How far could it be from here to Mendocino as the crow flies, six or seven miles? But that road meanders along the bluffs, down the ridges to ford how many streams, back up the opposite ridge, meander some more. Mercy. It took us all day." Her face quivered. Tears welled in her eyes.

"One can scarcely call it a road in most places," Willie

sympathized. "You have had an adventure. Think how happy I am you are safe and you are here."

"I was afraid I would never get away."

"Get away?" Willie asked. Elizabeth dropped her head to her arms and sobbed out the story. Willie listened. The afternoon passed. Elizabeth talked and cried, talked and cried. Alex woke, played, ate again and went back to bed. Willie hardly had time to appreciate his recovery as she turned to tend her distraught friend.

Elizabeth told of her life in San Francisco and of her new friends. They were carefree and gay and filled their drawing rooms with laughter. It was a relief for Elizabeth to forget about her neglectful young husband thousands of miles away.

"I was lonely. The men thought I was beautiful. One man especially wanted me. It was good to be wanted again. Needed. By the time I learned he was a Confederate deserter it was too late to leave him. He did things to me, Willie. Things I never knew a man could do to a woman. He made me do things. Things. I couldn't stop. He didn't seem sophisticated and romantic anymore. He was afraid and he made me afraid."

"What was he afraid of?"

"Dead men. He had horrible nightmares. He thought they were coming for him. He thought he was still there, at the battle he had run away from. He can hear his friends calling him back. But they were all killed and he can't wash their blood from his vision. He seldom slept, but the dreams chased him even when he was awake. He tried to escape them in me, in violent lovemaking, but I couldn't hide him."

"Why didn't you leave him if you were afraid, Lizzie?"

"I was more afraid to leave. He had a raging temper. I was afraid what he would do to me, what he would do to himself. He would fall apart if I left. Finally he wouldn't even let me leave his flat he was so jealous. I knew I had to get free. He threatened to kill me if I left. One time when he went out drinking with his friends I slipped out and got a schedule for a schooner to Noyo. I kept my bags packed under the bed, waiting. Luckily, the day of departure he slept late. I stole away to the schooner, to Noyo, to you."

"Does he know where to find you."

"No. I don't think so."

"Does Cletis write you?"

"Not in over a year. Two maybe."

The evening was late and they were both exhausted. They made up a bed for Elizabeth and she fell asleep straight away.

Willie was concerned to hear Elizabeth's story, but not surprised. She had known Elizabeth was lonely.

It is hard to be strong woman when you are lonely, isn't it Blue Feather? Willie thought.

For days Elizabeth lay about, walked on the beach, talked some and ate little. After a few weeks she stopped by the hospital clinic one day and helped out for a while. That evening she was a flurry of activity, going over old notes, planning and reading. She had heard much about the changes and developments in nursing procedures that were taking place in the war theater. She had received letters and reports from her nursing associates there. She was eager to implement some of the innovative ideas. Now she could be of service. She could move forward. That night she wrote a long letter to Cletis, her first in many months.

"Honey, when is the last time you got mail from Miles?" Elizabeth asked.

"Not since Vicksburg. He was all right then. He had Marcus and Daniel with him." Willie stared out the window at the first sunny day they'd had in a while. "He is very far away, isn't he?"

"Willie, you've got to get out of this house sometimes. I think my living here is great for me, but it's making matters worse for you!" Elizabeth said. "Maybe you are less likely to indulge your solitude with me here, but now you can easily arrange never to go into town."

It was true. Willie stayed home. She had become more resilient emotionally, but more of a recluse socially. She did not go into town all summer. There was no letter from Miles. She devoted herself to the care of her son, and while he played with the others, she walked. She walked for hours through the countryside and along the bluffs. She walked to edges she had to pray herself back from.

She did not notice the seriousness of Pahto's increased interest in the horses until he raised the stakes. By then it was out of her hands.

22

"I can no longer tolerate that dull look in your eye," Elizabeth said. "You must come with me and Blue Feather into town to shop and do errands. We have more summer weather in these fall days than we do that entire foggy season we call summer."

"I do need some fabric and buttons for a winter coat for Alex. But will the shops be open on Sunday?"

"It's Saturday, honey. Get ready."

Willie hitched up Glory, and the three women took the buggy into town with Alexander perched on the front bench helping Elizabeth drive.

As they came to the ridge above the river, they could see the race track and the milling crowd at a distance. A chill prickled at the back of Willie's neck when she thought of Pahto down there.

All summer long Pahto had worked with Rojo, the big sorrel, who grew lean and hard under his care. Willie knew Pahto had been riding him hard even though he made sure the horse was well cleaned of any traces of telltale sweat before he turned him loose in the paddock after a workout. But she was surprised when she learned he planned to enter Rojo in a race today.

"How can he afford the entry fee?" Elizabeth asked.

"He gets money from somewhere. He is able to contribute more to the support of the rancheria than I am these days. I don't ask. Rojo seems his as much as mine. What could I say?" She said nothing.

Rojo was older than most of the horses that raced, but he was strong and fit. After the rigorous workouts through the end of summer Pahto began to change the training regimen. He rested Rojo more and kept him sharp with shorter faster workouts.

The main advantage Pahto and Rojo would enjoy was their unity. Pahto and the sorrel achieved the singularity of purpose that horse and rider can sometimes know. The timing was right. The blend of training and rest had left them each hungry. Pahto had only to ask with a slight touch of his leg and the horse responded. Nothing interfered with them. The sorrel kept his ears turned to the rider—yes, yes, and now?

They came to the starting line poised and tense. At the gun the burst of power from Rojo's hindquarters nearly took Pahto's breath. He sat the horse with balance and control. They moved as one past the other riders. Pahto tasted the freedom of the win. It was not until he cantered the big sorrel back to the finish line after the race that the taste turned bitter.

He did not see it coming, the absolute consequences of what he had tried to do. He had not anticipated the angry drunken men who had lost money and the race to a wild heathen black Digger no different from an animal himself. Long Tree and Young Jack, who rode double on Long Tree's horse, brought their mount in close to Pahto. The race director worked his way through the crowd and pressed the winner's purse into Pahto hand.

"You'd best take this and leave quickly now, boy. And don't be coming back around here. This here race is for white men. You and those other two bucks take off now before things get ugly."

Pahto rode slowly through the crowd who cursed and reviled him. When they grabbed at him and tried to pull him off his horse, his friends moved up on this left and rode shoulder to shoulder with him. On his right side, he used his riding crop to strike at a man with an angry flushed face who would not let go of his leg. The clamor rose, the three riders were encircled. Someone fired a gun into the air. Someone else slapped Rojo's flank. The big horse reared; the snarling crowd fell back and the Indians escaped. They galloped off up river, angry shouts and gun shots fading behind them.

They did not return to the rancheria. They would not be safe there. They would camp tonight where they could not be found. And then what? How much danger were they in?

The three women talked and laughed their way along the wooden sidewalk. Alexander was engrossed with his stick of horehound candy but still managed to step carefully over the cracks between the boards. The gaiety of their party drew greetings from everyone they passed. Their shopping adventure was over and they were walking back to where they had left the buggy.

They had to pass the River Hotel saloon where several men who had come into town after the races that day were leaned against the railing. Willie recognized Nate, who she knew frequented the races. He was wearing the same red hat as he had three years ago when he had accosted Pahto and been chastised by Miles.

Willie picked Alexander up. "Let's hurry past here!" she said in a hushed voice to Elizabeth and Blue Feather. They lowered their eyes and walked quickly toward the buggy.

It was of no use though, for behind them they heard, "Well, if it ain't the little lady and one of her Digger friends."

Whistles and calls followed them. The men accompanied each vulgar remark with snickers and grins, keenly amused at their own wit.

The women had just reached the buggy when one of the men grabbed Blue Feather from behind. "Look at this squaw all prettied up like a white woman."

"Get your hands off of her!" Elizabeth screamed at him. Willie set Alexander down and reached into the rig for the buggy whip. It cracked through the air and took a piece of skin off the face of the man who held Blue Feather. He let her go and threw up his hands to protect himself. Willie did not stop wielding the whip until the man backed out of her reach and Elizabeth restrained her from pursuing him.

Elizabeth and Blue Feather put the terrified Alexander into the buggy and got in after him. Willie stood with the whip cocked behind her. Anger pounded in her temples. She could not hear her friends begging her to get in the buggy.

A large man of ample girth swaggered out in front of the others. "We already run off them Digger outlaws you keep out there. We just come from your place looking for them, but they're already gone. We'll see to it they stay gone. It ain't right you women live with them Injuns, no men folk about." He approached Willie slowly. "I remember you used to be willing to play cards and have a beer with white men. Why don't you give me that whip and come in and..." Cra-a-a-k! The whip drew blood on his hand as he stepped near.

"Do not interfere with me. You hear me? Do not interfere with me and do not interfere with my people." Menace hissed through Willie's clenched teeth. She spoke slow, trying to make her threat encompass more than this confrontation. The big man stopped his advance. No one spoke. Willie climbed into the buggy. Elizabeth retrieved the whip from her and used it to drive Glory hard for home.

The rancheria was in an uproar when the women arrived. Everyone spoke at once, rapidly, and in Bokaima. As Willie unhitched the buggy and turned Glory out into his paddock, she listened to the story of what had happened here. It was hard for Willie to keep up with the fragmented accounts. Alexander clung whimpering to Willie's neck.

"What are they saying, Willie? I can't understand," Elizabeth pleaded.

"Pahto got into a fight or something at the races. He was with Young Jack and Long Tree. Then six men on horseback came here looking for them. They yelled at everyone a lot, searched through all the buildings and pushed Old Chief down. They said they'd come back if they don't find Pahto."

"Where is Pahto?" Elizabeth asked of the frightened group clustered in the dusty farmyard. "Where is he?" No one responded. They looked at each other, at the ground, at the air.

Finally Blue Feather answered for them, "We do not know."

Darkness, the evening chill and the demands of a hungry child drove Willie indoors. From the porch her final comments were a plan for the next day.

"Decide on two, three or four of you to go tomorrow with me and Elizabeth to the fort tomorrow to bring this to Captain Hall's attention. We need his help."

"He will not protect us if we are not on the reservation," Old Chief reminded her.

"We will insist."

Once inside, Elizabeth sank into a chair, her head in her hands. "Doggone the war! I wish Miles were here," she said. "Or even Cletis, I guess," she added as an afterthought.

"Well, they're not and we must decide what we are going to do. Come here and help." Willie was lighting the fire in the cook stove and fixing bread and butter to quiet Alexander. Elizabeth fed him his supper while Willie rummaged around in the back of the closet in her room. She came back to the front room and put a large canvas-wrapped bundle on her writing desk. She carefully removed a shotgun from the wraps. She spent the rest of the evening cleaning the weapon and refreshing her memory about using it.

Alexander had never seen a gun in the house before and was impressed. The day was full of curious events. Willie concentrated on her grim task. She knew her tension was making Alexander more uneasy.

"Come, my lamb, kiss me goodnight and go with Aunt Lizzie. She will read you a story from the book Papa sent you. Mama has work to do tonight. Don't be afraid; Mama will take care of everything." He went with Elizabeth, chattering all the way. Willie could hear Elizabeth read the familiar story while Alexander provided commentary.

23

Mama will take care of everything. There's a deceit, Willie thought. But he needs to feel safe. How I'm going to actually pull it off is not something he needs to worry about. It never seems possible to keep him safe enough anyway. How? Where are the instructions? The rules? Love your neighbor as yourself. Are those men my neighbors? Even them? Doesn't seem like it from here.

"Willie," Elizabeth broke into her thoughts. Alexander had fallen asleep and she found Willie by a window, settling in for a vigil. "Maybe you and I should take Alexander and go stay with someone in town tonight."

"And leave them here alone?"

"Of course not. You're right. But then maybe we should go to the fort tonight and get help."

"They wouldn't come."

"What are you going to do?"

"I'll watch for a while. Then I'll go to bed. You go and sleep now."

Exhausted by worry, Elizabeth went to bed. She left

Willie sitting there in the great chair, staring out the window, keeping watch. Hours passed before Willie's eyes grew heavy. She had almost drifted off into sleep when a woman's scream brought her suddenly to her feet, her heart pounding, her hands clammy on the cool metal of the shotgun. "Elizabeth, come quick!" she called.

Elizabeth rushed to her side at the same moment a large man stomped across the porch and tried to open the bolted door.

"Who is there? What do you want?" Elizabeth yelled.

There was no answer from the man. He put his shoulder against the door, trying to force it open. There was more screaming from the rancheria houses across the yard. Men shouted to each other and Willie could see their shadows running between the homes. Willie knew she had to go out there. She threw open the bolt on the door and confronted the man standing there. His face was drunkenly contorted as he tried to form his red swollen lips around slurred words Willie could not understand.

He lurched into the room toward the women. Willie raised the gun and leveled it at the intruder. He stopped to consider this development, while continuing his ranting, "No black bucks gonna live with no white women. And I don't want no squaw."

"Leave!" Willie's fear poured furious power into her voice. "Now!" The man stepped back. She cocked the shotgun. He muttered curses and stepped back again, warning her to put the gun down. She advanced grimly as he retreated unsteadily. He missed the porch step and fell tumbling to the ground. Willie stood at the top of the steps with the shotgun pointed at him as he lay in the dust, moaning.

More wailing and screaming accompanied the sudden illumination of the night with the wild glow of fire. Willie was frantic to remove this man from her path so that she could figure out what was happening in the rancheria.

"Go on! Get on your horse and get out of here."

"You women probably ruint by them black bucks anyways," he said as he limped to his horse, mounted awkwardly, and rode off.

"Elizabeth! Stay with Alex! Go inside and bolt the door!" As soon as she heard the door's bolt thrown she ran across toward the rancheria. She could see the redwood bark roundhouse was burning. Flames crackled and reached to the treetops.

She saw several figures silhouetted against the flames, but could not make out who they were. The fire had spread to the roof of the frame house her father and Old Chief had built. When she got closer she could see six men standing in front of Sun Ray's cabin, gesturing wildly and yelling to one another. Willie stood frozen. She took refuge behind the garden wall before they could see her. She crouched low and crept along the wall until she could hear their voices clearly.

"Would you hurry up, Will. We ain't got all night."

"There's another one here, Nate," another man yelled from Sun Ray's doorway. "You can have her."

"Nah, shut up Leonard. I want this one, all fancied up."

Willie peeked over the wall to see one man getting up from the ground and adjusting his clothing. Lying at his feet was Blue Feather, the dress she and Willie had made together torn away to expose her breasts.

"She's all yours Nate," the man called Will said. Nate threw himself down on Blue Feather. She screamed again and struggled away from him.

"Ah-h-h!" Nate yelled. "Shit! The bitch bit me!" He grabbed her around the throat while he drew his pistol from his belt and beat the side of her face with it. She stopped struggling. He tossed his pistol aside and broke into her body. The men watching cheered encouragement to Nate as he grunted over her.

"Yeah, Nate! Look here at Nate. He gets that stupid look on his face when he comes. I must've seen him fuck a hundred squaws and he always gets that stupid look on his face. Look here at him."

Willie was paralyzed with fear. She crouched behind a rose bush. She could just make out by the light of the blaze the red of the first winter rose. She could not shake a recurring urge to yawn and rub her eyes, wake up from the nightmare. But she was here and she had no choice but to stand up and face them and get them off Blue Feather. Nate was getting to his feet when he saw Willie approaching with her shotgun held against her shoulder. His welcoming smile faded when he saw something behind her.

It was not until the horses were nearly upon her that she heard their thundering advance. As she leapt out of their way, she saw the three riders were Pahto, Long Tree, and Young Jack. They rode fast into the rancheria, each with an army-issue rifle in his hand.

Gunfire exploded. Willie ducked back behind the wall. In the melee two of the intruders ran for their horses, trying to mount and run at the same time. They rode past Willie with terror in their faces. One more horse soon followed with two riders clinging to its saddle. Two men and three horses did not get away.

Willie was still hanging onto her shotgun, but now it felt awkward and foolish in her hands. She laid it down under the bush. She ran to where Blue Feather lay on the ground.

"Blue Feather!" Willie spoke to her. No response— only the moans of an wounded animal and unseeing eyes. One side of her face was torn skin and bloody flesh. Her eye was swelling shut. Her jaw hung loose. The spent semen of four rapists ran down her leg and into the dust. Willie tried to cover her bare skin. Blue Feather began to tremble with a bone-shaking chill as her moans turned to cries. Willie rocked her in her arms by the waning warmth of the burned-out buildings.

Round Face Woman was inside the cabin tending Sun Ray, who had been raped but not beaten. Pahto was racing around, giving orders and securing three of the attackers' horses. One had been left behind by one of the riders Willie had seen riding double. The other two had belonged to the men who lay dead, shot by Pahto and Long Tree.

Pahto conferred with Old Chief and the other men of the tribe. Then he went to where Sun Ray lay and spoke to her and Round Face Woman. His voice was calm and reassuring. He came to Blue Feather and put his hand gently on her broken jaw. He turned to Willie with anger.

"It is because of you this has happened," his voice cracked. He spoke slowly in Bokaima, "It is because of you, trying to make our women white women. It is because of you they have been exposed to this danger. You led them into your town, led them away from the covering of the tribe. Your man has gone. You are not covered. He has left his woman and son unprotected. Who covers them? Pahto! Pahto protects the boy. But you bring danger to us all."

He rose to his feet and looked down at Blue Feather with wet eyes. Long Tree approached leading Rojo.

"We must go now," Pahto said. "Soon they will return with soldiers." Pahto stared at Willie. Did she understand? Did she see he had no choice? He gestured to the defeated tribe and asked her with bitter desperation, "Who will pay for this? There is no honor here!" And now he too must leave her. With a light spring he mounted the sorrel and the three men disappeared into the sheltering forest.

"Washo! Washo!" Willie called for Sun Ray's oldest

boy. "Go to my house Washo and get Elizabeth. Tell her I need her now."

A red dawn stained the horizon as they moved the wounded women into Willie's house.

24

Elizabeth's skills shone in the circumstance. She set up the house like a kind of infirmary. She assigned tasks. Wounds were cleaned and breakfast was prepared. She moved with clarity. Beds and pallets were laid throughout the house. Round Face Woman kept the children occupied. Willie sat with Sun Ray and Blue Feather. Blue Feather still did not speak. Elizabeth wanted to send for the doctor to look at her jaw, but Blue Feather looked terrified at the suggestion and Old Chief refused to let anyone go out. Pastor Justus heard what happened and came to the house. Old Chief said he could not come in. Willie spoke to her father's old friend on the porch.

"A posse of militia and civilians have gone after the Indians who killed the two men," Justus told her. "You must bring Alex and Elizabeth and come stay with me and Annalee. It is not safe for you here," he said. "At least let me take Alex."

"It's the Bokaima who are not safe. A few of us are riding in to talk to Captain Hall. We must get help. Won't you come with us?"

"Yes, certainly, Wilhemia. Of course. Anything I can do."

"Is Captain Hall at the fort?"

"Yes, he did not go out with the posse."

"They are deciding inside now who will go to meet with him. Wait here, please, and we'll travel with you."

Willie went back inside and dressed Alexander for the ride into town. She was afraid to let him out of her sight. Only when she could touch him did she feel he was safe. She could not think of letting him go home with Reverend Justus.

It was late morning before the procession arrived at the fort. Willie, Elizabeth, Alexander, Reverend Justus, Round Face Woman, Old Chief and his two brothers piled into two rigs—Willie's and the pastor's. Except for Justus and Alexander, who had slept soundly through the fracas, few of them had had any sleep.

As they rode across the green parade ground, they saw the troops untacking and stabling their horses.

"Evidently they have returned without Pahto," Elizabeth observed.

Captain Hall, accompanied by his aide, received them in his office. They all crowded into the room. Hall affected a waxed mustache curled up at the ends and his head bobbed back and forth when he talked as though he were being conciliatory. He looked only at Reverend Justus when he spoke.

He confirmed that his men had been unable to track Pahto. "Is this the family of that murdering buck?" he asked Justus. He would not look at Willie, but she rose from her seat to answer him.

"Seven men came to our rancheria last night and attacked us, Captain," she said. "Women were raped and beaten. Those same men harassed us repeatedly yesterday. Pahto was trying to protect us. We appeal to you for protection. You must chastise those men and let Pahto rejoin his family."

"Well, now. That's not in my jurisdiction, young lady," he responded, looking at the wall rather than at her. "However, Pahto can come in whenever he wants and face the charges against him."

Old Chief stepped forward and faced the Captain. He drew himself tall and cast his eyes down to look at Hall. Old Chief spoke and Willie translated. "Our young women have been dishonored. Who will pay? Who will redeem this transgression?"

Old Chief's question eluded the captain. "Pay?" he answered. "I've seen those squaws charge two bits for the same thing every night down at the river. You want payment?" He reached into his pocket and flipped a fifty-cent piece through the air. It fell with a hollow clatter at the feet of Old Chief. Willie did not translate.

"Now I want you all to listen up." Hall stood up behind his desk and spoke to the delegation. "If that buck ever shows his face around here again we will hang him."

"Captain Hall!" Reverend Justus was indignant. "These people have come here in good faith to appeal to your authority. You must give them a fair hearing. And the young man can never come in if he has to face a lynch mob."

"If you're going to coddle these people, do it on your own time Reverend. Now if you want to come to me with a delegation of reasonable men, not a rabble of hysterical girls and ignorant Indians, you are welcome to return. I will not listen to the demands of these people."

"Your bigotry is appalling," Willie said to him. "I shall report your irresponsibility to your superiors and to state legislators who are my friends."

"You don't have any power around here anymore,

young lady," Hall said. "So don't get all flustered. Times have changed. Your old man has been gone for a long time. Nobody cares about these pathetic half-human Diggers anymore. For your information, orders from my superiors are to clean out all the remaining wild Indians north of the Ten Mile. We'll about have finished with that by the time this militia unit is picked up by the Panama next month and this fort is abandoned. So all these useless Indians are on their own from now on. No more handouts.

"In the meantime, we are going to round up all the Jackson rancheria Indians and incarcerate them up here on the reservation. They've been harboring outlaws down there for some time. Now they've killed two men in cold blood. Those bucks're going to be hung if they're not hunted down and shot first, every murdering one of them and all who travel with them."

Elizabeth jumped up to argue against Hall's tirade while Willie translated the gist of his remarks for the Bokaima. They became agitated when they realized the scope of the threat. Round Face Woman began chanting. Alexander hung on Willie's skirt and cried. Old Chief and his brothers talked heatedly amongst themselves. Elizabeth continued to rant at Hall.

Hall sat back down and leaned back in his chair. He smiled smugly at Willie and said over the din, "Like I said, lady, you have no power here."

"We will go now," Old Chief announced.

They trooped outside in confusion. The Bokaima wanted to leave and return to the rancheria. Reverend Justus offered to take them home while Willie and Elizabeth went to the office of the Indian Agent at the reservation.

"I can't think that will do you much good, Wilhemina," Justus said. "Should I go with you?"

"No, please take them home now. Lizzie and I will be

right along. Thank you for your help today. I just feel we must make an effort to get some intervention here."

Alexander could not stop wailing. Willie decided to send him home with Round Face Woman. The situation here was too mean. Willie knelt down to speak with him.

"Go with Round Face Woman now, my lamb. I will be home real soon." She wiped the tears from his cheeks with her skirt and smoothed his hair. He clasped his hands behind her neck.

"I want you, Mama." His big blue eyes made her smile. Miles' eyes.

"You look like your papa you know." He nodded in agreement. He had heard that before.

"Papa is all gone."

"He will be home soon." Alexander began crying even harder. Round Face Woman stopped chanting and put Alex in the buggy.

"Come, Little Coyote. We are going away from here."

"We'll come along as soon as we've seen the agent. We need to get some help," Willie said. The plan seemed so futile she felt she had to explain herself.

Round Face Woman settled Alexander on her lap. "Agent will not help," she said. "You should come with us now."

Alex was comforted by the hands of people who loved him, but still he leaned over the edge of the buggy and called to Willie, "I want you Mama."

"I'll be home soon," she called to him. She wanted him too. She wanted to rock her baby and sit with her husband by a cozy hearth and wonder at the ways of the world outside.

She did not want this. They were standing in front of the fort headquarters building where Miles used to work. The fort had fallen into disrepair. Fences leaned to the weather, the whitewash of their pickets overcome by the moss-green of the lichen. The grounds lay littered with abandoned equipment.

"Willie, let's get going," Elizabeth broke into her reverie. "The days are getting short; it'll get dark soon. We must go on." They climbed into the buggy and headed to reservation headquarters.

Willie was silent during the short ride. "We have to do this," Elizabeth continued. "Even if we get no satisfaction today, we must make the official complaint. Then we can continue to make life unpleasant for them all until someone takes some appropriate action."

Elizabeth did all the talking when they got to the agent's office. She filled out the report forms the agent handed her. The afternoon light waned. Willie sat silently. She watched the two Indian women the agent kept as his wives as they moved about in the shadowy recesses of his quarters. The agent listened to Elizabeth, but his blank expression confirmed her and Willie's fears. What did he care? He was struggling to sweat out his alcohol overload of the evening before. The room reeked of it.

"I can do nothing to protect your bucks who kill white men. You all could've come to me in the first place. Maybe I could've helped then. Not now. You say it was white men attacked your squaws, but how do you know? You didn't see them did you? And how do you know who set your fires? See, if I try to indict these men without proof, they'll be real upset. Now, you've filed your written report about all your allegations so I'll try to look into it, but you ladies should know better than to live out there alone with those Indians. They are savages. You don't know when they'll turn on you and revert to their wild state. They ain't the same as us."

Willie's knuckles turned white where she gripped the edge of her chair. Her eyes were cold on him. Even him? Is he my neighbor? Willie wanted to bash his flaccid face. She saw all her dreams of a seamless melding of the cultures obliterated in the dark soul of this one man. Elizabeth who still counted on civility put her hand over Willie's, hoping to still her. It did not work.

"You live with Indians, you pig," Willie said through clenched teeth.

The agent sucked his breath in sharply, his eyes finally opened enough so that Willie could see them. "Well now, men can handle these things better than women, can't they? You haven't done a real good job down there doing it your way, have you? Trying to tell other people how to live. Your big britches old man going off to a war so he and the rest of the Yankees can tell someone else how to live. Then you ask for my help. It'll never happen, lady. Now get out of here."

His Indian wives stood in the shadows watching Willie. Their faces reflected fear and shame. What hope had they but this man to take care of them? Their own people were long gone. So were their chances of anyone redeeming them, taking them home. There was no home. They knew it. Willie knew it. Elizabeth pulled Willie from the room.

They drove in twilight past the homes and shops of the town that was growing up around the mill. There was no place for the Indians to live with grace here. The townspeople had petitioned the governor to do something about the Indian problem. Indians were begging on the street corners, clothed in rags, unbathed. The men were drunk, the women diseased, the children unfed. They were a pathetic eyesore. Couldn't he do something about the Indian problem? Move them somewhere where they could be taken care of. Put them in homes or on farms where they could work for their keep, learn the ways of civilized men. Get them off the streets of our decent town.

Willie felt sick. Neither she nor Elizabeth talked on the way home. Willie just wanted to get back to Alexander and to Blue Feather. She always knew going to town was a mistake.

They drove into a deserted homestead. Willie's house was empty. The rancheria was abandoned. No one was home. They were all gone, their belongings were gone, packed and gone. Elizabeth ran frantically from empty building to empty building looking for someone, anyone, but Willie stood still in the middle of the yard. They had left and they had taken Little Coyote with them.

"No, no, no!" she cried. Only the empty buildings were left to hear her protest the approaching night. "No, no, no!" she shook her fists at the first stars.

On her knees, her forehead in the dust, she could only whisper, "No, God. Please, no."

25

Now all of her thoughts focused: Find her boy, fetch him home. For a few miles she traveled east on a trail she knew well. By the time she had to navigate less familiar territory the sun rose and she was able to find the logging road that cut north across the Noyo. From there she knew she had only to find the trail to the east that would take her upstream and inland. This was the trail Pahto would follow to take the Bokaima back to the hills that were their home. At least, Willie thought, he would begin here. He might leave the trail if he thought they were being pursued.

The trail she sought was an ancient highway from primary inland villages to the summer camps of the coast. The Pomo people were not a tribe, but rather a related group of bands, similar in language and culture. Each group's territory was defined by the watershed of a river or stream where they lived, hunted, fished and gathered food. They may have had little or no contact with neighboring bands only twenty miles away, and may not have understood the language when they did have contact. When relationships with neighbors were friendly, hunting and gathering rights were exchanged and goods traded.

Rights to pass on this main highway trail were traditional and easily negotiated. Bands like the Bokaima lived in their homes in the inland hills most of the year, traveling to favored beaches during the summer season to collect salt, sea vegetables and ocean fish. Permission would be granted from one tribe to another if passage through their territorial watershed were necessary. Such traditions had been abandoned in recent years. Many tribes, in fear of the safety of their children and of their own lives, no longer traveled. Many more no longer existed.

The trail east was still well marked though, and Willie found it by midday. She skirted the edges of the violent scars of the logging operations. Along the river the forest was stripped clean from the earth. To her left where the forest was not in reach of the river-bound logging operations, the redwood forest flourished. To her right, there was nothing.

Into the afternoon, her mind drifting, sleep-starved, hazy, Willie rode. She cried for the barren ground and her own barren arms. Look what they have done to the land! She had argued with her young men about the forest. Only Daniel had understood.

"But they own it," Marcus had protested. "It's their land. They have rights to do what they want with their own property." Miles had fallen asleep with his head in her lap while the others argued.

"It is not their land," Willie said. "Some of it is. Some of it they bought dirt cheap or leased the right to log it, but a lot of that land is not theirs at all. They just go in and log it. They've been doing that all along. They are the ones who build the mills. They own the saws. That's it. The mill at Noyo sits on reservation property."

Daniel agreed with her. "Some way or another they have managed to finagle the money to finance the saws, set up the mills, go into the forests and take everything out. Nothing lives where they have been. No salmon spawn on rivers that are being used to run log braces downstream."

"I have worked in logging camps all along the coast and I logged in Finland when I was still a boy," Rune said. "I have seen the limits of a forest. I cannot understand these mill owners. The mill owner in Mendocino told me that these forests are so large that we can never cut down all of the trees. He figures there are enough trees for his lifetime. He has men working for him who come from very poor places who do not object to the fact that he pays them so little while he takes out so much."

"Yes," Daniel agreed. "And soon they will have railroads going deeper into the forest where they can't reach now because they can only log close to the rivers that they use to get the logs to the ocean ports. Already at the Caspar mill they are talking about putting in a rail line so they can reach deeper into the forest."

"It is true," Rune said. "But it is a good country and a man can make a living. My friend is going back to Finland soon to bring his bride here. He will fall the big trees and make a home here."

"And you, Rune Kalevala?" Willie asked. "What will you do now?"

"I have accepted a job with Harpers. I am going back to cover the war."

"Now you're in for it, Rune!" Daniel laughed. "Willie doesn't even think soldiers should be going to war. And you're a civilian!"

"The war is ugly, Willie, I know that. But I am going to chronicle the war, not encourage it."

"Sounds pretty innocent, doesn't it?" Daniel chided.

"Of course he's not excited about the assignment at all, are you Rune?"

"Our observer of humanity doesn't want to actually get his hands dirty, but he still wants to breathe the action," Marcus said.

Rune raised his glass of ale and said, "Victor Hugo wrote that, 'Life itself is a battlefield with its own obscure heroes.'" The three men grew raucous; Rune, as usual, laughing the loudest. The imminence of the war kept them keyed up in apprehension. Only Willie did not laugh.

"Uh-oh. Willie's getting mad. You guys are gonna wake up the Major." Rune's attempts to charm her were failing.

"Will you write a great war novel then?" Willie asked him.

"Don't be so hard on them, Willie," Miles stretched and rose, awakened by the argument. "Men have jobs. We do the best we can to be honorable in them." He fetched a cup of coffee from the pot that sat on the back corner of the warm stove. "I remember in 1850, Telegraph Hill in San Francisco was covered with tents that were home to thousands who had come west looking for gold. Some went back, some stayed. There is a city growing there now and the people there need lumber for housing. Can't they harvest some of your trees, my love, for their homes? It is a very large forest. You can ride for days and never see the end of it." He put his arm around her and laid his hand on her belly to feel the baby move.

She yielded her protests to his touch. Maybe the forests were large enough to withstand man's greed. Maybe war could be noble.

Perhaps she had been too hard on them back then, but now it was even more difficult to see the purpose of it all. Although it appeared that after the deaths of hundreds of thousands of fighting men the South faced certain defeat, the Union was only winning at a cost in lives that was twice that of the Confederacy. The North had always had more men to throw into the fray. And where were they now, her young men? Her dream lover, where was he? Wars and fighting had left her in this predicament and she resented all warriors for it.

Finally she could ride no further. She halted and slid from her horse at the edge of a clearing near where the trail would wind into the forest. One advantage to riding the edge of clear cuts was there was light. Once in the forest it would be darker, harder for her to orient herself.

She secured Glory with a long tie so that he could graze on what he could find. When the sun fell below the trees the air chilled, but she decided not to make a fire. She was more exhausted than she was cold. And she wanted to conserve her precious phosphorus matches. She ate some of her bread and then climbed into her bed roll with all of her clothes on. She drew a blanket over her head.

Sleep did not come right away. She worried that she had been awake for so long—staying alert, keeping sleep at bay—that maybe she was trapped here in this bleary-eyed watch, sleep no longer available. But even as she fretted over such a fate, slumber stole her away and dreams swept clean the corners where the dust of days collected.

Footsteps! Her eyes opened wide, but she lay still, listening. Who was it? Was someone there? A rustling step approached her. Her heart pounded. She turned to confront the intruder. Her movement startled a possum who scrambled back into the cover of the forest. It had been pawing inquisitively at her saddle bags that lay some distance from her. She would have to remember to keep her pack closer to her when she slept. Or maybe hang it from a tree. She could barely make out Glory's outline from where she lay. The night was dark. Cloud cover had returned. There would be no frost tonight. She pulled the blankets back over her head and found sleep again.

It was not until she heard Glory stirring in the early morning that she woke again. She slipped out of her bedroll. With careful barefooted steps she led Glory to a fresh spot to graze, then scurried back into her warm bed to assess her situation.

Too bad I didn't pack any coffee, she thought. Even though they had many more people than horses, Pahto knows where they are going and I have to figure it out. Still, I should have some advantage with speed—they are carrying wounded. I must assume they will use this trail. Will they leave someone bringing up the rear to watch and see if there is anyone following? Should I travel on the trail or just keep myself in relationship to the trail, possibly avoiding their discovering me? But then there would be no chance of my finding any sign of their passing. But they won't leave any sign.

She knew the Bokaima way, when they broke camp, was to leave the area scrupulously clean. It was a ritual based on the belief that an enemy could use any personal item left behind to poison its owner. Pahto would leave nothing behind, she knew.

Because if you did Pahto, if you left any remnant behind, I would use it. I would smell it and track your scent. I would curse the shred and your every step. I would chant over it and breathe fear into your heart. Damn you, Pahto!

Anger warmed her. With purpose she rose and saddled Glory. While she watered him at a small stream nearby she ate a little bread and filled her canteen. They took the trail that led into the redwood forest. This was a silent, twilight world. The giant trees let only dappled hints of sunlight through to the ground below. Few live branches grew below seventy-five feet up the trees, which were two- or three-hundred feet tall.

Willie and Glory passed between soft-barked trunks that were ten or fifteen feet across. The red of the thick fibrous bark and the decaying fallen needles gave a rosy glow to the forest floor. The lack of sunlight penetrating the towering canopy meant little else grew there. Gone was the ocean's background roar. Sounds and sunlight were muffled out. It was difficult to determine which way she was going because she could not fix on the sun.

The temperature in the forest stayed even as Willie traveled by day and camped at night. It stayed cool but never froze. The redwoods lay in a thin strip along the northern California coast, seldom further inland than fifty miles. They were restricted to this area by their dependence on the fog that clung to the western slopes of the coastal mountain range.

The problem she faced in the forest was finding feed for Glory. There was little forage for him. She sought out the creeks and streams where often the land opened up and a small meadow could be found. She discovered a perfect spot to camp one afternoon. It was at the base of an incline where the trail would turn steeply uphill. The redwoods had begun to share the landscape with fir. Forage was plentiful here in pockets in the rocky terrain. It was early in the day to set up camp, but she thought she could use the time well to tend her gear while Glory grazed. Pahto would not stop, she knew, but she had to. She had been on the trail for five days. Her anxiety had left her little appetite before, but now she found herself hungry, and the lush mountain meadow was inviting.

She loaded the shotgun with one of the cartridges. She sat silent, unmoving, behind a log that overlooked the stream bed. She did not have to wait long before a family of plump quail scurried single-file out of the underbrush. Willie rose swiftly and shot. The family flew with shrill calls back into the woods. They left two of their own behind. Hunger makes a good hunter out of a novice.

Willie made a fire and gathered huckleberries to mix with a flour and water batter that she fried into skillet cakes. The quail cooked up tender on a spit over the coals of the fire. Willie ate, rested, and ate some more.

She bathed in the chill water of the stream and then washed out her shirt and socks and lay them out to dry. The sun was behind the trees now, but she would let the damp clothes dry draped over the saddle bags tomorrow as she rode.

Once the saddle bags were repacked she laid her head against them and relaxed with almost a sense of contentment. I will overtake you soon, my lamb, she thought with peaceful assurance. A warm fire, a full belly—she slept deeply.

She never heard the men steal into the night and lead Glory away.

26

She woke in the early morning light and stared at the unfamiliar surroundings, trying to orient herself. She knew something was wrong, but could not immediately figure it out. Then she realized—Glory was not stomping around restlessly, waiting to be moved to water and fresh forage. Willie sat up and looked into the shadows where Glory had been left tied to a tree. He was gone.

She put her boots on quick and searched for him, hoping maybe he had pulled loose and wandered off. No such luck. He was gone. She had tied him securely, she knew. He was just gone. She slammed around the campsite in anger, throwing things, cursing and talking aloud to herself.

It was Pahto. I know it was Pahto. He came and took my horse. He knows I am following him now. I suppose he thinks without Glory I'll turn back. Well, I won't, you rat! I'm coming after you, godammit! The saddle...where's my saddle?

She had not noticed if the saddle was still there where she had left it thrown over a fallen log. She ran back across the clearing. But no, it was gone too. Of course. The bridle, however, was still lying where she had left it near her campfire after cleaning it the night before. Glory and the saddle had been on the other side of the clearing from her. Nothing had been taken that had lain near her.

Once her fury cooled, she centered her thoughts on a plan of action. She inventoried her gear and determined how best to use what remained. She had the shotgun. It would be heavy to carry. Would it be worth the trouble? She would need it for game. She had only a small amount of flour remaining and leftovers of the quail. She wrapped the meat carefully. There was no need to carry the pan. She could cook up the rest of the flour into cakes now and leave the pan behind.

She cut the saddle bags in two with her knife. Out of the canvas of one of the bags she cut long strips. Then, using leather and buckles from the bridle and the canvas strips, she stitched them together to made a knapsack. The reins from the bridle would tie her bedroll on to the top of the whole affair. She chose carefully which things to bring and which to leave behind. Of the three shotgun cartridges left, one had broken open. If she could use the other two profitably, perhaps packing the shotgun would be reasonable. She would have to reassess that decision at the end of the day. Maybe she could use one of the shells on Pahto.

She cooked up skillet cakes with the rest of the flour, ate a few and packed the rest. She drank as much water as she could and filled the canteen. After some adjustment, she settled the awkward pack onto her back. The shotgun definitely was a nuisance. It was strapped to the outside of the pack and flopped about as she walked.

She stood in the center of the meadow near the smoldering fire and the pile of discarded clothing and gear. The air was still. Heavy clouds hung on the mountain. It was time to go but her feet held fast to this spot. Not even a horse for company now. The grief she had tried to contain broke free in a rush of tears. It was the first time she had cried since Alexander was taken. She felt hopeless and alone. The makeshift pack hung haphazardly from her shoulders.

Pahto, Pahto. Don't leave me here!

Whimpering still, she struck out on the trail. The going was slow. Although she was used to taking long hikes, carrying a heavy pack uphill was intense. She had watched the Bokaima carrying heavy loads on their backs in their large conical baskets supported by a tump strap across their foreheads. She witnessed their stamina at a swift pace over long miles—the same strength they would use to distance themselves from her.

By the end of the day Willie had to admit that she would not be able to keep up this way. Her pack was much too heavy for her to maintain a decent pace. She was exhausted. Her shoulders bled from the crude straps of the knapsack. By twilight she fell into her bedroll without even eating. She loaded a cartridge into the shotgun and laid it close to her. She did not know whether she was close to water so she conserved her canteen supply. She slept fitfully. Her legs ached. Her feet burned with blisters.

Before dawn she took the shotgun and walked downhill from the trail until she found water. Where the trail approached the creek, she lay in wait for a fellow creature to come for water. She let a deer come and go. The air was chill and the ground frozen, but she stayed still, motionless. She lay shielded by a bank of lacy five-fingered fern. As the sun rose, ice crystals sparkled in the lichen growing on the rocks she leaned against. Willie spent her last two shells bagging a large cottontail and a small raccoon. She had them skinned and cooking by the time the sun was up.

Now the shotgun could be discarded. She chose the most practical clothing to wear and abandoned the rest. She fashioned a scabbard and wore the knife at her waist. One more remodeling of the pack left it lighter and more efficient. She hung the rabbit skin on the outside of the pack to dry. She could make use of it later. By late morning she was on her way again.

The trail was still well marked. She bypassed small side trails without investigation. She must stay on the main trail for now. It was evident that this road had been trod by many feet recently, but there was still no sign that it was the Bokaima who had passed here. But she knew they had to come this way through the mountains. This was the pass. She walked on.

By nightfall she had not gone far. The trail had climbed and dropped and twisted. She ate most of the rabbit. She found berries and ate the tender curled tips of the bracken fern. She went to sleep hungry and woke hungry. Each day she traveled lighter. Once she ate the last of her meat stash, she no longer had food to carry. She walked with hunger always now. Midday she found a huckleberry bush and ate a great amount of the small blue berries. Picking them was time consuming however, and she pushed on bringing only a small stash with her.

The leaves of the winter purslane were the easiest forage for her to find. Rune had called it miner's lettuce.

She searched for arrowhead plants in a marshy area near a slow-moving stream she came across. When she found a patch, she gathered a pile of the edible roots—tule potatoes. She made camp near the stream and roasted the potatoes in the coals of her fire. She made a salad of purslane, fern tips and berries. Hunger and impatience drove her to retrieve one of the tule potatoes from the fire before it was quite ready. She burned her fingers breaking it open. She ate ravenously, fetching one after another of the roots from the fire.

At the end of her meal sprinkles of rain sizzled in the fire. She sat unmoving, watching the rain extinguish the fire.

Her stomach protested the extravagances of her meal. She felt weak when she threw the poncho over her as the rain began to pour. Her skin was warm and clammy. Her stomach groaned and turned. She tried to stay dry by covering her head with the poncho, but that made the air stuffy and she was uncomfortable. She had to leave her face outside her makeshift shelter. Only the last wisps of smoke from the fire escaped the downpour.

In wrenching heaves, Willie threw up her dinner.

The rain was cool shocks on her upturned face. She sought its comfort—carefully, carefully turning her poisoned body whenever she could move between relentless bouts of vomiting—and lifted her face to the rain thankful for the wet drops on her thirsty tongue. Can you see me, Miles. I cannot find my baby boy. Miles, Miles, come now.

She was kept long in that night. Some nights are made longer and darker than others, morning's entry forbidden. That morning there was no dawn, only a steel-gray light that allowed her to find her damp gear. Her hands shook as she made sure the wrap on the matches was secure and she packed the few remaining tule potatoes. The sight of them cast her stomach into another fit of vomiting, but she packed them anyway. They were the only foodstuff she had; she might need them. That done, she dragged herself back to the trail, her mind capable of only that. Her body struggled to keep up.

The trail was slippery. The rain was the only thing consistent. Her thoughts were not. In moments of clarity she reviewed her situation and committed her course. Other times she was crippled by despair as she lay crumpled by the roadside, her stomach ridding itself of the few sips of water she took from the canteen. Then she walked on. Some kind of equilibrium was achieved. A kind of steady unsteadiness.

There were no options, so she had no fretful debates with herself. There were still signs that she was on a well-used trail, so she knew she was not lost. But she made little headway. Rain washed away her footholds. She was an inadvertent spectator in the arena where climate and geography stand against each other. Wind and rain steal the mountain, bit by bit, into the streams and to the valleys below.

Animal tracks and droppings indicated she shared the trail, but she saw only glimpses of retreating critters now and then. They could hear her coming. She talked to herself. And coughed. A tightness in her throat made each breath difficult. When darkness made forward movement impossible, she slept under an overhanging rock. In the morning she ate a cold tule potato, drank water, and kept it down. The rain poured. She had learned to keep a supply of thimble berry leaves in her pack to clean herself after relieving her bowels along the trail side. She tried binding the soft leaves with strips of canvas around her feet to protect her raw blistered feet. She walked on. Fever blurred her vision.

Everything seems so thin to me, she thought. I feel hollow. A shell. I am thin; my skin is thin. My breath wheezes and rattles around in my hollow bodyshell. Hallowed bodyshell.

The sky cleared and the sun broke through at midday. Sunlight sparkled in the drops hanging from the brim of her hat. It warmed her back. It glinted off her fevered headache. She found a walking stick and used it to keep her balance.

Dear God! What is the worth of all this work if this deadening despair still steals away the very air. What? "Hello!" People there...a village. "Hello! Hello!" she yelled. "No, no! Don't run off."

Four elk lumbered through the tall meadow grass and ran off into the oak woods. There were no people, but there were the remains of a small village. The huts had been burned down. Willie walked around the charred rubble. At the edge of the village the round dance house was mostly intact. The entrance had been caved in, but the building had not been burned. She pushed aside the tumbled entranceway and crawled inside. The smoke hole in the roof let in daylight. Once her eyes adjusted to the dimness, she found the room to be sound, stripped of all reminders of its previous inhabitants, but sound.

There were unburned pieces of firewood left in the fire pit in the center of the room. Willie scavenged for kindling. She would need a fire. Now that the storm clouds had blown over, the night temperature would drop. She found a mouse nest near the entrance way, its tatters of fibers perfect tinder. The room filled with smoke before the fire found its draft in the ceiling. Soon she was warm. She took off her wet clothes and propped them up to dry.

Her teeth chattered and fever chills clenched her muscles. The taste in her mouth was harsh and unfamiliar, metallic. She wrapped herself in her blanket and lay as close to the fire as she could. Her hands could not recognize her naked body. A disguise of skin draped over hopeful bones. Is this a woman's body? Then where is the man? Does not one imply the other? What perspective can there be, alone?

As the fire quieted, the only sound she heard was her pulse rushing in her ears. Her breath burned across her upper lip. Shapes took form in the shadow, gained life from the flickering flames and then died in the darkness. She was afraid to sleep. Fever dreams lurked there, lying in wait for her to slip beneath the surface of consciousness.

I am made of trembling glass. I mustn't sleep, for then I'd dream and my own screams would break me.

27

A fit of coughing woke her. Her fever had waned in the night and she slept until the sun was high enough to cast light through the smoke hole onto her blanket. The fire had burned out and the air was biting on her bare skin as she dressed, but her clothes were warm and dry. She moved slowly, her breath a labored rumble. Her boots also had dried by the fire. The leather was stiff and she dreaded putting it against the raw skin of her feet. She cut the rabbit hide into pads for the bottoms of her boots. Then she rested. Each flutter of activity cost her. She was reluctant to leave this cozy shelter, but her empty canteen prompted her.

Willie stood outside the round house squinting into the sunlight. The smaller rain puddles that were shaded from the sun were iced over. A movement caught her eye. Something small, familiar, swung from a tree in the center of the circle of burned huts. She tried to make it out. Her head was muddled but she was sure it had not been there yesterday. She walked over to it. The crunch of her steps on the ice recalled her to last winter: Alexander had been so sick; outside the ground had been icy, brittle under her feet when she went out for wood. She had been afraid then, too.

The small basket that she had used to carry flour in her saddle bags hung from a charred leafless branch—the basket she had discarded days ago on the trail. Blue Feather's basket. She stood before it, transfixed. Two winters ago Willie had watched when Blue Feather had intentionally woven a small interruption in the pattern of the basket, a break in the perfection necessary for letting the evil spirits out.

She snatched it out of the tree and spun about quickly to catch sight of the one who put it there. She stood alone.

"Alexander! Blue Feather! Are you there?" Only the scrub jay called back.

"Pahto! Pahto!" Stillness answered. "Pahto!" No one was there.

But he left the basket for me, she thought. A sign. He retrieved it from where I left it behind, how many days ago? He probably got the shotgun too, for whatever that is worth. But this! This basket is real. Not a dream. This is not a dream. He knows I am following and he left me a sign.

She was giddy as she gathered her gear and got on her way. It was slow going. She wanted only to maintain forward movement at this point, but even that seemed too much. She rested as much as walked. Only small sips of water could be swallowed past her raw and swollen throat. The trail still meandered on a steady grade up the mountain. She gasped for each breath. Continuing seemed futile.

Maybe the basket was a trick, she thought. Make me think I'm on the right track. A trick. I could go back. Find a different path. Go back. Find Miles. He would know the way.

Shadows grew long. Her canteen was empty. She left the trail to find water. The woods were shrouded with gray-green moss hanging from the oaks. Her legs stumbled on the rocky ground. She leaned her hand against the hillside to steady herself. Water dribbled over her fingers. A small spring escaped from the stone hillside. She knelt down and used a stick to dig a hollow spot to place her canteen to catch the trickle. The water was cool on her burning cheeks. She rose to her feet. The ground shifted menacingly. Which way was the trail? Shift, shift again. She could not find footing. Her teeth chattered as fever chills shook her body once more. She managed to wrap the blanket and poncho around her and find a log to huddle behind. She never noticed the rain, or the people who carried her away. It all seemed a dream. She thought they were angels. Singing angels.

Days and nights flowed together, unheeded. Willie was barely aware of the smoky dark shelter she lay in. Gentle women's hands ministered to her and their soft voices lulled her.

The day came when the fever and gripping pain in her chest lessened. She sat up and took notice of her surroundings. She was in a small rough sleeping house. Two women sat just outside by the entrance way, one old, one young. They noticed Willie stirring and the younger woman came to her. A shy girl with downcast eyes and a tentative smile, she touched Willie's cheek with familiarity, smoothing the bedding and cooing softly as though Willie were her child. The older woman left and reappeared with warm food. Willie reached for it gratefully.

A tule potato! Oh, dear. She smiled at the two women who watched over her proudly. Oh, dear.

She figured the tule potato had probably not been responsible for her getting so sick on the trail, but its involvement was gruesome. She was not sure she could eat another. She tried a few cautious nibbles, which satisfied her caregivers. They brought her warm herb-flavored water to drink. Willie tried to speak to them using the few words she knew from various languages and dialects. They discussed her attempts between themselves, but they could not understand her, nor she them. The only word they recognized as similar to theirs was that for child. With hand gestures and pictures scratched in the ground, she made them understand the object of her quest. At least it seemed they understood. They nodded their heads reassuringly.

She tired soon. She gave up trying to talk and submitted herself to their attentions. They made her lie back down. They washed her hands and face all the while singing softly. She drifted back to sleep.

This band who rescued her shared their food with her; but it was evident they had little to share. As Willie gained strength, she was led outside, barefoot, to eat with the others. Eleven bedraggled adults watched her with curiosity. They looked half starved. They apparently had no winter stores. They had no weapons that Willie could see. There were no children and no young men. They must have lost a number of their band. The old one who seemed to be their headman did not have traditional trappings of status. She guessed he had only assumed leadership recently. The old woman who was Willie's guardian had more authority in the group than he had, but it was he who was wearing Willie's boots.

This camp is a hiding place, she thought. These people are refugees.

Willie watched the women discuss Willie with the others. After much gesturing she concluded they all understood she was looking for her child, a boy. She thought if she could identify the Bokaima to them, they could probably tell her where to search. But it was difficult. They averted their eyes from her and shook their heads. She had no way to talk to them.

Once again the fine design of the small flour basket caught her eye. It was in the hands of the old woman who was gathering the left over food morsels from the meal and putting them in the basket. The eating time was over and the adults began to leave the circle. The old man had her boots, the old woman her basket. The Bokaima design would speak for her. She needed the basket. She reached out for it. The old woman withdrew it quickly, holding the stash of food close to her chest. They would share with Willie but she could not help herself. The basket was in use.

Willie spoke with animated gestures, trying to get everyone's attention, "Wait, wait. Don't leave yet. Wait! Listen! The basket. My baby! My Child! My child!"

She began repeating the only word she knew that they understood. She pointed to the basket and drew the pattern on the ground, pointing back and forth and repeating, "Child, child, child." She gestured to the hills and appealed to them for directions. Three of the women and two men knelt and examined the basket. They conferred with each other, looking at Willie from time to time with worried glances. She figured these people had seen trouble at the hands of white men; her presence here probably looked like more trouble to them.

Her women guardians were speaking with strident voices, arguing with the others. The younger of the two women narrowed her eyes and shook a threatening finger under the noses of the men. Willie recognized that attitude and appreciated the sentiment. The girl left the group and came to Willie. With her shy smile she beckoned to Willie to follow her. From a vantage point at the top of the hill near the trail the girl pointed across to the hills on the other side of a river canyon, showing Willie where she would find the Bokaima. She removed her ragged leather moccasins and gave them to Willie. She stood with Willie looking out over the distant reach of forest. She tried to speak but tears betrayed her voice. With one hand on her grieving breast she repeated the word "child," shaking her head, weeping, mourning a loss.

Her own baby was gone. She touched Willie's cheek once more and turned back to her people, leaving Willie standing there alone.

28

The path shown her turned north off the main trail she had been following. It dropped back down to the edges of the redwood forest. This path was old and easy to follow, but it often meandered without obvious aim. Willie assumed it was not a thoroughfare, but perhaps an access to various favored hunting and gathering spots. It did meander. She had a good sense of direction. She generally knew where she was in relation to where she had started and where she was heading, but this trail did not seem to maintain relationship to anything. Several times she had to suppress a panicked lost feeling. Eventually, once she became familiar with the peculiar nature of the path, it began to make sense to her and she relaxed and trusted it.

The mountain people had been kind to take her in and tend her until she got well; even though they had sent her on her way abruptly like an unwelcome stray once she was able to travel. The circumstances of their lives put limitations on their ability to extend their circle of caring.

Hill tribes were a sturdy and resourceful lot, she knew.

Their simple lives were always one step ahead of poverty. Neighboring tribes who settled in the valleys generally had more wealth and social networks, but the hill tribes were resilient and independent. Perhaps if they could stay out of the way of the white man long enough they could find a way to survive unmolested. If starvation does not overtake them first.

Willie had recovered her health during her stay with the mountain tribe. She received directions to a possible location of the Bokaima camp. She lost her boots, blanket, poncho, knife, canteen, and jacket. And the small basket, again. She had her heavy sweater and the same clothes she had been wearing for...how long? And of course the moccasins. Never had she traveled so light. The day was overcast, but no rain threatened. It was even balmy.

Maybe a spell of Indian summer, she smiled to herself.

The soft floor of the redwood forest was gentle on her moccasin-clad feet. She strolled easy. Streams and springs appeared regularly, allowing her access to water. A family of deer continued to browse and barely acknowledged her passing. Why would they? She had no power over them now, no weapons, no tribe. She was trapped in the moment just as they were. But they knew what they were about. They were in complete obedience to the rules for deer. Unthreatened, with ample forage, a comfortable herd—they were satisfied. They were unmoved by the beauty of the forest. But she, a woman alone, she walked outside everyone's circle. Was it really the circumstances of war that left her here, or was it the inevitable result of following of her own desire?

Is that it then? Was I following my heart, stubborn and willful? That's why I am wandering alone, looking for my child? No. No. I know it is not true. Like the deer, I have no choice here. I am obeying laws beyond my understanding too.

My love might be greater than my understanding
of how to work things out, but even if I were to die before I
found Alexander, and he were to grow up not remembering
me, my love would live in the heart of his soul. He would grow
up with the strength of a love that is beyond memory.

A sense of peace rested on her. The closer she drew
to the foothills pass that was her goal, the more assured she
became.

Time was lost here in the orderly forest, in the
reasonable meadow. She was ten-thousand years old. She was
everywoman. She was everywoman's heart looking for lost
everychild. Hers was the passion of everywoman. Hers was
the grief of everywoman. She could not look for Miles, she
could only wait. The inevitability of one flesh would reunite
them. She looked for Alexander, she had no choice. There was
nothing to figure; there was only walking. She knew where the
Bokaima were now. She had only to walk.

She was out for an afternoon stroll: now, ten-thousand
years ago—the same. She would gather her family, build a safe
nest, wait for her husband to return from the war. It was the
best she could do.

When the shadows stretched across the meadow she
was passing through, she knew she must find shelter for the
night. It was still early, but she was afraid she might lose her
way in the fading light if she kept walking. There was more
light in the meadow than in the forest during twilight, but
there was nothing there to afford shelter. So she chose the
edge of the forest and found a fire-scarred hollow at the base
of a redwood tree she would be able to curl up in.

Hunger gripped her gut. She walked about the
immediate area and gathered redwood sorrel. Her stomach
churned. She sat on a large flat rock that caught the last rays of
sun and chewed on her sorrel. Her fingers traced the patterns

of moss on the rock until she was struck with the realization that these were man-made patterns. She jumped off the rock and studied the patterns. The light faded fast, but she could see stick figures of people, animals, hands, and other symbols that she could barely make out. The rock was grown over with moss and lichen. The etched glyphs must be very old. She looked forward to the morning when she could study them in better light. For now she must curl up in her tree hollow and try to get warm.

She was too cold and hungry to sleep. She lay alert, vigilant. She hoped her tree was not also the home of some other, larger forest creature. She poked her head back out of her hole to find a stick to arm herself with. She listened to the sounds of the falling night.

What she heard was voices. Voices she recognized. Voices on the path, passing her way. She crawled out of her hiding place and ran stumbling back across the meadow to where she had left the trail. She could see their backs retreating into the woods ahead of her. Long Tree! Young Jack!

Should she call to them, or should she follow quietly? A cry froze in her throat, her feet held fast to the path. She had never actually considered how she would contact the tribe and retrieve her boy, and now the consequences of her bold approach unnerved her.

In the final muted glow of the evening she could see the two men pause at the edge of the clearing, then turn and face her.

29

They led her into the woods, one before, one after. Each was well armed. Neither said a word. She supposed that they still knew no English, but they did not respond when she queried them in Bokaima either. She babbled, regardless, a litany of supplications alternated with threats.

They came out of the woods at the edge of a circle of brush huts; but before she had a chance to scan the layout of the village, they thrust her through the doorway of a roundhouse causing her to stumble into the large room and land in an indignant heap in the dust. She was aware of other people standing at the periphery of the smoky fire-lit room, but she only saw the figure looming over her. Pahto! At last.

She gathered herself to stand and face him. Round Face Woman came to Willie's side offering her a hand up. Pahto backed Round Face Woman off with a movement of his hand and a stern look. She retreated.

Willie brushed herself off and rose slowly. Her gaze never wavered, nor did his. They spoke in Bokaima.

"I have come for my boy."

"You are in my camp now."

"I know that."

"I am headman."

"I can see that."

"Old Chief says that you made passion walk. He says you redeem Little Coyote with passion walk. But you are in my camp now."

Willie did not fully understand the words he used, but she paid it no mind, thinking only to make one thing clear to him. "I want Alexander."

She could not read his eyes. He was sure of himself, she could sense that, but she could not get a sense of his purpose.

She stepped in closer to him and spoke in English, "I want my boy, godammit, Pahto, you bastard. Where is he?"

Pahto turned to Round Face Woman and with a wave of his hand sent her from the room. Now he leaned in close to Willie. The air between them was raw. He took her upper arm in a firm grip. She made a effort to pull it away.

"You are in my camp now," he repeated. He released her arm. "Go to Little Coyote."

She dashed from the roundhouse in pursuit of Round Face Woman. She saw them near the campfire. Alexander was crying and Round Face Woman was telling him about his mother's arrival. He looked up, saw Willie, and, after a moment of stunned disbelief, ran to her.

"Be careful how you hold him. He is hurt." Pahto spoke from behind her.

And then the boy was in her arms. Her hands avoided the wounds on his back while she caressed him, carried him, kissed his wet dusty face and soothed his tender broken heart. She burrowed her face past the smell of smoke in his hair to find the scent she hungered for. Her tongue tasted the sweet sweat at the curve of his throat.

When his sobs turned to whimpers and she regained control of her voice, she tried to examine the wounds on his back. It was difficult because he would not turn loose his arms from around her neck.

"Let me see, my lamb. Let Mama see what happened to your back."

The mention of the wounds led him to a new wave of crying, but he let her examine him. Two fresh bleeding open cuts lay across his back. Willie knew what this was; she had seen its scars on other backs. Gahagaha. She cast an accusing look at Pahto. He turned away and went into the roundhouse with his men.

"When was this done to him?" Willie asked.

"This day," Round Face Woman answered.

"Gahagaha will help Little Coyote," Old Chief tried to explain to Willie.

"Pahto!" Willie yelled after him.

"It was not Pahto who cut him."

"Who did then?" Willie sat on the ground, rocking Alexander. She began to relax the tight hold she had kept on herself during her search. Emotions spilled one over the other; relief, joy, anger swarmed through her thoughts. She was furious at these folks who were her dear friends. They stood around her concerned and helpless.

"Who?" She demanded.

"I did," came the slurred, throaty answer from behind her. Willie turned to accuse the criminal.

"Blue Feather!" Willie mouthed the beginnings of words she could not empower with sound. Blue Feather watched Willie with eerie silent eyes. It was only her eyes that Willie could look at, even though the scarring had distorted the brow and lid of one eye that wandered while the other stayed fixed on Willie. Blue Feather's face hung misshapen and lax. Her jaw had healed in a rigid, unaligned position. She had no control over it. Her voice was a husky rattle. Alexander clung to Willie more tightly yet.

He was afraid of Blue Feather. Willie shook her head, not understanding, appealing to her friend for an explanation.

In Bokaima, Blue Feather spoke in bursts of words Willie could barely make out. "Little Coyote did not thrive. I cut him there. Gahagaha. We do not have enough food for the winter. Gahagaha will help him be strong and bring good fortune to us. This is good for all Bokaima." She stepped backward and disappeared into the shadows.

"A shaman!" Willie whispered in awe. "Blue Feather wears the shirt and the feather of a shaman. What has become of my friend?"

Willie turned to Round Face Woman and Old Chief, who looked concerned and nodded in sympathy.

"She speaks to me as a stranger. How could she do this to my baby?"

Willie had never known what to expect when she arrived here. She knew upheaval and desperation were certain to lead to changes in relationships; Blue Feather's and Pahto's new positions in the tribe did not surprise her, but the intensity of their feelings toward her did.

"How come you have cry drips in your eyes, Mama?" Alexander asked her in English.

"Why darling boy, Mama is just so happy to hold you and look at your sweet face. I missed you and I am very happy to see you."

Alexander put his hand to her cheek reassuringly. "I cried for you Mama."

"I know you did my lamb, and I have been trying to find you. We are together forever now, no matter what."

Alexander examined Willie's clothing, which was strange to him. Sun Ray brought warm food. She sat with her arm around Willie in unassuming friendship. Round Face Woman and Old Chief sat with her also, and others came and went, curious and welcoming. They filled her in on their entire adventure, how they returned to this place, an old hunting camp site of theirs. Willie had to slow them down from time to time when she had trouble understanding their words.

Old Chief still decided where they were to camp, hunt, and gather. He had power still to mediate disagreements. But Pahto was headman. He saw to their protection from threats from outside. Blue Feather danced and dreamed and prophesied. She saw to their protection from threats from inside. No English was spoken. No white ways were allowed... or so Pahto and Blue Feather claimed.

Pahto and Blue Feather were in disagreement about that. Pahto believed they needed the power of the white man's weapons and the speed and mobility of the white man's horses, but they did not need her white-man-influenced dances and dreams. Blue Feather thought there was no chance for survival if they engaged in fighting with the white man with white-man weapons. She believed in the power of faith; she dreamed of a savior.

"Pahto said you would come. Blue Feather did not think you would make it so far as you did," Sun Ray said. "She tried to stop you. She says you put us in danger."

"Blue Feather says we must not let the poison of the white man touch us," Round Face Woman explained as she brought water to Willie.

"But why the gahagaha?" Willie asked.

"Pahto said no. Blue Feather said if we did not do this there would be trouble soon. The white soldiers would come for us. She said the boy was too sad. He would die," Round Face Woman added.

"Of course he was sad! He was taken from his mother to a strange place."

"That is what Pahto said. Blue Feather did the gahagaha when Pahto went out hunting today." Round Face Woman wanted Willie to understand everyone's position.

"But what about you all? Where were you?"

"We helped Blue Feather. We held the boy down while she made the gahagaha with the shell," Round Face Woman answered.

"He must not look up at the oak trees during the gahagaha or the acorn harvest will be poisoned," Old Chief explained.

"We tried to make him feel safe and not scared," Sun Ray added.

"But why? Why didn't you stop her? I was so close."

"We did not know that. Only Pahto knew where you were. I think maybe Pahto was searching for you today. We must do what Blue Feather says. She has dreams that tell her what to do. She dances through the night until the dreams come. She knows what is best for us now," Sun Ray explained. "It was white men who hurt us, Willie." Willie met Sun Ray's eyes.

"I know, Sun Ray." Willie kissed Sun Ray's cheeks which were tear damp now also.

"Gahagaha will be good for Little Coyote," Old Chief repeated with authority. "Passion walk gives him back to his mother. I have said this. Blue Feather hears me."

"What is passion walk?" Willie asked. "Pahto said that too."

"You walked a dark trail alone. You can redeem Little Coyote. Now he is yours again. I have said this. Gahagaha will protect him." Although Old Chief presented his dictate in an lengthy authoritative chant, he tried to speak slowly and simply so that she might understand all his words. She tried. "The white man has not done right," he continued. "We were poisoned living with white man. Little Coyote had no father.

We took him with us so he can be Bokaima. Blue Feather dreamed about great Bokaima leader with blue eyes. But you made passion walk. You redeem him. I have said this."

The Bokaima sitting around the fire marked the end of his speech with calls of "O!" Old Chief took up his pipe, a long wooden cylinder that flared at one end to accommodate the pungent tobacco he packed into it. He lighted the herb with an ember from the fire. He held the pipe upright above him and tipped his head back. He put the tapered end of the pipe into his mouth and drew the smoke into his lungs. After a time he shared the pipe with Round Face Woman.

In the flickering shadows at the edge of the camp Willie could see where Glory stood quietly in his hobbles.

Late that night as Alexander slept curled in the curve of his mother, Willie tried to unravel the tangles of intentions. She was thankful for the grace that allowed her this, to lie with the soft touch of tousled hair on her face, but she knew she and Alexander were not safe here. Their presence probably endangered the whole tribe. Once the whites in the settlements in the valleys south and east of here learned a white woman and child were being held by a wild tribe, neither she nor Alexander nor the Bokaima would be safe.

Anxious thoughts tumbled as she awaited sleep: The Bokaima are my good friends, but now we are also enemies. They are hunted like beasts in the wilderness and they know I am not one of them. I will never be Bokaima. They will never be white. Now must I think of them as my enemies? I cannot trust them; they cannot trust me. I tried to teach them white ways; they want Alexander to live the Bokaima way. They want to live their old ways; I want to return to mine. The weather will be harsher yet on the trail back once winter settles in. There is no way I can make it to the coast with Alexander. I have no idea where any other white settlement is from here. By now the word of our being missing is probably known everywhere and we are already being hunted.

Fear sabotaged her thoughts. While she struggled to make sense of it all, rain began pelting the hut; at first a sprinkle, then a downpour. It would be a long time before anyone entered or left these hills. It rained all that night and every day until the solstice. Four weeks of unrelenting rain.

30

Sergeants Buckner and Finn rode with Colonel Early along the tracks east of the train station. The taste of smoke still drifted in the air, but no fires were visible now. Atlanta's siege-ravaged streets lay quiet in the brisk November morning. Her citizens had been evacuated. Many lived in makeshift shelters in camps scattered in the countryside. Families who had relatives nearby who would take them in were lucky, even though often it only meant company for their hunger. The Confederate Army had demanded all the crops and young men the farms had to offer. Now the Union troops would eliminate any ways and means the city of Atlanta could use to support the Confederacy. Banks, warehouses, rail lines would be destroyed.

"We just spent the last two months repairing these lines Hood's rebels tore up when they abandoned the city. We've been spending every waking hour trying to keep our supply lines open. Why're we tearing them up now?" Sergeant Finn asked.

"We'll be turning loose of our own supply lines,"

Colonel Early answered.

"What? Say that again real slow, Colonel," Daniel said. They had all grown accustomed to the unusual maneuvers of their unorthodox leader, General Sherman, but cut their precious supply lines? Daniel and Marcus stopped their horses and waited for the explanation. Rumors were thick around the encampments in and around the city about what Sherman would do next. Miles had brought these two men out here away from the rest of his company so that he could talk to them privately.

"We won't be chasing General Hood's army up north. We'll cut ourselves free of our supply lines and our communications with the rest of the army. Sherman's going to leave General Thomas and General Shofield to contain Hood. We will march through Georgia to the sea. We'll forage from the countryside and confiscate the supplies that would otherwise go to the Rebs. General Sherman plans to dismantle the economic support the South needs to continue this war."

During recent months Miles' voice was seldom free of this grim tone he spoke with now. He rarely let his anger show, but he never smiled. "Once Vicksburg fell it was foolish for Jefferson Davis to continue to fight this bloody war. Now that Atlanta has fallen, it is criminal. Sherman wants to march through the South and convince them to cease. He will bring the South to her knees."

The three men stood quietly, looking east along the tracks trying to see clearly the events that awaited them.

"We'll tear up what's left of these tracks and any tracks we encounter on the way. We'll lay our own roads and bridges where we need to," Miles explained.

"Who will try to stop us?" Marcus asked. "General Lee?"

"I don't know what kind of resistance we'll encounter.

I don't think there is any kind of army in there, and Lee has his hands full with Grant."

"You mean we're going to fight civilians?" Marcus challenged. "Who is the enemy here?"

"The war is our enemy. All Johnny Reb wants is to go home, just like us. Once we cut away economic support for the military and moral support for the troops, we will defeat that enemy." Miles stared into the distance. "Then we can go home."

"What about mail?" Daniel asked. "How're we going to get mail?"

"No mail. We won't be able to get word in or out until we get to the coast and we connect up with the rest of the Union Army. Sherman is right now trimming down and building up his army to sixty thousand healthy war-seasoned men. We'll be in two wings, marching in four columns, more or less parallel but never in a straight line. We'll feint one direction and head another. No one will know for sure where we're headed, not even us. We don't know where we'll come out. Some say Richmond; some say Pensacola." Miles turned to the two younger men. They had become lean and hard on this campaign. He would see to it that both would receive field commissions before this march to the sea began. He relied on them. Colonel Early's unit was assigned to protect the road builders and engineers as they built the necessary bridges and roads for this army's march. Marcus and Daniel were essential to the company. They did not require a lot of direction in order to get the job done.

They waited now for the rest of what he had to say. They knew the look when he had something difficult to say, his eyes squinted as though he were trying to squeeze out thoughts too harsh to speak.

"I am going to ask General Sherman to relieve me from this campaign," he said. "It's my last chance to ask him to grant me a leave. I must get to California, if only to see them for a few days. It has been too long. I must see them. I have it worked out; I can travel quickly, get Willie and Alex settled in San Francisco, and get back in time to rejoin Sherman when the army reaches the coast. I wanted you men to know." A muscle quivered at his jaw and throat. He wheeled Slats around and cantered back to general headquarters.

General Sherman was agitated already when he received Colonel Early. He paced as he talked, his hands clasped behind him. His red hair was an unkempt tangle; a stubble shadowed his face. He was excited about the march. He had been waiting for approval from General Grant for his plan. Sherman now fired questions at Early. He knew the momentum of his army was dependent on Early's being able to protect his road builders.

"General, there is a matter I need to discuss with you." Early had to capture Sherman's attention away from his planning. It was not difficult. Cump Sherman was a severe man, but devoted to his men. Once he became aware Early had other business on his mind, he stopped his pacing and sat down. He poured them both a drink and waited.

"What is it, Colonel?"

"I need a leave to see my family, sir."

"In California?"

"Yes, sir."

"We have tried to make sure men have had leaves to see their wives and children between campaigns, you know that. But California is too far. And this march is too important. I need you. We all want to go home." He leaned forward and refilled Early's glass. "You might as well appeal against the thunderstorm as against the terrible hardships of war."

A rosy evening light filled the large room of the old Atlanta home that served as Sherman's headquarters. Orderlies and aides talked and laughed in the hallway outside. The sharp warmth of old bourbon spread across the back of Early's head, loosened his joints and brought color to his cheeks.

"When did you last see your family?"

"Not since the fall of sixty-one when I was ordered back here. I have never seen Alex."

"How old is your boy then?"

"He'll be three in the spring."

"When my boy Will was three, we were living in San Francisco. It is a vigorous age. He could hold his own with any three-year-old in Frisco! Remember?"

"I remember that big half-broke roan you put him up on."

"That horse was broke! I gentled him myself. You recall the day we ferried our horses across to the east bay and rode all the way to Mount Diablo? That was long before you had that long-legged mount you ride now."

"I rode that gray mare. Tough little horse; she got old on me."

"I would have liked to have stayed in San Francisco after my banking house there failed. I wanted to open a grocery store, you remember? Banking is a disreputable business. Honesty is not at a high premium. I sometimes think we should eliminate modern economics and return to a system of trading with beads and shells." Both men laughed. Sherman filled their glasses once again. He grew somber with memories and whiskey. "But asthma was about to kill me, and my wife was never happy out there. I would like to have stayed in California. The world wouldn't let me."

"Nor me, sir."

Sherman leaned forward in his chair and said, "Stick with me, Miles. I want to end this war and I want to do it without losing a single man. Not a single man. We've lost too many of these boys." His eyes drifted off to losses too heavy to bear. "Help me make short work of it Miles and we'll all go home."

"I understand, Cump." A thick calm throbbed at his temples. "It's just that I've never seen my son."

Sherman's stiff posture broke. He rested his forehead on his hand. "Of all my children, Will was closest to my heart. It's been two years now since typhus took him."

"There are times I grieve for Alexander as though I have lost him. I am preoccupied with worry. My wife and son are alone."

For silent moments the two men shared this longing for their sons. Sherman raised his head. "What can I do? Is the army seeing to their needs? Is their allotment check enough?"

"A lack of money hasn't really been the problem, but provisions are. And they are too far away from San Francisco for the Presidio to offer them any protection. I am concerned for their safety. The situation where they are has deteriorated, but my wife is...," Miles paused, searching for the right words, "...fiercely loyal. The mail takes so long already and now we will have no communication at all."

"I can contact the Presidio and see to it that they send someone to Fort Bragg to check on them and attend to their needs," Sherman said.

"Perhaps you should request a detachment go up there and bring them down to San Francisco where they can be looked after."

"I'll do it straight away, I promise. I'll send a telegraph message before we leave Atlanta tomorrow. I'll get you home soon, Colonel." Sherman sprang to his feet and resumed his pacing. The griefs of the past were left behind. He plunged forward into analysis of their present circumstances and his theories about the South. "These rebels have fought a war trying to preserve their old ways."

"They want a revolutionary means to conservative

ends," Early commented.

"That's right, but it doesn't work that way. Win or lose, life in the South will never be the same again. I can make Georgia howl! Once we pierce the shell of the Confederacy, we will find it hollow inside. The California Gold Rush helped bankroll the North for this war. When the panic of fifty-seven crashed my banking house and others all over the country, it left the South unscathed because the South was already so poor. But the North recovered and grew wealthier; it has financial, industrial, population resources. The South remains poor. They give a show of luxury, but it is at the mercy of slave labor and the perpetual poverty of the general population and the exhausted soil. The Confederacy is a shell, I tell you, and slavery is a lie told by bullies."

Sherman fixed his gaze on Early. His eyes flashed as he leaned across the table strewn with maps. "I don't want to lose one more soldier to this war, Colonel. Not to a battle or an ambush. Not to combat or a sniper. You understand the kind of security I want."

"Yes, sir. I do."

"No fortifications. No trenches. I want to move forward with impunity. Entrenching makes troops timid."

"If we encounter a sizable resistance?"

"We'll out-maneuver them. Just as we've been doing. I'll take care of that. I can wheel these sixty-thousand men to outflank any army. Sam Grant can throw his whole army against whoever stands in his way without hesitation. He's a master at it. I can't stand the losses. I'll only do it if I must. I'd rather roll right past them. War, at best, is barbarism. I want to see victory, and I want sixty-thousand men to see it with me. You will help me?" This last was less a question than an order.

"I'll want a share of that new supply of repeating carbines. I want all my men to have them," Early replied.

"I've already taken care of that."

"I need field commissions for two of my best men."

"Certainly."

"You'll send men to fetch Willie and Alex?"

"I'll have the message on its way to the Presidio tonight."

They were interrupted by loud voices outside the open door to the hallway. Two orderlies rushed inside followed closely by three cavalry officers. The orderlies had been unable to restrain the officers from bursting into Sherman's presence. Now the room filled with the smell of their heat and excitement.

Their company had been sent to escort five hundred prisoners to a rail head where they would be transported to the Northern prison, Camp Douglas near Chicago. When the escort got back to Atlanta, they rode along the great columns beginning to form up for the morning's march.

"General, at the end of the columns there seems to be about five miles of Negroes. They got everything they own tied to their backs; some of them are packed twenty to a wagon. They're planning to follow you to the promised land. They told me so, sir," a young major reported breathlessly.

Early drew himself back from the intimate comfort he had drifted into and joined the impromptu discussion of the problem of the refugees. Liberated slaves had been flocking to Sherman for weeks.

"We found three men who could be identified as leaders of some sort. We brought them to you, sir. They are Negro preachers!"

"Excellent, Major. Bring them to me."

The three chosen black representatives of the freed slaves came into General Sherman's presence in awe, but their manner was easy, confident.

"Do you understand what this war is about?" he asked

them.

A older man with a head of gray hair answered him, "Yes I do, sir. I been looking for the angel of the Lord since I was knee-high. We know you be fighting for Mr. Lincoln, but we know that when you win, we be free."

"Then I want you also to understand that I cannot take you with me. I wish you all to remain where you are and not load us down with more mouths to feed, which would eat up all the food I need for my fighting men. I can receive a few of your young, hearty men to be paid as workers, but if you follow us in swarms of old and young, feeble and helpless, it would simply load us down and cripple us in our great task. Our success is your assured freedom. I wish you would tell this to all your people so that hunger will not hinder our progress."

"We would rather live in tents by the roadside than live another night as slaves, but we will wait here until your victory." The men were jubilant with the prospects of their new freedom. They were elated to confer and cooperate with the great General Sherman and his staff officers who had gathered in the room.

"I am leaving a regiment behind to hold Atlanta. They will help you set up a camp. My aide will direct you to the general headquarters with a letter from me."

The men shook Sherman's hand and left the room with hope and resolve. They would not be able to convince all of the refugees not to follow their liberators, however, and a column of freed slaves would still be following the Western Army when it marched out of Atlanta at dawn.

It was dark when Early rode back to his camp through war-battered neighborhoods. Fires burned again on the far side of the city and the sky glowed red. Many of Early's men were awake, talking quietly around campfires, sharing stashes of coveted foodstuffs. Colonel Early checked with his staff on their preparedness for the early departure, spoke briefly to Marcus and Daniel to tell them of their impending commissions and that he would be with them on the march, and retired to his tent.

He fastened the tent flap closures and lay in his bed. Once again the air had leaked out of his India rubber air pad. Comfort evaded him. He would like to have wept but could not. He had not lied to his old friend Cump; he was worried about his family. But he had left out the part about this grinding pain. This ache. He had no peace for wanting her.

In the distance he could hear a Negro woman singing in deep slow tones. She sang praise to God. The refugees were impoverished and homeless, but not hopeless. They were not alone. Not like him.

If I could be by the strength of her, God help me.

"War is cruelty," Cump Sherman had said. "You can't refine it."

31

Sherman meted out harsh punishment to civilians within his reach who aided rebels. Homes that served as bases for guerrilla activity were burned. Homes that were suspected as serving as bases were burned. When Sherman came upon the wealthy plantation owned by Confederate General Howell Cobb, he ordered that nothing be spared. Former slaves as well as soldiers carried off quantities of corn, beans, peanuts, sorghum and provisions of all sorts. Bonfires consumed the fence rails and kept the soldiers warm.

Sherman sat in the big house of an abandoned plantation and read a letter from General Hood, who had opposed him in the battle for Atlanta. Hood railed at him for invading Southern territory, and especially for interfering between master and slave.

You came into our country with your army, avowedly for the purpose of subjugating free white men, women, and children, and not only intend to rule over them, but you make Negroes your allies, and desire to place over us an inferior race, which we have raised from barbarism to its present position, which is the highest ever attained by that race, in any country, in all time.

Sherman was perturbed by the tone of Hood's letter, but his men were growing increasingly angry as they encountered this rebel attitude. The Union forces heard reports that any black prisoners taken by the Confederates were shot. The abandoned homesteads Sherman's men encountered along the march often housed slaves left behind by fleeing owners who took the valuable and able-bodied slaves with them and left the old, the young, and the sick behind to fend for themselves. The slaves had been told horror stories about the Union troops—that they would burn men alive, drown the women, roast and eat black babies; that the Yankees would put holes in the men's shoulders, attach harnesses and force them to pull wagons. But the warnings had little effect. The slaves swarmed to their liberators wherever the march led. They danced and sang in celebration. A column of a thousand former slaves followed the army. Even though very few of the families on the farms they passed owned slaves, the troops also began to see themselves as an army of liberation. They told themselves they were not conducting a war against civilians, but a war against bigotry. They allowed themselves to see the citizens and the countryside of the South they passed through as their enemy.

Not only General Hood, but Jefferson Davis, president of the Confederate States of America, and all the newspapers of Georgia called on the citizens to fight against Sherman's army and sabotage its every advance. Some of Sherman's men were killed by land mines placed in the road before one of his columns. From then on Sherman had a group of prisoners walk directly in front of the march. Whenever Union soldiers were killed by snipers, he had an equal number of Confederate prisoners executed. Every effort was made to secure an appropriate prisoner for this end, one whose home state was the same as the sniper's presumed home.

The foraging for supplies began in an orderly manner. Squads of men, each led by an officer, rode out from the two great wings of the marching army. They were passing through countryside whose harvests had long been appropriated to feed the Confederacy's hungry troops. Since early in the war President Jefferson Davis and his Confederate Congress had encouraged planters to replace cotton and tobacco with food crops. The economic base of the Confederacy was planted on the lands of wealthy farmers, consequently they had been largely unmolested by the Confederate quartermasters. The small landowners however were ravaged by the imperatives of the secessionist cause. Women and children—their husbands and fathers away at war—were barefoot and destitute, while fine stately homes were still well stocked with hams and hominy, chickens and eggs, coffee and sugar. Sherman's army did not hesitate to take advantage of this distinction.

The foragers learned their craft well. As they learned where the silver was buried, their military protocol disintegrated. They became known as bummers and they foraged from rich and poor alike supplies that were necessities to the marching army as well as supplies that were merely luxurious booty.

A good forager became an asset to a company—the men ate well and traveled comfortably. Foragers also acted as scouts and reported back any instances of guerrilla resistance, sightings of companies of rebel outriders or the discovery of a supply cache destined for the Confederacy quartermaster.

Sherman issued a special field order directing the foragers to take only what was needed to maintain ten days of provisions and not to enter any residence or commit any trespass. Sherman's quartermasters became adept at loading supplies while on the march so as not to lose their place in the column or hinder the march. They were always shifting the loads in the wagons, keeping several empty, so that when they came to a bummer squad's stash of forage stacked alongside the road they could load up and regain their place in the column quickly. Their wagons were kept full and the teams well-fed.

Sherman insisted that foraging be done by regular parties, properly detailed by their brigade commanders and that all provisions be delivered to the quartermasters for fair distribution. Nonetheless, it became impossible to police the line between foraging and thievery.

Colonel Early never did like Bummer Bob, even before he became Bummer Bob. He never wanted to work. Only food motivated him. During the Atlanta campaign, when their supply lines had been cut, Early tried to motivate him: "The sooner this road gets built, the sooner you get to eat." But even then Bob was figuring better ways to procure food. Once the army launched the march through Georgia, Bob took to foraging right away. He kept Early's men well fed.

He rigged his pack mule with cages so he could bring back live fowl, only some of which were eaten. Men throughout the column were fond of cockfighting; Bummer Bob kept them supplied with game cocks. Fancy men and gamblers among the troops gathered for the fights, betting and drinking until dark.

Early's men often found it difficult to participate in the carousing—not because they did not want to, but only because it was difficult to manage. They ranged far in front of the columns, protecting the road and bridge building crews, and far at the rear of the columns, where the bridges were burned and the tracks torn up.

The engineering crews were ingenious at building

as well as destroying. When they had approached Atlanta they built an eight-hundred-foot railroad bridge over the Chattahoochie River in four days, but now temporary pontoon bridges thrown across even the widest rivers were usually all that was necessary since they no longer relied on railroads for supplies. The army crossed the river and the pontoons were drawn up behind them. Railroad lines that had been destroyed by rebel saboteurs were repaired so quickly there was no delay in the march. Boggy roads were lain with logs side by side to corduroy them, strengthening them enough for the entire army to pass unimpeded. The rail lines behind them were torn up, the rails heated over fires and then bent in knots around trees so that they could never be used again—Sherman's neckties the men called them. Sherman had studied engineering at West Point and took particular interest in the work of the engineering crews.

Sherman directed the columns in a meandering route, keeping the leaders of any opposition guessing as to his intentions and his destination. He headed toward one city before wheeling about and entering another. Even his own men wondered at the time about their purpose, but they were devoted to "Uncle Billy" and complained little.

Marcus and Daniel did manage to find some time to participate in the gambling and gaming. Bummer Bob gave them the pick of the birds he stole from nearby homesteads. A young Negro boy handled their birds for them.

"Henry, this new bird is sick. I don't want him in there with the others," Daniel instructed the boy one day. The columns were moving slowly, but along good roads. The engineer crews and Early's men stayed in their camp forward and off track of the march, tending gear and staging cockfights.

"Bob, where'd you get that scrawny bird. He

maybe looks like a fighting cock, but he's half dead," Daniel complained. The bird made feeble attempts to attack anyone who passed his cage.

"He was all right when I brought him in yesterday," Bummer Bob slurred through a mouthful of tobacco. "I think that woman I got him off of has some birds hid up there, but I can't figure where. That there one used to be a good fighter, but she give me him cause he was sick, I guess. I'm going back up there today, I expect."

"We'll ride with you," Daniel offered.

"We will?" Marcus was looking forward to doing nothing.

"She's a right pretty woman alone on that place. Only about half hour ride from here." Bummer Bob offered this information through half-opened eyes.

"The Colonel won't like this at all," Marcus cautioned.

"He won't even know we're gone if we get moving," Daniel said.

A half hour later, the three men rode into the yard of an impoverished homestead. There was no livestock to be seen. Storage shed doors stood ajar. Broken furniture lay about the yard. At the house a curtain fluttered through a shattered window. The wind drew dust devils from the dried up flower garden.

Two small boys spotted the men and ran crying to find their mother. As the men approached the house she walked slowly onto the porch and confronted the men quietly.

"I've nothing left," she said, stone-faced.

Bummer Bob wiped a dribble of tobacco juice from his chin whiskers. "We want them cocks you got here somewheres."

"I have no fowl of any kind, sir." There was a little fire in her voice now. She raised her hand to sweep a lock of auburn hair off her face. The gesture struck Daniel like the memory of loss. The woman stood her ground against three armed men, with two sobbing boys clinging to her skirts.

"I know you got them birds, lady, and we come for them now."

"We have nothing. No chickens, no grain, no cow. You've taken everything. Why don't you Yankees get out of here now."

"A teenage girl passed around the door, which hung awkwardly half off its hinges, and joined the woman on the porch. Bummer Bob gave a low appreciative whistle. The girl held to the shadows, but the men could see that her face was bruised.

"We don't mean you harm, ma'am. We don't want your food. We are looking for game cocks," Daniel said.

"We are willing to pay fair price for them," Marcus assured her.

"Lieutenant!" Bummer Bob hissed at him.

"It doesn't matter what you want. We have no food, we have no cocks."

Daniel dismounted. The woman stepped back to the shelter of her doorway.

"We mean you and your family no harm," Daniel repeated. Marcus dismounted also and the two of them walked around the farmyard, inspecting the sheds, with Bummer Bob riding along beside them barking anxious protests. When the two men went into the house, Bummer Bob waited outside. He finally dismounted and lay in the shade of a tree. He was asleep there when Marcus and Daniel finally came out. The two boys jumped and tumbled around Daniel's feet. The girl smiled shyly. The woman thanked Marcus for repairing her front door.

"You boys get cleaned up now and we'll be back straight away with some good victuals for your scrawny bellies." Daniel grabbed the boys around their ticklish ribs.

"Shit! You two have lost your minds." Bummer Bob spat a brown stream onto the ground.

"Watch your language in front of the women folk, Corporal, and don't spit where these barefoot babies will be walking," Daniel reprimanded.

"Jesus!" Bummer Bob muttered. They all three mounted and rode off, the children running along after them in the dust.

32

Marcus and Daniel had hurriedly put together as much food as they could carry discreetly. Bummer Bob refused to return to the woman's farm with them.

"Y'all are crazy and I ain't going with you." He waited until they left before he told Colonel Early.

Marcus and Daniel rode off on their adventure with light hearts. Perhaps an evening of chatting and laughing lay ahead. They could tell her of home, of Fort Bragg, of their friends there. They forgot about the war for those few minutes. They forgot as they rode along with gifts for innocent civilian victims of a cruel war. They forgot.

They forgot until they halted their horses at the edge of the yard. Stillness greeted them. Dust hung suspended in limpid air. The broad moment began slow and finished sharp. A bullet caught Marcus in the shoulder just as his spurs dug into his horse's flanks to call for a quick retreat. Too late. More shots brought Daniel's horse down as Marcus fell from his. Daniel grabbed his carbine as they scrambled for cover behind a water trough.

"Where are they?" Marcus's words pulled tight from his throat.

"The house."

"Who the fuck is it?"

"I don't know."

"You see anybody?"

"No, just guns. You all right? This the only place you're hit?" Daniel tried to tie a bandanna around Marcus's wound.

"Yeah, I'm all right. Let's get out of here, get over to the shed where we can get a better shot. We can't see anything here."

"They can't see us either, though. If you can run, we can make it to the shed."

Low, quiet, and quick, they dashed for the back of one of the out buildings. Marcus stumbled inside. Daniel dragged him behind a broken bale of old hay. Blood poured from the hole torn in his arm. Footsteps scampering into the shed drew the bead of Daniel's gun. In his sights stood the older of the two boys. The younger boy peeked from behind his brother.

"You boys go on out of here," Daniel warned them.

"Here they are! In here! I found the Yankees!" The elder boy ran out while the younger stood watching, wide-eyed.

"Shit!" Daniel moved to the door to cover his position, only to face guns approaching from all sides. The woman and her daughter, both carrying heavy, unwieldy muskets and accompanied by a dozen Confederate soldiers armed with Kentucky long rifles, surrounded the shed. Marcus moaned weakly in the corner. Daniel let his carbine drop to his side. The smell of blood and decaying hay made him light-headed.

Daniel retreated into the shed as several of the soldiers and two officers entered. The women followed. The small boy stared at Marcus who continued to lose blood. The soldiers who disarmed Daniel wore patchworks of uniforms, none the same, no recognizable insignia. A large man with captain's bars on his collar faced Daniel with cool menace. He addressed the girl.

"These the ones that hurt you?"

The girl shook her head while her mother answered. "No. Them others come before these two and before the fat one looking for fighting birds. I told you that."

"Any more of you Yankees coming around today to help yourself to our women and our food?" he asked Daniel.

Daniel stood silently. Marcus muttered something and Daniel made a move to go to him. Three rifles persuaded him otherwise. He was taken outside.

"Tie this one up and put him on a horse. We'll take him back to headquarters. They'll want to talk to him." The captain went outside and told the men to prepare to ride out.

"Is the other one dead?" a soldier asked him.

"Not yet."

"You want me to shoot him?" the soldier asked.

Daniel's protest was silenced with a rifle butt.

"Get this one on a horse first," the Captain answered.

Daniel was being mounted onto an unsaddled unshod horse when the report of rifle fire coming from the woods beyond the farmyard brought all the unmounted men running to their horses. One rebel soldier lay on the ground. More shots dropped two more.

Colonel Early held his men under cover where they could pick off the Confederates in the farmyard from safety. The mounted rebels under attack fired wildly into the woods giving cover to those trying to reach their horses. Two more men were hit. The Confederate captain grabbed Daniel's horse and led him to the center of the yard. He held a rifle to Daniel's head as he rode out at the head of his battered company.

"Hold your fire!" Early yelled to his men.

With Daniel as his shield, the Confederate captain led his men out of the farmyard. When the rebels were almost out of sight, Early sent half his company to follow them at a safe distance. "Don't let them see you. See where they take Lieutenant Finn."

Early rode into the farmyard with the rest of his men to rescue Marcus. He dismounted and approached the shed where Marcus lay. A woman and a girl emerged from the shed and leveled their old muskets at him. Early stopped and slowly raised his hand to restrain the men behind him. Both women fired at Early. The older woman's musket was wildly inaccurate and the bullet missed Early. The girl's gun misfired, flashing in the pan but not taking in the chamber. A volley of shots from Union carbines shot both women down.

Two boys ran from their cover and wailed over the bodies of their mother and sister. Early ran inside the shed and found Marcus unconscious but still alive. Shards of bone protruded from the flesh of his upper arm. Early re-wrapped the wound and stopped the bleeding.

"Is there a wagon and harness around here we can rig to take him back?" Early shouted to the men who stood guard outside the shed.

"Stay with me Marcus," he whispered to him. "You're all I have now."

"We'll find something, sir," a soldier replied and ran off, glad for a task to aid his fallen comrade, glad to remove himself from the horror of the dead women and crying children.

A wagon was rigged and Marcus was transported. The children were taken kicking and crying to a neighboring farm.

The detail of men that had followed the fleeing Confederates returned, unable to rescue Daniel. When Daniel's abductors had neared their headquarters, reinforcements of their comrades rode out to escort them in. The squad of Union soldiers was outnumbered and had no choice but to retreat. They rode hard back to the farmyard but found it abandoned, dead bodies lying in the waning sunlight. A cavalry patrol came out to find them and bring them back to the safety of Sherman's invincible corps. They rode away from the farm in a dusk aglow with the flames of the house, the shed and every building they could torch.

33

Colonel Early sat on a canvas camp stool, his elbows heavy on his knees, his head down. General Sherman sat in front of him.

"Where do you think the bastards come from? What's their home state?" Sherman asked.

"I don't know. Sounded like Texas from what I heard of their voices. Looked like raiders. No proper outfit," Miles responded. He studied the back of his hand where Marcus' blood had darkened and dried.

"We'll send a strong battalion after them before dawn, but I'm sure you're right—they are raiders and they'll have moved out by then. Lieutenant Finn will be far out of our reach." He called toward a group of men standing outside the tent, "Templeton! Templeton! You out there?"

A Captain of the Guard who oversaw the contingent of Confederate prisoners had already been summoned and was waiting outside. He entered Sherman's command tent.

"Captain Templeton, you find in those prisoners of yours two Texans and two officers and have them shot. At first light."

"Yes, sir." Templeton left the tent and conferred with aides outside.

Early was still mulling over Sherman's remark that the raiders would soon have Daniel out of reach. "Can't we track them down?" he asked.

"Lieutenant Finn may not even be alive, Miles. If he is, they can move him faster than we can chase." Sherman stood now and paced the short breadth of the tent, frustrated by this circumstance.

"What about Lieutenant Buckner?" he asked. "Will he pull through?"

Miles rubbed the back of his hand. His friend's blood fell away in bits and flakes. "The medics say he has a chance. If he does pull through, it'll be with one arm."

Captain Templeton reentered the tent.

"General Sherman?"

"Yes, Captain?"

"General Sherman, sir, we have no Texan prisoners."

Early did not raise his head or look up, but he spoke before Sherman could respond, "Make it Georgians."

Sherman nodded his affirmation to Templeton who retired wordlessly, his orders clear.

Sunlight slipped through cracks in the loose boards of the barn, and dust from the dirt floor where Daniel lay danced on the shafts of light. His one good eye opened. He drifted out of a fog of semiconsciousness. The ray of sunlight seemed close enough, if he could turn toward it he could get warm by it. From deep in his protective fog he tried to reach out. He lifted his head and arm, ready to turn. Pain seared through his body and he fell back. Back to the cold floor. Back to the fog. His eye shut. He would not go there. Pain is there. No more. Stay back. Deep. Away.

Consciousness bounded by fears can go no further. Voices drifted in from outside the wall and fell on Daniel's ears, but he heard nothing.

"We're not going to get anything out of him today."

"Or any other day. He ain't worth the trouble. Nothing he's said is any help at all. I say we shoot him."

"Yeah! That fucking Sherman shot our boys when they was prisoners."

"We'll hold him until he recovers and we can question him again."

"He can't walk. He hasn't come to since the questioning we gave him day before yesterday. We can't take him with us. You'll have to take him with you if you want him. We want to shoot him."

"I'll need an escort to take him to the Andersonville prison camp. We'll hold him there."

"Andersonville! He won't live long there. What's the point?"

"The point is, he's all we've got. It's important we find out General Sherman's destination and route if we are to stop him."

"If General Sherman was to go to Hell, he'd corduroy the road on the way. You find out where he's heading, what're you gonna do? Blow up a tunnel in front of his army? Shit! He carries a spare tunnel with him. The likes of you ain't gonna stop him. We need Robert E. Lee down here. Lee could stop him."

"Nonetheless, Captain, I'll take the prisoner to Andersonville with me. From there I will report on your situation to President Davis."

"Jefferson Davis! Fat lot of good that'll do us."

"Captain, you are flirting with treason."

"Treason! Treason is Jeff Davis hanging us out here to dry. No supplies. No reinforcements. We can't stop Sherman's whole army by ourselves."

"You just keep General Sherman worried. Hound his edges. We'll lay a trap for him once we determine where he's going."

Daniel watched sunlight through the veil of his lashes. No more than this. Being still. Only his breath to disturb the air. When their boots touched the dirt floor, clouds of dust swirled through his sunlight and he drifted back away. Not to feel. When they reached to move him they blocked the light completely and he was gone.

"Colonel! Colonel!" Marcus called softly to Miles who had fallen asleep in the chair next to his bed in the hospital tent.

Miles woke startled, his heart beating hard, orienting himself to danger. He was surprised to find Marcus smiling at his confusion.

"Marcus, you're awake." Miles rearranged himself in the chair, remembering where he was.

"I have been awake, sir. You're the one who's been sleeping. I thought I'd better wake you before you fell out of that chair."

"They told me your fever had broke last night, but you hadn't been able to sleep in the hospital wagon over these roads."

"I don't know what's worse, traveling over roads that the Rebs tore up, or traveling over roads you boys have fixed." Marcus was weak, but alert.

Miles had despaired of his friend ever recovering from the amputation. For two weeks, every evening after camp was set up he had sat with Marcus as he thrashed with fever and delirium. Now, to see him awake and joking, Miles was relieved.

"I never could trust what those medics were telling

me. They kept saying that once the 'laudable pus' took over, the wound would start healing. It never looked 'laudable' to me; it looked and smelled putrid. You haven't been very good dinner company."

The two men smiled and watched each other in silence. Miles reached across for Marcus' good right hand and held it until awkward tears threatened both of them.

"You won't have to move for a while, we're camped outside of Savannah, which has fallen to us. We should be able to set you up in a hospital in town soon. We've reached the Atlantic Ocean. We have contact with the Union fleet off of Fort McAllister. We'll be getting supplies soon, mail I hope. We should be able to get you out of here and on home."

"Where's Daniel?" Marcus asked.

"I don't know, Marcus. We've made inquiries, but so far we just don't know. There have been no more prisoner exchanges. The South is short of fighting men. Grant and Lincoln don't want to supply them with released prisoners to get back in the fray. Our boys in Southern prisons are just left to wait it out." Miles was restless and had trouble finding a comfortable place for his large frame in the confines of the small tent. "We picked up two Yanks who escaped from Andersonville last week. They were half dead. Skin and bones with sores all over their bodies. Now that we're this close to Andersonville, I hope we'll see all our men freed. President Lincoln's just been reelected; maybe he can bring this thing to an end."

It was the most words Miles had spoken in a month. His men were a tight disciplined unit. None of the roads or bridges or tunnels his men secured had been damaged by rebel attack. Not one man from any of the engineer crews they protected had been lost. Colonel Early watched over every aspect of his unit's operations, but it took very little talking to get the job done. Now for a change he was chatting.

"I don't think they are the enemy, sir," Marcus said quietly. "You told me and Daniel that back in Atlanta. Johnny Reb ain't the enemy, the war is. That's what you told us. We have to see our fellow man as less than human in order to see him as the enemy, worthy of our less than human treatment of him, that's what you told us."

"I guess we're enemies now." Miles stood at the tent entrance and watched the rain. "Two weeks until Christmas. I hope we get mail by then," he said.

"You heard from Willie?"

"No."

"There's a whole stack of letters from her in a mailbag somewhere. They'll find their way here. I'll be able to ride my horse soon, Colonel. I believe I'll stick around until we find Daniel. I don't want to go home without him."

Miles settled back down next to Marcus. "I don't know if any of this country's wounds can heal. We're a young, muscular, hungry country, but instead of building we're fighting among ourselves. The South won't ever be able to forgive us for what we've done here. This war isn't being fought like any war before it, not any more. We started out army against army, but once Lincoln declared the slaves emancipated the whole South became the target. We've devastated their land, left women and children homeless. General Lee holds his army in defense of Richmond: What's the use? The South may be able to stand the fall of Richmond, but not the fall of Georgia. Not like this."

"Lincoln will see that they're given a way to stand up again, sir. Give him a chance. There'll be lots of roads that need building, that's for sure, and there'll be a lot of men that need work." Marcus' words began to slur and his eyelids drooped.

Miles sat quietly until Marcus fell back to sleep. How could he have so much hope and I have none, Miles wondered. If I could be by the strength of her, know she is safe...

34

Christmas Day, 1864
Savannah, Georgia
My Darling Wilhemina:
  Winter has stopped Sherman's army for a while here in Savannah. It will probably be a few weeks before we are able to march north. General Grant is dug in outside Richmond boxing Lee in. But they won't be able to make any big move this winter either. Marcus and I have dry comfortable lodgings in town. We have become separated from Daniel, but I hope we will be reunited with him soon. I believe spring will bring the end of this war.
  We will leave a wake of desolation behind us when it's over though. I don't know what will become of these people. The white folks think Sherman is the devil and the Negroes think he is Moses, come to redeem them. Thousands of Negroes followed us through Georgia. The logistics of supplies and mobility are difficult with such a large group of dependent camp followers, but it is hard to figure out what to do about them. Sherman is in negotiations now, trying to

hammer out a plan to give each Negro family forty acres of land and a mule to work it. He says we've liberated the land and it ought to belong to the man who works it, not the man who sits in the big house profiting by the labor of others. Sounds like your father. But I think, once we pull out, the whole situation will deteriorate even further. The rich white men will regain power and they will never willingly allow Negroes to own prime farm land.

Once we turn and march north, I fear our men will know no restraint in their treatment of South Carolina. They are tired of war and want to go home. They hold South Carolina responsible as the mother of secession. They are horrified at the condition of the Union soldiers who escaped from Andersonville and found their way to our corps. The men are angry, and their loyalty to Sherman (they call him Uncle Billy) is strong. They will follow him anywhere.

I talked to a Southerner who is camped out with his family on the courthouse lawn here. He and his sons had built up a piece of land nearby and worked it themselves. Now he has nothing. He is burnt out. His home, the fences he built when his boys were young, the sheds he added over the years, his fields, everything.

But his plight only sharpens my concern for you and I hold it against him, somehow, that we are apart.

Daily I expect letters from you. We had no mail until we reached the coast, but that is sporadic and none from you. Cump arranged for someone from the Presidio to check on you, but we've heard no report from them either. It is unsettling to have no word of you at all. I would prefer to be on the march again where I know what I am supposed to be doing. Then I can keep busy with my tasks and avoid the fears and worries that haunt me when I can only wait.

Bravery is the mark of the man, I know, but I am no longer brave. I only can find a kind of fearlessness that comes from defeat at the hands of fear.

There is little to do here. The men await supplies and mail, mend gear, get re-outfitted. The supply of replacement clothing is limited, of course. My riding cloak you mended is still holding up, but everything else I have could stand your attention. I do get joshed about the edge of red silk you used to patch the cloak's lining, but when that flash of red from under my cloak catches my eye I can see you sitting by the window with your sewing basket, the graceful sweep of your needle, your laugh, "Miles, I cannot sew when you're doing that!" But I couldn't keep my hands off you.

I know I shall touch you again soon. Kiss Alexander for me.

Your loving husband, Miles.

Early walked back from the docks where he saw his letter to Willie safely aboard the ship carrying outgoing mail. He had questioned and accused every person he could find who knew anything about incoming mail. His inquiries gained him no satisfying answers. His frustration and anger exploded and he knocked over a large bag of mail, spilling its contents onto the damp floor of the mail room.

"That won't help us any, sir! Those letters are for other men who want them just as much as you do yours. Why don't you just take it easy and get out of here. When we get the letter, you get the letter."

He did not believe them, but he left anyway. No one could possibly want mail as much as he did. They had not located his mail yet; he had no confidence they ever would. His temples pounded as he strode along the side streets to where his unit was garrisoned. Soldiers lounged in the taverns that were still in business. Game rooms had been made out of deserted store fronts.

Early found a group of his men huddled under an awning, planning a Christmas Day meal. Marcus and young Henry, whose attachment to Marcus had only increased since Marcus had lost his arm, were in animated conversation at the edge of the group. Marcus pressed some money in Henry's hand and the boy ran off down the waterfront street.

"Colonel," Marcus greeted Early. "Wait until you hear this! Henry has found someone with a good stash of tobacco. He's going after some for me now. It's just down the street. He'll be right back. And listen! In this little tavern across the street, you'll never believe what they've got. Just guess. You'll never guess." In the face of war heaving threats at his loved ones, Marcus had replaced his customary taciturn manner with joviality. He surrounded Early with upbeat chatter in an effort to keep him from sinking further into the despair that held him. Today Early looked worse than ever. Creases pulled on his face and dark circles lined his eyes. Marcus took him by the arm and led him across the street to a small tavern.

"Over here, have I got a surprise for you. In this place they've got, get this, peach pie! Ha ha! Somehow they had some canned peaches they've hoarded and now they're selling peach pie. It's a bit expensive, but they take trades. Of course they make their coffee with godawful chicory in it, but look here! Pie! It is Christmas, isn't it? I haven't had any yet, I was waiting for you to get back. No mail yet, huh?"

The tavern was empty of other customers. Marcus and Miles sat on three-legged stools at a bare, stained table next to a window.

"They say Jubal Early ate here. Think of that. Kin of yours, a Confederate General, ate at this same place, maybe even this same table. He gave the folks in Washington a hard time last summer, quite a pounding. Now he's up against Sheridan, I hear. Sheridan'll take care of him, what do you think?"

"I think I've never heard a man talk so much, even you. Where's this pie you've been going on about?"

"They're not real happy about waiting on Yankees here, but they'll come around. They're lurking in the kitchen. We'll just wait them out. Henry's not back yet, anyway. I promised him a piece of pie." Marcus drummed his fingers on the table. The colonel's gloom made him nervous. "Jubal Early is a Virginian. I was born in Virginia, but I don't have any people there any more. I was raised up in Maryland."

"Jubal never wanted secession. He felt he had no choice but to join the Confederates once Virginia seceded." Reluctantly Miles was drawn into conversation.

"I wonder about all the boys I've known who are Rebs now. Johnson and Dillon served with us in Fort Bragg. Cletis, he was a good friend. They're all Rebs. Gibson, the guy that first set up Fort Bragg, he's a Reb, but I never knew him. He even named the camp after Braxton Bragg, and he's a Reb general now. You knew Bragg too, didn't you?"

"Yeah, I served with him in the Mexican War."

"How do you suppose it would be if we were to see all those boys when this thing is over?"

"It'd be just the same as if you and I were to sit with Daniel again. We'd tell war stories and eat pie. We were all career soldiers. We aren't like all these civilian soldiers who came into this thing not understanding soldiering and the code of the warrior. It will be hard for them to forgive. We would just be glad to be alive and sitting with friends," Miles' voice trailed off and he stared out the window.

"Code of the warrior, huh? That sounds, I don't know, lofty. Code of the warrior...sounds..."

A cheerless woman approached their table and asked Marcus what they wanted.

"Yes, ma'am! We want peach pie and coffee, please."
She retreated without responding, her face

expressionless. She and a burly man spoke quietly to each other at the back of the tavern, moving slowly.

"They're probably going to be making more money off of all these hungry and thirsty soldiers than they did before the occupation. You'd think she could look a little less sour," Marcus said.

"They'll never be happy about it," Miles said.

Rain drizzled outside the window as the sun, angling to slip through the clouds, made the wet panes sparkle. Henry burst through the door and a gust of cool air blew across Miles' face. The boy carried a handful of large cured tobacco leaves, which he laid triumphantly on the table in front of Marcus who thanked him with a little one-armed roughhousing. As Miles watched them, tenderness softened his despair. Henry sat down and relayed every detail of his quest to Marcus. The rich smell of tobacco filled the room. Marcus grinned.

The proprietress returned and set two servings of pie down on the table. The forks clattered on the plates.

"Thank you, ma'am. We'll be needing one more piece, please," Marcus said.

The woman breathed in short gasps. "I might not have much choice but to serve you all," she said, "but I'll never serve pie to no nigger boy. And he can't sit in here neither."

The burly man came out from the back and stood watching. Marcus was still grinning. He looked down at his plate. His smile broadened in amazement, and his eyes opened wide. Miles and Henry followed his eyes to the plate. What they saw on the chipped, cracked saucer was the smallest piece of pie any of them had ever seen. Marcus looked back up at the woman, then back at the miniature pie segment. He picked up his fork and scooped up the pie and put the whole piece in his mouth at once. Henry whooped and laughed as Marcus managed to chew and swallow the pie without losing a crumb.

The woman's jaw tightened. "The nigger cannot sit at my table."

Marcus appealed to her, "Look, lady, we didn't come all this way for the boy to be put out like a dog on Christmas day. We'll pay for the goddamn pie." His smile was gone.

Early rose slowly from his stool. Despair reclaimed his face. He walked to the back of the room. He brushed past the man and grabbed an entire uncut pie from the pantry shelf and brought it back to the table and placed it in front of Henry.

The burly man fetched a shotgun from under the counter and approached the table, cursing Colonel Early, Yankees, and niggers. Early kept his eye on the man and moved to the door and opened it. He called to the group of his men who still loitered raucously across the street.

"Yes, sir!" They responded. His sharp tone hurried them to him.

"Disarm this man and make sure there are no other weapons here," Early ordered. "Station guards, inside and out, until Henry finishes his pie." The men moved quick. They took the man's shotgun and searched the tavern. Armed hostile civilians were a danger to them all. The fact that their commander had been threatened was especially alarming.

Early turned to the woman. "Lady, there are sixty-thousand men out there who say this young man can eat wherever he wants."

The tavern filled with Early's men. Marcus and Henry fought over their pie. The men decided they had found the perfect place to stage their Christmas party, so near where their unit was garrisoned.

Miles stepped out into the rain and walked to the converted warehouse where Slats was stabled. He saddled up and rode up to a hilltop at the southwest edge of the secured periphery of the Union-held territory around the city of Savannah. Through the rain dripping off the brim of his hat, he looked in the direction of Andersonville. Since Daniel's body was never left for them to find as a reminder of the fate of captured Yanks, Miles hoped they had taken him to the prison camp at Andersonville. But the infamous prison was out of his reach now. All during the march across Georgia many of the men had harbored the hope that Sherman would turn toward Andersonville and free the Union troops imprisoned there. That was no longer possible. Sherman had needed to drive to the sea to make contact with Grant; now he would turn his Army of the West north to join Grant's Army of the Potomac and secure the South's final defeat.

Miles turned away and rode back down into Savannah.

35

"I don't know, Brother Samuel, that boy's been here two months and he ain't said a word yet. We don't even know what his name is or what outfit he's from." A young man with fair features beneath the layer of dirt addressed an older man whose unkempt shock of coal-black hair shot in spiked rays in all directions around his head.

"I know what his name is Brother William," Samuel responded. "It's Daniel. He told me that yesterday after prayers. It's only been the past fortnight that he's been able to keep any food down to speak of. He's getting better. Since I've been collecting rain water for him to drink, his dysentery's not been so bad. He's getting stronger." The three men were sitting on the ground in a makeshift tent that provided scanty shelter from the rain. Samuel helped Daniel to his feet and encouraged him to take a walk. The walks around the muddy, filth-infested compound frightened Daniel, but the movement brought feeling back to his limbs.

"And another thing," Brother Samuel said, "he cried when he told me his name. That's a good sign. That means he's feeling the Lord's hand on him." Samuel held Daniel's arm as they walked, more to keep him moving forward than to support him. Daniel had grown stronger under Brother Samuel's attentions.

"I'm taking him over to the Providence Spring to wash him with the pure waters of God Almighty before the guards come to hand out the transfer cards today," Samuel said.

"They won't be giving him no transfer card," Brother William said. "They're giving them to the boys that's been here longest, and I've been here longer than him, and you been here longer that most. Besides, he got kicked in the head too many times before he even got here. I don't think he knows where he's at or the way home."

Brother Samuel guided Daniel around the trenches, puddles, and open sewers that traversed the Andersonville compound. Even though the rains could not wash away the stench, they could overflow the sewer trenches and flood the camp with disease-carrying excrement. Still, walking through it was easier than finding a dry place to lie down. Daniel's bare feet were swollen and red, but he showed no sign of their being sensitive to the rough ground.

"Yes sir, Brother Daniel, things are looking up now. Why, you never saw this place at its worst. Last summer there were thirty thousand men here, and they were dying two hundred a day. The food was bad, but the water was worse. That little stream there going through the middle of camp was all there was and it wasn't fit to drink.

"That's why, come August, the Lord dried that stream up and we had no water at all except the vile liquid the guards brought to us. It was the wrath of God, we knew that. Myself and the other brothers who fear the Lord, and there were hundreds of us believers, we started a prayer vigil. We prayed night and day; we prayed without ceasing, just like it says in the Word. On the third day the Lord brought water from the ground. A fresh underground spring burst forth spontaneously with pure sweet water. Providence Spring! Praise the Lord. And all things will be restored in him. Amen.

"So many boys were dying from disease, starvation, beatings and bullets that even Jeff Davis's Reb congress got wind of how horrible it was here. They sent some men up here and ordered that we all be relocated to better camps. Now there's only a few thousand left here and there will be more transferred today. None too soon for most of us. There's still too many boys dying every day."

They arrived at the spring where a leaky barrel was propped at an angle to collect the thin flow of fresh water.

"Yes sir, all will be restored in Him!" Brother Samuel took small handfuls of the precious water and washed Daniel with it. Daniel submitted to Brother Samuel's gentle hands and never took his eyes off him.

"Brother Daniel, do you know what that means, what God has promised us in his Word? All things will be restored? Everything which was lost will be found? We've all lost a lot who have come to this place. We've lost our freedom, our ability to feed ourselves, our health. Some have lost arms and legs. Back home some little children have lost their daddies. Our hearts are struck with pain when we lose something. There is an emptiness where that thing we were attached to used to be. But, praise God, when we put our faith in Jesus Christ, all will be restored!

"Does that mean that Brother Pete's leg will grow back? Or that those little babies' daddies will come back? No sir, not in this life. But it does mean that they are restored even now, by faith in Jesus Christ. He will enter our hearts and fill the empty place. He will fit there perfectly. We will understand that all things work for good for those that believe in him. All will be restored. He just wants us to love each other the same as he loves us. Greater love has no man than this, than he lays down his life for a friend."

Brother Samuel talked and talked while he washed Daniel and smoothed back his tangled hair. The muscles in Daniel's face contorted and quivered and tears dampened his cheeks. Brother Samuel talked.

"In sixty-three I was in a prison camp in Salisbury, North Carolina. Myself and two brothers escaped from that hellhole, only to be captured and sent here. Then we found out what hell was really all about! But anyway, when we were in Salisbury, you know what we did? We played baseball. You ever hear tell of baseball?"

Daniel nodded. The soft memory of a baseball game was as soothing as the cool water of the spring.

"Well then you know. You get a ball pitched and you hit it with your bat as best as you can. You make your way around the bases, trying to get back home safely before those other boys catch the ball and tag you out. But you've got all the brothers on your team. They're trying to help you get home. And you! You try to help them get home. Even if you hit a fly ball and get put out, you maybe helped someone else get home. The brother gets home safe, and you'll get another chance in the next inning. I was happy playing with the brothers in the baseball game. That's when the Lord told me to escape and try to make it home. It wasn't until after I was captured and brought here that I found out where the only truly safe base is: God's mercy.

"You are washed clean now, brother, I guess you don't need to hear any more preaching," Samuel said softly.

Daniel laid his head on Samuel's shoulder. The two men sat on the barrel's edge and watched as a guard unit rode through their section of the camp, handing out transfer cards to men whose names were on their list. As the riders approached, Samuel and Daniel rose to face them.

"Samuel Austin?" the captain of the guards asked.

Daniel retreated a few steps before Brother Samuel's hand caught his arm.

"I am Lieutenant Daniel Finn," Brother Samuel answered, "and this man here is Sergeant Samuel Austin. He does not have the ability to speak."

The guards' suspicions were muted by their callous indifference. The captain handed down a transfer card with Sergeant Samuel Austin's name on it. Brother Samuel grabbed it quick and handed it to Daniel.

"He's much obliged, sir," Brother Samuel said.

36

After three days on the march, Daniel began to drift back into his fog. The soles of his bare feet were raw with cuts and scrapes. He had no idea where he was being taken. He had been reluctant to leave Brother Samuel and the tattered tent they shared; now he was remorseful. Circumstances had not improved.

The line of prisoners straggled rather than marched. Each prisoner's wrists were bound, but the men were not tied to each other. The countryside they passed through was poor. Women, children and old men watching them pass could feel little vindication. Were these sickly, emaciated skeletons of men the same indomitable Yankee monsters who have been terrorizing their homeland? Smug satisfaction at seeing the brutal warriors brought to their knees was shadowed by the shame of witnessing their degradation. As the prisoners walked through the muddy streets of one small town, a young war widow who ran into the street to spit on the prisoners was tolerated but not cheered by the silent crowd who stood aside to let the defeated men pass.

Twice the prisoners passed Confederate units marching in formation in the opposite direction, north to join General Johnston in Jeff Davis' last attempt to stop Sherman. Confederate ranks everywhere were thinned by desertions, and these units were no exception. Many of their comrades-in-arms had returned to wives and farms that desperately needed them. Plaintive letters drew them home. Many others wanted to lay down their arms in the face of endless bloodshed and butchery. In the ranks of the Confederates who passed by the line of prisoners the morale of the men was further eroded by the sight of the stumbling ragged Yankees and the stench of their festering sores and rotten clothes.

The Confederacy was bankrupt. That the South could field an army at all was due to the resolve of the resourceful soldiers who remained for honor.

Daniel began to fall to the back of the line, unable to keep up. A mounted guard prodded him with a bayonet.

"Move Yank! You laggards are a nuisance. If you can't keep up any better than this, they should have left you at Andersonville." The guard reached down and grabbed Daniel's hair. "Listen, shithead! You keep up with the others, or else as soon as we get out of sight of these townspeople I'll shoot you dead. You seen me do it before. Now march!" He pushed Daniel forward; but the guard's threats could no longer pierce the fog, and the bayonet pricks lost meaning. Daniel fell to the ground.

"Get up, shithead!" Prod. Prod.

"Hold there, sergeant!" A Confederate soldier who had observed the incident approached the guard. He wore the regalia of a cavalry officer. Supple leather boots reached above his knees. He sported a plume on his casually slouched hat whose brim was pinned up on one side. At the waist of his jacket he wore a tasseled belt. Looped braid on his lower coat sleeve indicated his field officer rank and he wore a

major's star on his collar. Until the Union's Western Army
came east, the Confederate cavalry were unequaled by their
Union counterparts in horsemanship and fighting skill. They
were usually outnumbered, but they made up for it in bold
position, daring attacks, and their unnerving rebel yells.
Their commander General Jeb Stuart often said, "We must
substitute esprit for numbers."

The officer broke ranks with his company and
approached the rear of the line of prisoners. Daniel lay in the
muddy road. A light rain blurred the speckled blood stains on
his shirt. The guard had dismounted and stood over him.

"Leave the man be," the rider insisted. "Who is in
charge of these prisoners?"

"I am myself, sir. Sergeant of the Guard
Humpston."

"Sergeant Humpston, I am Major Carter of the
Nineteenth Virginia Cavalry. You have a prisoner here who is
familiar with the security defenses of General Sherman's army
corps. My company is riding to join General Johnston's army
which will soon engage Sherman. I request that you turn this
prisoner over to us for questioning. I will take him off your
hands and assume all responsibility for him. He evidently
cannot keep up with your line of march anyway, and we can
make use of him." Two other cavalrymen dropped back and
joined Carter.

"Yes, sir. I'm happy to help the cause anyway I can.
Yes, sir. This shithead's no use to me. No, sir." He prodded
Daniel once more. "Get up, Yankee. There's officers here come
for you." When he reached down with his bayonet to prod
the prisoner again, Major Carter leaned from his saddle and
seized the guard's arm.

"Leave the man be, Sergeant Humpston. We'll take
care of him from here."

"You'll take care of him. Yes, sir. Looks like he's been

taken care of already. I'll be needing a signed receipt for this man, saying you took him off me."

Major Carter signed a receipt for "the prisoner Sgt. Samuel Austin" and waited until the guard marched off with the column of prisoners before he dismounted and hurried to the prisoner to cut free his bound hands.

"Daniel! Daniel! Can you hear me? Look at me Daniel!"

When Daniel raised his face from the cool roadway he exposed the white scar that ripped from the top of his head to his cheek, ending just beneath his hollow, staring eyes. He peered through the fog. The image eluded his vision, but even his clumsy tongue remembered the name of the face.

"Cletis," he said with deliberate focus. "I need some help getting home." His eyes closed and his head sank back into the mud.

37

Young Henry kept himself well-hidden behind Marcus. He shifted his weight from one foot to the other, unable to keep still. He did not know who Secretary of Defense Edwin Stanton was, but he thought he must be a fearful man. He wondered at anyone who would dare to cross Uncle Billy.

Lieutenant Buckner and Colonel Early waited with Henry in an anteroom of the church where Secretary Stanton met with a group of black church leaders Sherman had invited to discuss the problems and needs of the former-slave refugees. General Sherman had just burst out of the meeting room in a fury. Now he paced the anteroom, alternately moving about with short bursts of energy and then pausing to glare out the window. His anger was barely contained.

Henry ducked closer behind Marcus when General Sherman stopped near Colonel Early and absently fingered the pages of a Bible lying on a wooden desk.

"Are you a believing man, Colonel?" he asked.

Early turned sympathetic eyes to his commander.

"My wife is a Catholic, you know," Sherman continued without waiting for a response. "She fears for my soul, but I cannot embrace it. The timidity. The acceptance of defeat. She wants me to duck my head. I believe God wants men to prevail over evil. Mr. Stanton is a evil man. He means me harm. He sees me as a threat to his power and he tries to use this Negro thing to defeat me."

"Negro thing?"

"He wants to prove I do not look to their well being."

"But they love you. And what of your plan to give the blacks the abandoned lands of the Sea Islands off the coast to farm for themselves?"

"He thinks it is a ruse and that I pressured the Negroes to praise me in his presence. He thinks I am secretly undermining the efforts of the abolitionists. He wants to maneuver these people to reveal evidence to support his theory. So, he ordered me to leave the room that he might assess their true response without my intimidating presence."

"Ordered you out?" Early repeated incredulously.

Sherman's face was scarlet with emotion and the muscles around his mouth twitched. "It is certainly strange that the War Secretary should question Negroes concerning the character of a general who has commanded a hundred-thousand men in battle, has captured cities, conducted sixty-five-thousand men successfully across four hundred miles of hostile territory, and has just brought tens of thousands of freed men to a place of security."

Just then the meeting room emptied and the murmur of pleasantries filled the anteroom. Stanton approached Sherman as though greeting an old friend.

"General Sherman! Yes! These men have given you their highest praise. They tell me your conduct and deportment toward them characterize you has a friend and gentlemen. They express confidence in you and think their concerns could not be in better hands."

Sherman could not completely conceal the glimmer of bitter gloating in his eyes. He did not speak as Stanton made eloquent statements loud enough for all to hear. Sherman ushered him with cool formality out to his entourage and saw him on his way back to Washington.

In the church anteroom the black church leaders were taking leave of each other with fraternal cheer. They knew they were facing troubled times, but they were relishing the taste of their new freedom.

A tall robust man dressed in the clothes of a farmhand, holding a raveled straw hat tied with a bandanna around the crown, approached Marcus, Henry and Miles and greeted them cordially. His large rough hand reached down and enveloped Henry's. Henry clung to Marcus.

The tall man was Henry's Uncle Wesley, his dead mother's brother. When Marcus had learned that Henry had kin nearby who would be attending this conference, he arranged to meet with him. Uncle Wesley was the preacher for a flock of former slaves who worked a plantation on an island off the southern border of South Carolina. He wanted to take Henry home with him.

"For true, the boy belongs with his own folks. He be needin' us. We be needin' him," Wesley told them in the melodious dialect of the islands.

"I've grown fond of Henry and I can take good care of him. This war will soon be over. I'll take him back to California with me. He could go to school. Learn to read and write. He's a smart and clever child. He deserves a decent chance," Marcus pleaded.

"For sure, them book-teachers only for the white folks hereabouts. But now we done been delivered; we be safe soon. But we need good boys to learn to read and write and start for teach each other and make learn true. This other country you want to take him to, California, how they treat colored folks there? Same as for white folks?"

Henry moved in tighter to Marcus, trying to merge himself with the large man's leg. Marcus studied the worn floorboards, looking for a satisfactory answer.

"Yes, there are dark-skinned people there," Marcus answered. "And no, they are not treated well for the most part. But they are not slaves, and many folks want to treat them well. Henry will be with me. I will take care of him."

"He always be a nigger boy though, yes? For true, we lose all our children if we lose our chance in days comin' to be raisin' up strong men to lead our people to good life with our white brothers and sisters."

Wesley's simple vision for his people and sense of brotherhood for all people brought Marcus's conflicts in sharp contrast. Henry sensed his weakening resolve and dug his fingers deeper in the grip he had on Marcus' thigh.

"The boy loves me and wants to go with me. I will take him to church myself."

"What church? Will this here church learn him up to be a proud leader of his people?"

Emotion swept Marcus. He shouted at Wesley, "Proud? Proud of what? What can you do for him? You have no land, no food, no homes, no hope."

Wesley did not yell, but his strong voice filled the room and rattled the windows. "The boy belongs with his people. He is our hope."

Henry bolted and ran from the room. Miles put a restraining hand on Marcus.

"Gentlemen," Miles said, "this does Henry no good. We are beginning our march north within a week. Let Henry travel with us for another month. We will look to his safety. Perhaps by then the situation will have calmed somewhat. We know how to contact you. We can all think about this and talk to Henry. By then we should be able to make a decision that suits everyone."

"I know you be righteous men," Wesley's manner softened and his tone was conciliatory. "We leave it in the Lord's hands now. For true true, I always be searchin' for my one lost sheep. Lord have mercy on us all."

38

Sherman's two-winged army lumbered through February and early March, bulling its way through the Carolinas. Dreadful marching country threw itself in Sherman's path and slowed him to a hard-won ten miles a day: swamps and rain-swollen rivers, bad roads made worse by spring downpours, a ravaged countryside that yielded few provisions to even the now-legendary grasp of the bummers. But nothing stopped Sherman. His men engineered crossings, built bridges, laid down corduroy roads, and trudged through swamps with rifles and boots held over their heads. They passed through Columbia, the capital of South Carolina, and left it burning behind them. Their relentless drive demoralized the South, producing a flood tide of Confederate desertions.

Robert E. Lee, still holding on against Ulysses S. Grant's siege at Richmond, ordered reinforcements sent to Joseph Johnston's army for a stand against Sherman at Bentonville, North Carolina. Sherman rose to meet him with a tough, masterfully coordinated corps who fought Johnston to a standstill. The intense and bloody battle left twenty-six-hundred Rebels and fifteen-hundred Yankees dead. But once the doomed Johnston was driven with his back against the river, Sherman held his army in check and refused to release them to crush the outnumbered Confederates.

"My boys have walked across water and through fire for me," Sherman said. "I would rather avoid a general battle now. Johnston is a master at withdrawing in perilous circumstances. He will slip away in the night and we will hear no more of him. They abandoned all their cities to get enough men to whip me but did not succeed."

Sherman's men smelled the finish line. They would not entertain defeat. Sherman led them north.

Sherman had left General Shofield behind at Atlanta with General Thomas to follow Hood's Confederate forces into Tennessee and keep them from turning back and interfering in Sherman's march to the sea. After the battle of Bentonville, Shofield's corps merged back with Sherman's great army, which now numbered ninety-thousand men. They bivouacked in sprawling camps stretching from Bentonville to Goldsboro, North Carolina.

Grant sent reports to Sherman advising him on the deterioration and imminent dissolution of Lee's army. Sherman made the short trip north to the Union supply harbor at City Point on the James River, where supplies, food, and arms were stacked in great piles, waiting to fill the eighteen trains a day that left City Point to supply the Union forces. There Sherman met with Grant and President Lincoln to discuss the fate of the country and Lincoln's desires for a bloodless winding up of the war and a reconciliation with the Southerners.

The men camped near the Bentonville battlefield enjoyed a respite from fighting and marching. They shared a truce with the Confederates while the dead were buried and the wounded attended to. The acrid battlefield stench was being replaced by the promising smells of the first days of spring. The dawn chorus of courting songbirds announced their reclaiming of their valley.

Marcus and Henry were outside Colonel Early's tent discussing the details of the final agreement they had made with Uncle Wesley. Wesley had consented to Henry's traveling out west with Marcus so long as communication was frequent and it was assured that Henry could return at any time he needed or wanted to. Henry and Marcus were silly with relief, even though Henry was trying to concentrate on the application of an ointment to Marcus' hair—one more battle in every soldier's fight against the insidious louse.

Inside the tent Miles Early listened to their chatter while he wrote yet another letter home. It had been so long since he had heard from Willie that his letters could not escape the monotonous refrain of worry and yearning.

"Lord of mercy, Henry! That is foul-smelling potion you got there. What's in that?"

"Miss Mabel give it to me. I don't know what it's got," Henry answered.

"Well Miss Mabel is a fine woman, but she's black, Henry. Maybe this is only for colored folks. I don't want no nappy wool for hair like you got."

"I think that'd be fine! Then people might think you're my daddy!"

"What about my white skin? You're black as nighttime."

"I'd tell them you got real scared when they took that arm off and your face went all white."

"I think it's time you rinsed that shit off my head, Henry you little brat, before I expire from the smell. Then you won't have no kind of daddy."

"It's almost all washed off now. Hold your peace. You the one with the cooties in your hair, not little brat Henry."

The sounds of their fondness for one another only sharpened Early's melancholy.

"Holy Jesus! Colonel!" Marcus shouted suddenly. "Colonel! You'd better come out here. Holy Jesus!"

Miles threw open the tent flaps and squinted into the bright colors of morning as he tried to bring the scene into focus. Three mounted Confederate cavalry officers riding behind a five-man Union escort were in front of his tent. Their horses snorted steam into the cool morning air. The riders had approached from the east and the rising sun framed their heads and left their faces in shadows.

The captain of the Union escort dismounted and addressed him, "Colonel Early, sir? These Rebs have passes and authorization from generals on both sides for a prisoner exchange, with the condition that they can deliver our Union officer to you personally, sir."

"Holy Jesus," Marcus muttered under his breath. "Holy Jesus." He moved to Daniel.

"Sir, if you want to receive this officer and this Confederate delegation, we will leave them here and wait over yonder," the captain indicated a group of Early's men that were gathered around a card game nearby. "You can call us if you need any assistance, sir. In one hour we will escort the Rebs back to their lines. This officer has been wounded, sir," the captain said.

"Thank you, Captain," Miles answered. Daniel sat motionless between the Union riders. "Lieutenant Finn belongs to my command. We will take him care of him from here."

The escort withdrew. Marcus and Miles stood by Daniel's side. Daniel watched them with a soft smile, but did not move. One of the Confederate officers dismounted and moved closer to them.

"Go slow with him, Miles. He is some skittish and he

rarely talks," he said.

Miles turned to face the familiar voice. "Cletis!"

"Holy Jesus," Marcus said. The three men greeted each other and then turned their attention to Daniel. They helped him to dismount and settled him into the big camp chair in Early's tent. Cletis' men waited close by outside.

Marcus kneeled before Daniel and looked closely at him. Daniel raised his pale thin hand to touch Marcus' empty sleeve. He stroked Marcus' face. His remembering was quiet.

"Henry! Go rustle him up some grub," Marcus said. Henry scurried off.

"What happened to him?" Miles asked Cletis.

"I don't know," Cletis answered. I found him being transported with a gang of about fifty prisoners. They were being evacuated from Andersonville. That's all I know and Daniel doesn't talk much. He tends to cry a lot."

Henry brought a bowl of stew, and Marcus fed it to Daniel.

"How about you, Cletis?" Marcus asked. "You look good. How'd you manage all this. I'm impressed." Cletis sat with Miles at the map table. Poignant years hung between the men, but just as Miles had predicted back in Savannah friendship warmed through the chill.

"It wasn't hard. Everyone knows the war's about over. They were willing to deal. And my men wanted to be able to say they rode right into a Yankee camp."

"We'll see they're fed," Marcus said. He called an aide in and directed him to see to Cletis and his men.

"This is the first we've seen of Sherman's famous Army of the West," Cletis said. I swear it took those Northerners in the Army of the Potomac the whole war to learn to ride, but folks down here think your Western Army cavalry have their boots glued to their saddles they ride so hard. They ride most as well as Southern boys," Cletis said. "And I thought you all would be fat from eating the fruits of our countryside."

"We did get a piece of peach pie once," Miles said. He told Cletis the story about Marcus and the one-bite piece of pie. Laughter slipped through the thin walls of the tent and drew smiles from the Blue and the Gray soldiers waiting outside.

When Cletis asked about Marcus' arm, Marcus told him about the skirmish when they had last seen Daniel.

"Hell, Cletis, you definitely look more fit than most hungry-ass Rebs we've seen," Marcus noted.

Cletis looked sheepish. "Well, truth is, I've got me a family. My wife—my new wife—Della and me and our two younguns live in east Tennessee. I go home a lot."

A chill breeze lifted the tent flap. Daniel shivered. Marcus' attention was drawn to Cletis.

"You what?" Marcus asked.

"I go home a lot. I get leaves, furloughs. Go home. We got a little farm. Della was working in an armaments factory when I met her. Lot of women work in jobs like that down here. But it got so you couldn't buy anything with the pay though, the money was no good. So, when the babies come, we bought a farm and she stayed home. I help out as much as I can. Her family's nearby and I go home a lot."

Marcus' mouth hung open slightly. His lips moved but he did not speak. Miles too was speechless, but a thin chuckle escaped his throat.

Cletis twirled his hat in his hand, round and round. A red feather swirled up from the band. Cletis tried to appear unruffled by their reaction, but he kept his eyes on his hat as it twirled a little faster.

"You were always such a good ole boy, Cletis," Marcus said. "I guess the chickens come home to roost." He shook his head in disbelief.

"What about Elizabeth?" Miles asked.

"Well, shit, guys. You know how it is. Elizabeth has her own life now. I've got mine. I haven't even heard from her in sometime. Actually, I was wondering if you boys knew how she's doing? Last I heard she was still worried about Willie and little Alex. I guess if you two are still here with nothing better to do than laugh at your old friend, they must've been rescued from that kidnapping all right. I suppose that business gave you all a fright, being so far away and all. They get home safe then?"

Cletis looked up from his hat, expecting an agreeable response. It was his turn to be shocked. All the color had left Miles' face. His eyes hit Cletis with a fierce look that made him draw back in fear. Marcus dropped the empty stew bowl with a clatter and stood over Cletis.

"Holy Jesus, Cletis!" he bellowed. "What the fuck are you talking about?"

But stools, tables, and Marcus all fell aside as Miles rose up, reached for Cletis with both hands and snatched him up by the shirt front.

Cletis' men outside were the first to respond to the shouts, and the Union escort was not far behind.

39

Icy rain fell on frozen ground in the hills where the Bokaima had returned. The Bokaima Old Ones had been the first people to camp and hunt in these hills and in all the hills and valleys of these western slopes, long before anyone called it California. They were here even before the waves of other tribes, speaking strange tongues and singing strange songs moved up the great valley and drove the Old Ones to a circle of isolated pockets along the edges of the territory, north against the Cascades and south against the Mojave Desert, and along isolated, inaccessible stretches of the coast. Too scattered to remember, distant, distant connections with the Old Ones faded from the tribal memory. Traces were left only in language and ritual. The memories lived in the place now. The place determined the way one lived. Place kept pure the memories of a people and their ways. When they were ripped away from these hills by the white man, they lost their power, they lost their bearings, they lost everything. They were forced to live like stray dogs on the edges of the white settlements, begging for handouts, watching their children starve, suffering their women to be sold or stolen, dying in heartbreaking numbers of white man's diseases. Even those Bokaima who were able to live in a protected rancheria lost power over their own lives.

But now the Bokaima returned to their hills. Parts were missing from their tattered tribal body. They limped, but they returned. They were back where they belonged. They could begin healing. The signs of the Old Ones on the earth would guide them. Each plant, each rock, each tree signified. From this place they could shape life, resurrect the old ways.

It was the beginning of First Moon Month. Old Chief had announced that the winter solstice was upon them. Willie sat with Alexander through that long evening when they were left alone, and told him the nativity stories as accurately as she could recall from the book of Luke.

She was having trouble keeping Alexander warm. The round bark house kept them dry, but the small fire was losing its battle against the chill night air. She slipped outside and grabbed pieces of branch wood from the pile outside and put them on the fire. The wood was wet and the bark house filled with smoke.

"Lie down, Alexander, and the smoke won't get in your eyes," Willie told him. "Soon the smoke will all be drawn up through the smoke hole and we can sit up again."

"Pahto said to talk to the fire and the smoke will go up," Alexander said. He watched the fire thoughtfully. "But you have to say it in Indian. It won't work in English."

"Did Pahto say it won't work in English?"

"No. But I know."

"Lie still and be quiet and I'll tell you a story."

"About Coyote?"

"No, not about Coyote. About baby Jesus."

A fit of coughing shook his body. Willie lifted away the deer hide that covered the doorway just above them. The smoke cleared and the fire blazed up and warmed the air. The house, fifteen feet across at the dirt floor, was supported by stout poles and covered with layers of redwood bark and branches and packed with earth. It was built over a dugout area a foot and a half deep. The doorway was at eye level from where she sat on the ground next to Alexander's bed.

Willie was reluctant to pile more blankets on Alexander because to do so she would have to borrow some from the other women's sleeping mats. Willie knew it would be many hours before the women returned from the dance house—if they came in at all this night—and they would not mind anyway, but she was trying to keep Alexander free of the vermin that infested everyone. She tried to pick his head clean of lice and she shook his blankets and clothing free of fleas daily. She was idly searching through his hair now, but the light was too dim to actually capture an elusive louse.

"Sun Ray says I mustn't scratch my head. If I scratch my head I will get cooties."

"Scratching doesn't cause cooties. Cooties cause scratching. Be still now, my lamb, and I'll tell you a story about Christmas."

With the door flap open she could see across to the dance house on the other side of the village camp. The Kuksu banner hung heavy and wet from its tall pole. The shouts and chanting songs coming from inside would occasionally build in fervor and someone would burst out of the dance house and dance in the cold rain.

Rituals are reshaped by desperate times. Willie noticed that women were seldom excluded from ceremonial dances these days. She knew it had been the exception in previous times to include them. Now Blue Feather was the only dreamer in the tribe. She had power equal to Pahto's.

Willie was clearly not expected to participate. She was happy to oblige. She did not want to join them. She was content to sit with Alexander and tell him about his father and about Christmas.

"Is Papa a soldier?"

"Yes, he is."

"Pahto said if the soldiers find us they will kill us all."

Just then two men ran from the dance house and headed down the hill to jump into the river. The voices of the other celebrants encouraged the frenzy of the men. The light from the dance house fire fell through the open door and across the rain pools, reflecting red against Willie's eyes.

Fear clutched at her chest and her mouth was suddenly dry.

"Hush now, Alexander, and I will tell you about when baby Jesus was born."

"Old Chief says the mountains and rivers are watching everything we do. They will punish me if we are bad."

Willie lay next to her frail son and with whispered assurances stroked away his worries. When the pus ran from the red inflamed gahagaha cuts, he had been feverish and fretful. When the wounds had finally healed, hoarse coughing spells began to plague him, leaving him weak and listless.

Each time her monthly bleeding began, Willie had to be confined to the women's house. She never resisted her confinement, but the first time it happened they tried to remove Alexander until she was clean again. She refused to turn loose of him. Old Chief had to intercede; he made an exception for her and told the others to leave her be with the boy. Sun Ray stayed by her and helped her tend him.

Alexander was quiet now, warm and relaxed finally, but still not asleep.

"I am very hungry you know, Mama," he said matter-of-factly.

"Yes, lamb. And in the morning I think we shall eat."

His sickly-sour breath fell soft on her cheek.

She told stories of mothers and mangers. Once he was sound asleep, she reached to the edge of their sleeping area and retrieved a bundle wrapped in rabbit skin. She withdrew a small wood horse she was carving for him. Late into the night she carved the soft wood with a broken blade she had found. The horse would be his Christmas present.

40

Willie woke with first light. Alexander's cough grated harsh in her ear. How could so simple a sound be so ugly, she thought. It felt as though someone had cuffed her on the ear. She wanted to say, stop coughing or you will never get well! Just as Sun Ray had implied that if you refrained from scratching you would stay free of lice.

Alexander's coughing did not rouse him, though. Willie rolled out of bed and slipped quietly from the house. She stepped outside into the stillness of a snow-covered camp. It must have snowed all night while she slept. She shielded her eyes against the brightness. The silence was broken only by the occasional rustling of a laden branch springing free of its burden of snow. The dance house was quiet. Everything was quiet.

Willie went to the campfire, which smoldered from the evening before. Old Chief had two quartz stones he could strike against each other to make a spark to ignite tinder if they needed to start a new fire, but it was so much easier if the fire from the evening before was still alive. She stirred the embers and fed them with small pieces of bark and twigs. Her feet were very cold and hunger nagged at her insides. She brought the fire up and walked over toward the dance house where there was a pile of larger wood. Her thoughts were preoccupied by hunger and cold; it was not until she almost tripped over her that Willie saw Blue Feather sitting in front of the dance house.

"Blue Feather!" Willie dropped to her knees in front of where Blue Feather sat. Her eyes were half open, but she made no sign of noticing Willie's presence. Snow lay like a shawl across her head and shoulders.

For three months Blue Feather had only spoken to Willie in the most formal and cool manner. Willie kept her distance and tended her own affairs. But now she wanted to reach across the abyss to touch her old friend. Willie remembered long ago having lain in her bed despondent. Miles had left. War had broken out. She remembered Blue Feather sitting on the edge of Willie's bed then, reaching out to her.

Willie repeated the English words Blue Feather had said to her that day, "We have mercy on us. We are strong woman." Blue Feather raised her eyes to Willie. A smile tempted her twisted mouth but tears filled her eyes.

"I will never have a husband now," Blue Feather said softly.

Willie brushed the snow from a spot on the blanket Blue Feather was sitting on and sat next to her. Willie reached over and brushed the snow from Blue Feather's bare hands, which were loosely folded in her lap. Willie took Blue Feather's hands in her own and tried to rub warmth back into them. Blue Feather submitted to her but stared straight ahead into the fire that Round Face was now tending as she walked stiffly about the camp paying no attention to the two women on the blanket.

Blue Feather wore a large robe of deerskins and a shredded redwood bark skirt. Underneath the skirt Willie could see Blue Feather was still wearing the cotton petticoat she had worn that day they went to town, gray now and frayed.

In her gravely voice, Blue Feather spoke in Bokaima, "In the days before the white man, a woman married only outside family, never to her cousin or her brother. A man and a woman liked each other, the price was paid, they married and she went to live with his people. That was where he knew the place, where to hunt, how to protect. This day, that is not possible. There is no place for us. The men have been taken away by the white man. Killed by the white man. Even you have no husband. White man has changed everything. You have a child. I will have a child and I too will have no husband. I will be. . ." She had to revert to English to express her thought, "I will be the handmaiden of God."

Willie was trying to grasp everything she was saying. "A child?" she asked.

Blue Feather turned the gaze of her good eye on Willie. "I will have the child of the white men who knew me," she said softly. "My son will be God's man. I saw it in a dream."

Willie put her hand inside the robe that covered Blue Feather and felt her swollen belly. The two women looked at each other. Forsaken, frightened, joyful. Emotions gripped them both. Tears made the broad scar on Blue Feather's misshapen face glisten.

"Does everyone know?" Willie asked.

"No. I will tell them today. It is the day of the renewal of the seasons. I have kept it hidden until now. I was afraid if I told before, hot stones would be placed on my belly and I would be given poison to kill the baby because he is the white man's seed. But it is too late now. He will live now. I saw it in a dream. He will save his people from the white man. God will be his father." Blue Feather's eye drifted and stared straight ahead again. Willie withdrew her hand and sat back. When Blue Feather looked back at Willie her eyes were once more cool and distant as they had been for the past few months. She looked hard at Willie.

"Do you remember Zephania of the Bible?" Blue Feather asked.

"No, Blue Feather, I don't."

"He told me that the day of the Lord is near." She stared at the fire and recited in a fervent monotone the passage she had memorized.

And I will bring distress upon men, that they shall walk like blind men, because they have sinned against the Lord, and their blood shall be poured out as dust, and their flesh as the dung.

Neither their silver nor their gold shall be able to deliver them in the day of the Lord's wrath, but the whole land shall be devoured by the fire of his jealousy, for he shall make even a speedy riddance of all them that dwell in the land.

I will also leave in the midst of thee an afflicted and poor people, and they shall trust in the name of the Lord.

This remnant shall not do iniquity, nor speak lies, neither shall a deceitful tongue be found in their mouth, for they shall feed and lie down, and none shall make them afraid.

Behold, at that time I will undo all that afflict thee, and I will save her that halteth, and gather her that was driven out, and I will get them praise and fame in every land where they have no shame.

"On Judgment Day only we," she gestured around the camp, "we, the faithful and shameless remnant, will be left," Blue Feather said. "In my dream I saw this. My child is not the seed of the white man. He is the seed of the spirit of the Old

Ones. He will free us from the bonds of the white devil." With that Blue Feather rose and entered the dance house where she resumed her droning chant.

Willie went over to where Round Face Woman puttered about the fire.

"Do you know already?" Willie asked her.

"Yes. Blue Feather wants to think we do not," Round Face Woman replied. Willie did not pursue the question further. Her attention returned to the problem of her son's lingering illness and immediate hunger.

Sun Ray was placing round boiling stones in the fire. When they were red hot she placed them in a tightly woven basket full of water and removed stones that had cooled, repeating the process again and again until the water boiled. Later today they would process the last of their stash of acorns but for now Willie took some of the hot water to make a tea for Alexander with angelica leaves she and Sun Ray had gathered.

Most of the hot water would be used to pour over a basket full of fat white wood grubs that had been collected yesterday. It was Willie's least favorite food. She had come to appreciate the chewy, sharp-tasting, slow-roasted larvae that were kept strung on a rawhide lace and snacked on throughout the day. And she had developed an appreciation for cooked grasshoppers. But the grub gruel—her unspoken name for it—was beyond the limits of her palate and her hunger. The gelatinous consistency of it caused her stomach to protest and her throat to rebel. It was difficult even for her to give it to Alexander, who loved it. She kept her feelings about the grub gruel to herself. Acorn mush was more to her liking.

As soon as she fed Alexander a fat piece of the black acorn bread baked in yesterday's fire and a portion of the grub gruel, she dressed him as warmly as she could and let him come outside to play with his Christmas horse.

She engaged herself in the processing of the acorns. Their acorn reserves were not large enough to last through the winter. Not only had the Bokaima arrived back in the hills late in the acorn gathering season, their gathering territory and opportunities were further hindered by their fugitive status and the ever-encroaching white settlements. They had been carefully rationing their supply but today would be the end of it. The women prepared to grind the last of the acorns.

Willie enjoyed the work of grinding. It was the only important job that came with its own component of rituals and rules that the tribe would let her do. As in everything else, though, they exempted her from most of the more complicated practices. She was happy to be relieved of the obligation of having to know when to give meal offerings to the four directions and the necessity of not letting children stand behind her. She wanted Alexander to have access to her, and she did not want to be compelled by custom that held no meaning for her. However, she knew that either they did not let her do anything important or they granted her some kind of tacit absolution for not observing necessary rites when they did. They treated her as though she were simple-minded and could not effectively conceive of these complicated abstract laws that governed everything they did. Somehow this special status would not bring harm to the village by her not properly adhering to the rituals.

Perhaps she was simple, she thought. But it was not that she was unable to conceive of the rules, rather that she was content without them—even though she suffered an element of isolation in her freedom.

She sat on a deerskin on a spot of ground where the snow had been swept away. She worked the pestle into the acorns. When the consistency suited Round Face Woman, Willie shifted the coarse meal into the hopper basket. The process of preparing the leaching bed for the meal was left to expert hands. She was content to grind. Soon the muscles of her arms tingled with exertion and a sweat flushed across her upper body.

She paused in her work to turn up the cuff of her shirt. A rash slashed across the inside of her forearm. It had been fine pink spots yesterday that itched annoyingly; today it was swollen and covered with blisters. Her whole arm ached. Even in the dead of winter she could get poison oak. Her sweat and the action of grinding had irritated it and now it irritated her.

As she stared at the pulsing rash, Pahto appeared and knelt beside her. She tried to pull her sleeve back down to cover the rash. Pahto grabbed her hand. He carefully exposed the rash and studied it. Willie resisted and tried to withdraw her hand, but Pahto kept his grip. He looked up at her with insistence in his eyes. She yielded and submitted her arm to his examination. He studied the rash some more, looked in her eyes again, then rose to his feet and walked to where Round Face Woman was laying the fine sandy bed where water would be poured over the acorn meal to leach out the bitter poison.

Willie watched as Pahto stood over Round Face Woman. Willie could not hear what he was saying, but she could see the anger flashing across the muscles of his face. When he had finished speaking he turned to look at Willie while Round Face Woman left her work and scurried off to the woman's house, intent on some mission Pahto set her on. Willie tried to concentrate on her grinding task and ignore Pahto's stare. He continued to watch until Round Face Woman returned and dressed Willie's rash. She made a poultice of dried strong-scented leaves that Willie did not recognize. Round Face Woman crushed the leaves and mixed them with earth she scooped up from under an oak tree and warm water.

"Pahto thinks Blue Feather has poisoned you," Round Face Woman said.

"It's only poison oak," Willie protested. "I've had it many times before."

"Yes." Round Face Woman said no more and Willie could not read what thoughts lay behind the impassive face she presented. Willie allowed her arm to be tended. The damp herbs brought immediate relief to the pain and itching. She looked up to smile her gratitude at Pahto, only to see him swing up on Rojo. He rode out of camp with Young Jack mounted on Glory.

Glory and Rojo were the only horses the tribe had left. They were in low condition; their ribs showed plainly through dull, rough coats. It seemed pointless to Willie that they were being ridden. A man could make better time on foot than on those sorry creatures. But she never spoke up about either horse. Not to Pahto or anybody else. Her father's horses.

Her father. He must know by now that she and Alexander were missing. Was he looking for her? He could never find her here, deep in these hills where trails were mostly memories.

41

When the acorns were ground and leached, the meal was mixed with water in a large basket. Sun Ray heated stones in the fire and dropped them into the basket. Round Face Woman stirred the mixture to spread the heat evenly and cook the mixture smoothly. Her stirring tool was a long thin branch that was looped back on itself, the ends bound together to serve as a handle. As the stones lost their heat in the meal, she scooped them out with the stirrer and scraped the meal off. Sun Ray put the cooled stones back in the fire and fetched hot stones from the embers to drop back into the cooking basket. Before long they had a basket full of thick warm mush.

Willie took an abalone shell full of the acorn mush to Alexander. He ate with his first two fingers held together like a scoop, in the Bokaima style. There was only enough mush for every person in camp to have one portion. Long Tree did not eat. While Pahto and Young Jack were gone, his job was to stay in camp to guard and protect. He would not eat until the other two men returned. He stood near Sun Ray, shifting his weight from one foot to the other, speaking to her in low tones. His knowledge of Bokaima speech was still very limited, but Sun Ray was patient with him.

The sun came out. The air warmed and the exposed snow began to melt. Alexander played with Sun Ray's children. They played a game of kicking a deerhide ball. They played an arrow throwing game that Willie thought was too dangerous; but they played it every day, and she finally gave up her protests. It was good Alexander felt well enough to play, but she watched carefully, even when she sat with Old Chief and Round Face Woman to gamble at dice-stones.

The shell money tokens the dice players won or lost no longer held any economic value outside their game, although their play was earnest as though they did. The Bokaima and their Pomo cousin tribes had been the primary suppliers of the polished shell money for the economic exchange system that had reached across California into the Sierra Nevada. Valuations broke through language barriers and enabled trade.

The Bokaima still owned many drilled disk beads they had manufactured from clam shells fragments, ground smooth, bored and threaded—one or two hundred to the string. The most cherished string held beads worn to a luster by years of handling and counting. But all were of little value now. The old trade routes were breached. Tribes they had traded with were gone. There was no one to buy their strings of money, nothing to trade. The thoroughness of the white invasion had neutralized the native economy.

And now the Bokaima were fugitives. No one wandered far from camp to gather tubers or nuts; it was too dangerous. Rabbit snares set close by were the only hunting that was dared. Long Tree would not use his ammunition for hunting because he might need it for defense.

Willie felt isolated. The Bokaima felt stalked.

That afternoon only the young ones ate. They were

given bits and pieces of left-over food, dried berries. The adults tolerated their light-headed hunger. The children sat around a large basket and scraped remnants of grub gruel that clung to its sides. Willie could not watch. Hungry as she was, it still did not look appetizing to her. She and Sun Ray took a gathering basket and hiked uphill a short distance from camp to search for bracken ferns and winter purslane. Long Tree followed, his rifle over his shoulder, keeping both them and the camp in his sight. Old Chief and his cousin fished in the stream nearby.

The women were walking back with a half-filled basket just as Pahto and Young Jack rode into camp in a flurry of shouts and feathers. A dozen live chickens were tied to a rawhide thong which Young Jack held high over his head. A fat calf hung across Pahto's horse. All nineteen residents of the village camp swarmed to cheer their return.

The women replenished the fires with wood the children collected. The men prepared the meat. Old Chief gave several small fish to Round Face Woman to clean.

When all hands were at work preparing the feast Pahto stood over Willie as she fed branch wood to the fire. She turned to face him. Pahto grinned at her. He had never grinned at her before.

"What is it Pahto?" Willie asked him. He stood with his hands hidden behind him. His eyes danced with anticipation.

The fire flared with the fresh wood. She swept her hair up and let the air cool the back of her neck. Pahto grinned. Her lips moved to voice a question that she left unspoken as Pahto swung a white cotton bag from behind his back and presented it to her triumphantly. It was a flour sack half full of fine wheat flour.

"Pahto! I..." But before she could speak he turned away abruptly and joined his comrades.

Flour! A sack of flour! Could dreams come true? She

had no leavening of any kind, and no time to grow wild yeast, but she could make lovely large round flat breads over the fire. She set to work immediately.

When the feast was prepared, everyone gathered together. They ate with a voracious, almost hysterical hunger. Laughter and jokes shared mouths stuffed with succulent meat and warm bread. Hands tore the last pieces of meat off the bones, but none took the other's piece. They shared and ate, ate and shared.

The fire was kept high. The laughing and eating gave way to dancing and singing. The dancers were hot, even in the chill night air, and they shed their shirts. Alexander, feeling better with a good meal in him, mimicked the adults. Willie sang and rocked back and forth with the rhythm, watching the dancers. She watched Pahto. His body was lean, his form economical. Each muscle was tight, each movement sure. She stared and swayed, transfixed, until she realized Pahto was watching her, too.

She stopped singing. She stopped swaying. She averted her gaze. A steely, somber stillness chilled her heart. She rose and picked up Alexander who protested only mildly as she carried him toward his bed. Pahto stood in her path. Panic climbed the back of her neck. Pahto put his hand on Alexander's head.

"You will sleep well tonight, Little Coyote." He spoke to Alexander, but kept his eyes on Willie.

"I want to dance some more," Alexander yawned.

Pahto's gaze bore down on her. She felt out of breath.

"I am going to put Alexander to bed now," she kept her voice firm. She looked down, avoiding his eyes. Firelight flickered shadows across the smooth skin of his chest. She watched a glistening bead of sweat tremble with the flutter of his heartbeat. His hand still lingered on Alexander. She ducked her head and brushed past him, his leg in her path unyielding, hard against hers. As she slipped away, his hand trailed from Alexander across her hand, along her arm and down her hip.

Willie hurried Alexander into their dugout house. She covered the opening behind them securely, so that no one could see in or out. It was dark inside and she had to feel her way to their bed. Alexander began to whimper at having to leave the merriment behind, but she quieted him. He was tired and even a brief spell of coughing did not keep him long from falling into a sound sleep.

Willie was not so lucky. She longed for Miles more now since she had Alexander again, more than she ever had before. Through the chimney roof opening, the full moon bullied her. She despaired. What hope had she? She had tried to hang on to the promise of Miles, but he was not here. What use was he? Or his promise? Bitterness is the taste of death and she felt herself sinking.

The hides she slept on did little to shield her from the ground's harsh reality. She had not treated her poison oak that evening and now it flared. Her hair was matted, her skin sticky. She imagined a bath. A long hot bath. She would rise from the steaming water and rub her skin with a thick Turkish towel. Crisp percale sheets tucked snugly around a soft mattress awaited her. And Miles. Miles. His demanding hands would free her from the grip of...free her...no...no... plunge her...further...

Shadows menaced her thoughts until with one last protesting jerk of her body she fell into an uneasy sleep that slipped along the edges of the rhythmic singing drifting to her ears from outside.

As dreams are shaped by fears, they are rescued by hope. A breeze blew cool across her face when the door covering was lifted to admit a figure silhouetted by the moonlight. He was trying to walk toward her. He could barely move for the great sadness that dragged at him.

"Miles," she whispered to him and held out her hand, inviting him to come to her. He lay down beside her. She looked to his face for reassurance. His features were vague and elusive. Was he slipping away?

"Stay," she pleaded. "Stay until the night is over."

His large dark form covered her, penetrated her. But the hunger was not relieved. She opened her mouth for his strong male smell. His lips were at her throat. His warm breath whispered demands in her ear. She tried to draw him closer. Cling to him.

"You have enough passion for both of us," his words lingered as he faded back into the moonlight.

The sharp, tight ache pulled her away from dream sleep.

42

Through the chimney hole Willie watched the moonlight fade to dawn. She could see the sky clear blue as Miles' eyes. *You have enough passion for both of us.* The words from her dream lingered, like a melody caught in her head. The other women had come in late and they all lay sleeping around her now.

She heard someone stirring about outside. She knew it would be Old Chief. She rose to join him. He liked fishing in the early morning. She followed him down to the river where he set to work. She sat on a flat rock, huddled in a sliver of sunlight that broke through the trees.

Old Chief was sucking on a bone left over from last night's feast while he pounded soap plant bulbs into a chunky paste. He sang quietly under his breath as he worked. Yesterday he had built a little dam part way across the river and now a still pool had formed behind it. When he was satisfied with his paste, he scattered it and a few crushed buckeye balls over the surface of the pool. He settled next to Willie and the two of them watched the pool silently. Soon one, then two, then four salmon floated to the surface—stunned and helpless, but still alive. Sunlight glinted off their silvery pink skin. Old Chief cackled while Willie retrieved the young fish with a long-handled basket.

"When Little Coyote wakes up he will have cooked fish for his morning meal. He will be happy!" Old Chief made Alexander's well-being his personal concern. He gave him pretty stones and a pouch to keep them in, a spinning top to play with, and rabbit skin moccasins he had made himself. He had tied a string of shell coins around the boy's ankle so that wealth would find him. Alexander loved the old man.

Willie fetched the last fish from the water and turned to smile at Old Chief. If all the country's problems would be left to men like Old Chief and her father, we all would be living peacefully, she thought.

The fisherman grinned back at her with pride and delight. Suddenly his eyes looked past her, over her shoulder. Something downhill in the distance caught his eye, frightened him. Surprised horror crossed his face. She saw the red stain burst from his chest before she heard the cracking report of the rifle.

She reached out for him as he fell to his knees. A dozen horses crashed through the underbrush, their riders driving them up the hill with shouts and spurs.

Willie pulled Old Chief to his feet and they stumbled toward a thicket nearby. She let him slip to the ground behind a broad tree she hoped would shelter him. She knelt and looked into his eyes. He was calm, but bewildered. She pressed a soft green pad of moss against his wound. She took his hand and placed it against the moss.

"Hold this tight. I am going to leave you here. I must go get Alexander, then I will come back to you," she said. His lips moved, but no sound emerged. He nodded his head and sent her on with a gesture of his hand. She ran along the bank as the horsemen crossed the river.

"There she is! There's the woman! Get her!"

Returning gunfire burst from the hillside above her. A man jumped down into her path from the embankment next to her. A startled scream escaped from her throat before she realized the man was Pahto. He grabbed her arm and pushed her behind him. He took careful aim with his rifle and shot the lead rider from his horse, which then reared in fright and bolted back down the hill, dragging its rider by a boot that had caught in the stirrup as he fell. The riders checked their advance.

"Shit! They got Arvin!" One of the men shouted.

"I told you the goddamn chicken thieves would be armed, goddammit," another yelled back.

"Move into those trees. We can circle in from there!"

The horsemen veered behind a protective row of trees. Pahto led Willie up the embankment to where he had left Rojo. He sprang up on the horse and pulled her up behind him.

"Alexander! I must get to Alexander!" she yelled to him above the din of shouts and gunshots. Rojo galloped into the camp. The Bokaima were milling about, running for cover or preparing to fight. Young Jack stood next to the smoldering campfire and fired arrows at the horsemen. He was shot down just as Pahto and Willie rode past him. Pahto wheeled Rojo around to get back to the fallen man. Another shot and Rojo went down. He fell slowly, which gave Pahto and Willie a clear chance to land on their feet near where Young Jack lay lifeless. Pahto stood and fired toward the invaders. Willie ran for Alexander.

Alexander stood in front of the brush house with Sun Ray and her boys. The children were all crying. Alexander threw himself into Willie's arms, crying. His little arms wrapped around her neck and his fingers dug into her throat.

"Mama! Mama! The soldiers! They will kill us!"

"They are not soldiers, Alex. We must run. Hang on to Mama, but turn loose of my neck so I can carry you."

Twenty yards up the hill from them from behind a rock outcrop Long Tree fired his rifle at the raiders. Sun Ray, carrying Wali and holding Washo by the hand, ran toward Long Tree. Willie followed close behind with Alexander. The children continued to cry. Suddenly Sun Ray fell to the ground, a death bullet passing through her body and killing Wali also.

Pahto and Long Tree shot Sun Ray's killer simultaneously. Alexander was screaming. Willie stopped in her flight to grab Washo, who refused to leave his mother. Willie dragged him away and up the hill.

Pahto stood in the center of the camp, firing deliberately at the horsemen who circled cautiously now. He waited until Willie had the children safely into the trees, then turned and ran toward them, bullets kicking up furies of dust behind him. Abruptly, Washo wrenched his hand from Willie's grasp and ran back towards Sun Ray.

"No! no! Washo, no!" Willie, encumbered by Alexander, chased down after him as Pahto ran uphill toward him, but they were too late. He was cut down by a barrage of bullets that killed him and ripped into Willie's leg.

She felt no pain, just a sudden jarring that tore Alexander from her arms and cast her toward the ground. She watched the rocky earth take a long time to rise to meet her. It was slick with mud and snow, and she slid along the hillside on her face. The gunfire sounded muffled to her ear. Alexander stopped screaming.

Pahto picked her up and slung her across his shoulders. "Run Little Coyote!" he shouted. "Run to Long Tree. Run quick. I am bringing your mother. You run."

Alexander ran. Pahto followed closely with strong strides unhindered by his burden. He placed Willie on the ground behind Long Tree's sheltering rock—ground that was also sheltered from the warmth of the rising sun. Willie's warm blood cut a crimson trough in the snow.

Pahto and Long Tree fired down at the horsemen. From above a rocky escarpment, fifty yards upriver, arrows flew towards the white men who were now taking cover.

"How many of us are left?" Pahto asked Long Tree.

"There are four there," he gestured to the escarpment. "Old Chief is down by the river. And us here."

"No more?"

"No more."

"How many are left of them?"

"Six."

Firing ceased from both sides. Pahto stood up for a better view.

"I will move down river to see better where they are placed," he said as he walked out, moving quietly, but making no effort to duck or hide.

Every time Willie tried to move, pain seared through her thigh and made her vision blur. Her left leg was ripped open in one clean line. She packed snow on the wound to slow the bleeding. She held Alexander close to her and tried to keep him quiet.

A shot cracked the quiet air and was followed by a volley of gunfire and arrows. And then it was quiet again. Pahto returned.

"Now they are five," he reported.

Willie heard shouting and calling back and forth between the white men as they determined who was left among them.

"Jake's hurt bad and I ain't seen Bud move since he went down," one of them called out.

"Those cattle-rustling sons-a-bitches must have twenty guns up there. You told me this would be a small bunch of starving Injuns," another complained in a frightened and angry voice.

"Well, they're the ones that got the woman and the boy. Leastwise we found them."

"Makes no difference, way I see it. She's running with them bucks by now anyway. She'll be ruint."

"That don't matter. We can still get the money for her."

"We'll go tell Jarboe and Mr. White, get more men, get some of them militia soldiers, and come back up here for the bastards. But we got to ride out now. Can Jake ride?"

"He can ride."

43

Old Chief was weak but still alive. Blue Feather and Round Face Woman had taken shelter with Sun Ray's two brothers behind the escarpment. None of them was injured.

Willie bound her leg with a piece of the flour sack and hobbled around with a walking stick for support. She watched over Alexander and Old Chief while the other two women prepared to evacuate camp. They meticulously gathered all utensils, personal paraphernalia and remnants of their presence so that nothing could be used by their enemies. Necessary items would be packed in carrying baskets. Everything else was burned.

The men hastily constructed funeral pyres. There was no time for the purification of the pyre builders or proper preparation of the dead. There were no strings of redemption beads. No death dance. No shaving of heads or wearing of pitch. They burned their dead and ignored the bodies of the white men that had been abandoned by their gang; although Long Tree salvaged the corpses' weapons and ammunition.

They were now four armed men, two women and

Alexander walking; Willie and Old Chief were lifted onto Glory's bony bare back. The men and Blue Feather took turns packing Alexander when he tired. Willie could manage the horse and ride well enough if she did not have to move her leg, but Old Chief was not able to hold himself up at all. Pahto tied him to Willie so that he would not slip off and Willie would be able to handle the horse.

Old Chief did not complain. Only occasionally did moans rumble from his chest. He responded to Willie's simple requests to shift his weight or move his leg, but otherwise he was silent. Blue Feather had been silent all along. She had not spoken a word the entire time she and Round Face Woman broke camp. But now, as she carried Alexander on her back and the small band left behind their old village and the flames of the funeral pyres, she and Round Face Woman began wailing death chants.

The horrors of the morning replayed themselves across Willie's memory in bright colors. Salmon mocked her from their basket trap. Stunned pink swirled to death red. How had she let her guard drop?

The mourning song allowed her to cry, finally. She slipped from shock to grief. Her cheeks, scraped raw from her fall, stung with salt of her tears. Old Chief lay against her back. When had he become so frail? His breathy voice formed the words of the chant, rested, sang again.

Round Face Woman and the men carried all the essential belongings on their backs in baskets, which were secured with tump straps across their foreheads.

The weather held kindly. They kept a quick pace through a chill but sunny day. They made only a brief camp that night and moved on the next day, eating what they could gather as they moved. Old Chief grew weaker. Willie was merely uncomfortable. Her wound seemed minor to her, but still she could not hike with the others and someone was needed to hold Old Chief on the horse as they climbed over the mountain. They were avoiding the main trails. The route they followed was precarious but less traveled.

Whenever they stopped, Round Face Woman refreshed the dressing on both Willie's and Old Chief's wounds.

Willie could see that the bullet had creased a groove across her leg before burrowing beneath her skin into her muscle. A tender exploration with her fingertips told her the bullet was still there. She could wiggle it, gently.

Early the next evening they reached a high valley to the east of the mountain they had climbed. They joined up with another band of refugees and escapees from the Nome Cult reservation who had set up camp there. Pahto and Long Tree moved comfortably among these new people. It was apparent to Willie that they were not strangers to each other and that indeed this encampment had been their destination.

The small Bokaima band kept to themselves at the edge of the camp while Long Tree and Pahto conferred with the strangers. Their voices carried back to Willie because they talked loud, hoping volume would overcome difficulties in language differences. It was a strange mixture of tongues Willie heard. Often they resorted to English, a language most of the leaders had at least rudimentary knowledge of from time spent incarcerated at various government camps.

Willie watched as the attention of the men turned to her. Voices grew angry but she could not understand what was being said. Alexander whimpered when the men approached them. The Bokaima ceased their activities and gathered near Willie. She struggled awkwardly to her feet. The headman of the strangers carried a rifle. He spoke to her in English.

"You will show the white men where we are?" he asked her.

"No. Of course not," she answered.

He swayed as he stared at her. The rank smell of stale alcohol-laden sweat wafted across the space between them. He leered at her. A stranger's face, a familiar leer. Pahto moved beside her.

"Why did you not let white friends save you?" the headman asked in English.

She did not answer. The question made her both nervous and angry.

"Why?" he demanded.

"They are thugs. My safety is not their objective."

"Thugs?" he repeated.

Willie knew he would not understand her words. She did not like the man. She could see her obstinacy was making him mad. "They are not my friends," she offered finally.

"You will stay with us?"

"No. I will return to my husband," she answered. Pahto stood closer yet.

The headman kept his eyes on her but addressed Pahto, "Where is her man?"

"He left her," Pahto answered.

"No!" Willie protested.

"He will hunt for her," the headman said to Pahto. "He will bring soldiers."

Willie was silent. They would all be in danger if this man found out that her husband was a soldier.

"He will not find her where I will take her," Pahto said. "No one will follow us in these mountains until winter has passed. By then I will have her out of his reach."

"She will run away, tell soldiers where we are," the headman insisted. He brought his face within inches of hers. She resisted the urge to retreat from his sour breath. "Will you run away," he asked.

"Walk, maybe," she answered.

The headman and his friends laughed. They encircled

her. Pahto put his hand on her shoulder.

"She has no man. I will be her man," Headman said.

Pahto stepped into the slim space between Willie and the headman. Headman raised his rifle.

"No!" Pahto said. "She is my woman now. We only need to stay in your camp until our wounded can heal. If you have no room for us, we will move on now."

The tension of the moment eroded slowly, until finally Headman stepped back.

"You may stay then. But we have no food for you. Your woman must not betray us. Our people leave this place before the next moon."

Alexander clung to Willie's good leg, making it hard for her to maintain her balance. Pahto tightened his hold on her shoulder. Headman slung his rifle across his shoulders and walked away with his men. Willie pulled away from Pahto's grip and turned to face him, bracing herself between Alexander and her crutch. The air chilled and snow began to fall in great powdery flakes.

Pahto smiled at her. "Walk maybe?" he mocked. "A passion walk? Through the snow with a walking stick and a small boy?"

"Perhaps."

"You could not."

"I reached my son walking."

"I let you."

They faced each other silently. Round Face Woman left them to tend Old Chief. Blue Feather took Alexander's hand and led him away. Long Tree and the brothers returned to their work on the shelters they were building. Pahto and Willie did not move.

"Stay with me," Pahto said.

"I cannot."

"He will not know where you are. He cannot rescue

you."

Her leg ached and her chin quivered. She was afraid. Her bond with Miles was tight, but the distance between them was great and mined with danger. How would they find each other? And how could this tiny band evade their pursuers or survive the winter? The image of Pahto during the attack walking calmly through rifle fire returned to her mind. And had he felt no threat from the leering headman? His coolness made her more afraid.

"Aren't you ever afraid?" she asked him.

"No."

"I am afraid for you. You and the others can't run like fugitives forever. The white men are not all bad. You know that. You must find a way to live alongside them."

"I cannot."

Snow settled in their hair. Long Tree called to Pahto for help with the brush house. Willie scratched her poison oak and returned to Alexander.

44

By the time the two brush houses were finished they were already dusted with a cover of snow. Pahto and Long Tree and the brothers settled into one house, the women and Alexander into the other. Pahto and Long Tree picked up Old Chief from where he lay under a sheltering tree near the campfire and began to carry him to the men's house. Round Face Woman intercepted them.

"Tolashi will stay with me," she told Pahto. Blue Feather and Willie looked up from where they were spreading clothing and blankets for bedding in the women's house. It had been a long time since Willie had heard Old Chief's Bokaima name spoken.

"He will stay with me. I will take care of him in the nights. You cannot," Round Face Woman told Pahto.

"Yes, then I will take Little Coyote into the men's house. It will be too much work for you. You will have a pregnant woman, a lame woman, and a dying man."

"No!" Willie said. She dragged herself through the low door and fumbled for her crutch. "No, Pahto. He stays with me."

"Our house is right next to yours. He will be close," Pahto insisted.

Willie drew herself upright and faced him. "No, Pahto."

"We can take care of each other, Pahto," Round Face Woman assured him. The boy is too young to be in the men's house. My Tolashi is too old."

"You have four men. It is right," Blue Feather called out to Pahto from the doorway of the brush house. "Four is right for men. Power is with four."

A light snow fell on them. Long Tree and Pahto were still holding Old Chief, who moaned in his half-consciousness and resumed his death chant. Blue Feather moved out of the way and the two men placed him carefully in the women's house and went to their own house.

The openings of the houses faced the fire, which the stranger band was keeping fueled. The flickering glow gave them enough light to arrange themselves in the close quarters. Round Face Woman sat next to her husband who still chanted but did not respond to anything the women said to him. Blue Feather sat in the rear of the small house and sang prayers. Willie covered Alexander with a blanket of rabbit pelts.

"I need to put something in my mouth, Mama," he said.

"I have one more piece of bread saved for you," Willie told him as she rummaged in her deerskin pouch for his favorite things. She brought out the bread and his carved horse. He clutched the horse to him and attacked the bread hungrily. It was dry and crumbled onto the blanket.

"Eat it slowly," Willie advised. She felt around on the blanket to retrieve the crumbs and feed them to him, occasionally putting one in her own mouth.

"I'm still hungry," he told her in a tired voice.

"Go to sleep now. We'll find something to eat in the morning."

"I'm not sleepy."

She stroked his hair and they listened to the camp sounds. Some of the stranger tribe was still by the camp fire drinking whiskey. Willie found their slurred strident voices unsettling and wished they would tire or pass out.

The two Bokaima shelters were built close together and she could hear the men talking in their house nearby. It surprised her that Sun Ray's brothers sounded like men; she had know them when they were boys, dogging her father around the farmyard. Charlie and Bill he had called them. He thought they needed English names to assimilate into the white man's world. She had never known their Bokaima names; they still called themselves Charlie and Bill. Alexander's breath evened into sleep; Old Chief's quiet chant blended with Blue Feather's.

Round Face Woman began to cry. "I have been good wife to him," she said.

"I know you have," Willie said.

"What will become of us?"

"I don't know. Sometimes I think we will be safe, other times..." Willie was speaking softly to Round Face Woman when Blue Feather's strong voice cut her off:

Do not be afraid what you are about to suffer. Be faithful even to the point of death, and I will give you the crown of life. He who has an ear, let him hear what the Spirit says. To him who overcomes I will also give him a white stone with a new name written on it, known only to him who receives it.

Since you have kept my command to endure patiently, I will keep you from the hour of trial that is going to come upon the whole world to test those who live on earth. I am coming soon.

Blue Feather paused before calling out the affirming "O!"

"O!" Round Face Woman echoed.

Blue Feather's voice returned to her low guttural chant. The revelers outside were stirring from the fire. Pahto appeared at the women's house door.

"It is Pahto," he said. He knelt outside the doorway and spoke to Willie. "Keep this with you," he told her and passed her a rifle. "You can fire it all right?"

"Yes."

"Tomorrow we will practice shooting." He returned to the men's house. The revelers retired to their own shelters. The night grew quiet. Only the death chants. Willie slipped into dreams.

She awoke to the old woman's mourning wails. Old Chief was gone. Blue Feather began the preparations for the death ceremonies. Round Face Woman submitted to her gratefully.

Although their ways were not the same, the women from the stranger tribe followed Blue Feather's instructions. At noon a pre-dawn hunting party returned with a deer. As everyone ate together, Alexander made friends with the two children from the stranger tribe. Willie was excluded from the death ceremony preparations. Her grief would be solitary.

She called Alexander to her. "I'm going for a walk and I want you stay here in the camp and play. Blue Feather will watch you. I want you to behave while I'm gone. I'll be back very soon." He nodded his head at each admonition, waiting for her to finish so he could go play.

"You'll behave?" She asked him. Another nod and he ran off.

She spoke to Blue Feather, "I'm going for a walk. Alexander will stay here in camp to play. Will you watch him?" Blue Feather only nodded but Willie knew she would watch.

Willie muttered to herself as she took the rifle and her walking stick and left the camp, "All I get is nodding. No one talks to me. Alexander knows more Bokaima than English."

Sun broke through the overcast. She hobbled out of the woods to a hillside clearing. The world was brilliant white. Her eyes squinted against the glare. She stood alone in the clearing and cried. She cried for Sun Ray and her children, for Old Chief and for Round Face Woman who was left alone. She cried for herself.

It was awkward to manage the rifle and the walking stick and cry at the same time. In the center of the clearing she spotted a large rock with a sloping flat top. She made her way to it haltingly, brushed away the snow, and pulled herself up on it. The sun warmed her and the surface of the white rock. In the distance she could hear the children's voices. Her grief spent itself and peace settled over her.

"Please," she whispered, "help me get out of here." She smiled watching a family of quail with their fancy hats scampering across the snow. Suddenly it seemed possible; she could find her way out. She could take Glory in the dark of night, she thought. Scrawny Glory. He would not be able to go hard, but with a good head start no one could catch them. And she had the rifle now. She could hunt. She would have to convince Alexander to be quiet. She could find her way out of here. It seemed she could. But if Pahto took them farther north, it would be impossible. She loved them all, but she needed to find Miles.

She planned as she basked in the winter sun. Where the snow began to melt away from the rock, she discovered grooves were carved in its surface. She scooted off the rock so she could look at them closely. There were symbols all over the smooth slope. She recognized shapes that had also been on the rock outside the first Bokaima camp. It had been dark then, and moss had grown over the glyphs. The outlines of these markings were crisp in the midday light. She stared at them, wishing she could read their meaning. It seemed like a message, and the rock a message center. She needed to get a message through. Miles, Miles! I am trapped here.

She began crying again. Her inability to read the stone was frustrating. It was not for her. Nothing here was for her.

She returned to camp. Alexander was sitting on the ground in front of the women's house, playing with the string buzzing toy Old Chief had made for him. Willie went to where Blue Feather was mixing herbs for Old Chief's shroud.

"I found a rock out there with picture writing on it," she said. Blue Feather did not respond. "What does it mean?" Her voice still caught in sobs when she talked. Blue Feather put down her work and looked at Willie. Her eyes were distant and guarded. She did not respond, but turned and walked away.

Willie limped over to Pahto who was loading his rifle and told him about the white stone.

"What does it mean?" He started to walk away from her, but she put her hand on his arm to appeal to him. He stopped.

"It reaches between us and the Old Ones," he told her. Then he walked over to where Glory was tied, took careful aim and shot him in the head. He called Charlie and Bill to butcher the carcass. Alexander ran to his mother crying. She stood transfixed as Pahto walked back over to her.

"Goddamn you Pahto."

"When you are well we will walk out of here to the caves in the old place. Where we are going is not good for a horse. Now we need the food." He returned to assist in the butchering.

She sat in the snow so that Alexander could crawl into

her lap. He was frightened and confused.

"I was being have," he told her.

"Being have, sweetheart? You mean brave?"

He put his hands on both sides of her face and spoke directly to her mouth, "You said, 'Little Coyote, you behave!' and I was have. Why did Pahto shoot Glory, Mama?"

"I don't know sweetheart." She kissed his worried face. "But I am glad you were have. Papa would be proud."

She rocked him back and forth, and watched her father's horse be cut into strips.

45

The days passed grim and calm. The Bokaima did not include Willie in the funeral preparations, but she was able to participate in the ceremonies. By now, she knew the death chants well. At times Blue Feather sang new chants from her dreams that no one else knew. The stranger tribe wailed, but they did not know any of the songs. Alexander accepted the proceedings with fascination.

Round Face Woman's hair had been singed off with a burning stick, and the stubble was covered with pitch. Gifts were placed on her husband's funeral pyre. Neither his English name nor his Bokaima name would ever again be spoken out loud.

Round Face Woman passed through the days with pain no one could relieve. Her life partner was torn from her and burned up on a funeral pyre laden with his special belongings. She placed her best feathered basket on the pyre. She winced when it burned. When the fire cooled she rubbed the ashes on her forehead. Ashes clung to the sticky pitch that covered her head.

"I can't remember how to walk," she told Willie. "The ground slips away. I have no weight to hold me down."

Willie held her, but she had no words to express her empathy to Round Face Woman. Willie had found walking to be difficult since her own husband had been torn away. But he was still alive and Round Face Woman would not understand a marriage separated by a continent, by years. The old woman and her mate had never been separated, and three thousand miles was beyond her frame of reference. In these mountains, Willie was a widow also.

By the time the days-long ceremonies were over, Willie was getting around without her crutch. The bullet was still in the flesh of her leg, but it did not interfere with her. At the fire pit one gray morning she saw two stranger tribe women watching her as she examined her healed-over wound. Throughout the funeral the women of the stranger tribe had become less wary of her. They approached her now and put their hands on her leg.

"The bullet is here," Willie guided their fingers to where they could feel and move the bullet. They were impressed.

"Oh! Oh! Poison bullet?"

"No, just a bullet."

"Our doctor can take that. He has no hurting," they explained in broken English. "Nothing he makes you eat. No poison. He calls out the bullet. Sucking doctor." One woman left to fetch the sucking doctor; the other led Willie to a gnarled oak at the edge of the camp.

"Sit here, under the oldest tree," she instructed. The sucking doctor crept up behind Willie to frighten the bullet and take it by surprise. It was Willie he surprised. She jumped and the women laughed.

The sucking doctor blew a bird-bone whistle at the

wound site. He danced and rattled around Willie and the tree and sang songs. The women beat rhythms with split-stick clappers. Willie submitted to their attentions. The doctor blew clouds of smoke from his pipe at Willie's leg; then he touched the scar and braced himself, leaning back as though he was pulling very hard against resistance. Suddenly he held aloft a spent shell casing which was celebrated and cheered as the offending bullet from Willie's leg. Willie was puzzled by the procedure, but she laughed along with the revelers as they enjoyed their triumph. Blue Feather approached the noisy gathering under the tree.

"Fools!" she scolded them through her twisted mouth. "Go away from her!" The startled women retreated. Blue Feather waved her arms at them. "Take your poison and go. Your medicine is poison for our people."

The stranger tribe yelled at her when they reached their side of the camp. "You are crazy woman," they said. "You carry the devil's child."

Blue Feather turned her anger to Willie. "What are you doing with them?" she demanded.

"They were trying to be kind, Blue Feather."

"Do you get pleasure from watching them act out their nonsense? And then laugh at them?"

"They wanted to help me. Besides, no harm was done."

"You don't know that, Wilhemina. You have no respect for their medicine, why do you submit to it? They are like children. You should not laugh at them!"

Pahto walked over to them. The two women became silent at his approach.

"Fighting in front of strangers makes us weak," he said quietly. "Submitting to them brings danger to us." Neither woman responded. Willie had stepped out of the safety of the circle. Blue Feather had not been tactful about bringing her back in. They both stood their scolding in silence.

"We must leave this camp soon and I don't want them to feel threatened by us or try to stop us," he said.

"Why would they try to stop us?" Willie asked.

"Because of you," Blue Feather answered.

"Because of me?"

"They have talked of selling you to the white man's ranch in the valley," Pahto explained. "But I do not think they will try that. Their men right now are planning a raid on another ranch to look for meat and alcohol. When they do that white men will chase them up here. We don't want to be here when that happens. I want us to be ready to leave as soon as they ride off."

"They will notice us packing up," Willie warned.

"We won't pack until they are gone. Just be ready. It won't take us long if we are ready. By the time they get back, we will be out of their reach and they will not trouble to follow us. And they will not be able to tell anyone where we have gone. No one will be able to find us." Pahto looked at both women to make sure they understood, then he walked away and Blue Feather followed him. Willie sat under the tree and watched the clouds threaten a new snow fall.

To be sold or to flee deeper into the hills; not much of a choice, Willie thought. Pahto must think my leg is healed enough for hard traveling. He is probably right. Get ready. Keep moving. Watch out.

Her hand explored the wound site. Her fingers could still wiggle the bullet where it had settled just beneath the skin of her leg.

46

"It is Ripe-seed Moon," Round Face Woman insisted.

"No. This is Flower Moon. The sun stays longer during Ripe-seed Moon," Pahto said.

"I hold the season stick. I know when the sun stays longest."

"The knowledge of the season stick passed with the heart of our old one during the Snow Moon."

"Soon the sun will stay longest time. You will see."

"You don't know, old woman. Holding the stick does not make it so," Pahto laughed affectionately and made a grab for the stick. Round Face Woman tucked it under her blanket.

"I see flowers and not ripe seeds," Pahto pointed out.

"We are not in our country. This is stranger country. This is not our river. Things are different, but the moon is the same. Ripe-seed Moon."

"It is not a river," Pahto corrected her.

"Flat-river," she insisted. "White Sister calls it lake." She used the English word. "Flat-river is lake," she repeated. Round Face Woman had never seen a large lake before and had no word for it; and although she, like the other Bokaima, rarely used a person's proper name, she had only recently settled on White Sister as her familiar name for Willie.

"I see flowers," Pahto called back to her as he walked along the water's edge to where the three other men were putting canoes into the water. Pahto, Charlie and Bill had never been in boats before, nor ever seen them used, except for the schooners at Noyo harbor. But this was Long Tree's home. He knew the water. He knew the name of the lake. He was teaching the other men how to man the boats and catch the fish. Long Tree's village on the south side of the lake was deserted; his people were being held on the reservation they had been driven to in the north three years before. Long Tree had escaped from that camp and had been leading armed attempts to free his people when he was captured and taken south to the Mendocino Indian Reservation.

But he knew where the good food gathering places were and he knew well how to fish. He knew where to find the two weather-beaten canoes moldering in their rocky hiding place.

Rocks were everywhere. A barren landscape of red-black porous rocks stretched to the north horizon. Trees and brush tried to hold their own in small pockets of loam to the south and on the hillside behind them. Long Tree told the stories of when the fire came out of the earth and threw the black rocks over the land and the hills trembled.

Blue Feather loved that story. In her slurred tones, she recited her favorite book of Revelation—

The second angel sounded his trumpet, and something like a huge mountain, all ablaze, was thrown into the sea. A third of the sea was turned into blood.

—and from there expanded on her prophesies about the revival of the Indian people, the faithful remnant.

"We have plenty of fish," Round Face Woman yelled to the men. "You have been fishing every day for the ten days we have been here. You do not need to fish today."

The men ignored her. They stacked their rifles on high dry ground before climbing into the canoes and paddling out onto the lake. Their boating skills were not yet mastered sufficiently to risk losing their weapons to the bottom of the lake. Their motions were more smooth now than they had been their first day out, but Long Tree still laughed at Charlie's and Bill's awkward efforts as they tried to race him and Pahto.

"They do not need to fish today," Round Face Woman repeated as she returned to her task of stripping and splitting long roots for weaving the large basket she had started. The dry clear air was rich with the chirping of birds and crickets. Blue Feather and Willie sat nearby, smiling at the banter and watching Alexander building a dam along the shallow water's edge. Blue Feather twirled shoots of angelica around two crossed sticks to make another charm to add to the pole of charms and feathers that stood spiritual guard outside the cave where their band had found refuge. Stood guard well, because the band was content here after their many weeks of hard traveling.

"Little Coyote!" Round Face Woman said. "I tell you about how coyote made this lak-ee?"

"Yes. Coyote vomit the lake." He balanced a rock on his teetering wall.

"I tell you what coyote make from pitch of a tree?"

"Potato bug," he answered smugly.

Blue Feather chuckled. Little Coyote's wall tumbled.

"You laughed and poisoned my wall, Auntie!"

Blue Feather reached down and pressed one of the crossed sticks of the charm into the silt in front of his dam. "There. No one can poison you now."

Round Face Woman continued, "Little Coyote, I tell you about the girl who became a red-tailed hawk?"

"I want to hear about my horse."

"You do not have a horse, Little Coyote," Round Face Woman said.

"Uncle shot him. I want Uncle to take me fishing."

"You make too much noise and scare the fish away."

Willie felt contentment warm her like the sun on her back. Blue Feather rose to her feet. She moved her heavy form with slow grace. She wore a skirt of tule reeds, the waistband slung under her swollen belly. Round Face Woman had made tule skirts for all three of the women once the band settled by the lake. She made them in the same manner of the redwood bark skirts she was used to. The skirts were comfortable, cool in the day and warm in the evening. Round Face Woman and Blue Feather wore nothing else, but their skin was burnished dark by the sun. Willie's skin burned and cracked. She wore the same shirt she had left home with in the fall. It was cool enough because it was shredded and threadbare now.

Blue Feather poured dried berry powder into a small basket and mixed it with lakeside silt. She settled next to Willie and began to spread the warm purple paste on Willie's face, neck and arms where the sun had blistered her skin raw. She worked it into Willie's brittle hair. During their trek north, Willie had used a sharp knife to cut off all her matted knotted locks. Now her hair was a frayed stubble. Finally Blue Feather patted the paste carefully on Willie's throat and chest which were inflamed with poison oak.

Willie submitted to her friend's gentle hands. She listened to Round Face Woman's stories and Alexander's arguments. The dark suntanned skin of her son's back was streaked with the slender silvery gahagaha scars. The gahagaha that bound them all together.

"I want to hear the story about my horse!"

"Horses are for white men, not us People, Little Coyote," Round Face Woman told him. "Horses and guns are from white men. Poison."

"I am a white man," he protested.

"You are not a man at all. You are little boy. You do not know all the stories of the People," she said.

Willie smiled at Alexander's irreverence. A tribe is its stories. Willie and Round Face Woman told Alexander different stories. Alexander listened to what suited him.

"Mama, Mama! I need Slats. Go get me Slats." He gave his carved toy the name from his mother's stories of his father's legendary mount.

"It is just there, Alex, in the cave, in your bed. Can't you go get him?" Willie teased. She knew he would not venture that far.

"I can't get him! I can't walk!" It was his favorite stall since they had stopped traveling. They had walked for many weeks to get here. They moved through stranger country none of them but Long Tree knew. They encountered no white settlements and made only cautious contact with other native bands they encountered.

They encouraged Alexander to walk when he could, but for the most part they took turns packing him in a burden basket with a tump strap across the bearer's forehead. Even Blue Feather, swollen with child, packed him. Even Round Face Woman, aged with grief and loss, packed him. When they needed quick pace, Pahto packed him. Little Coyote was the only young one they had now.

"I need him, Mama. I need Slats to play with me."

"I'll go get him, Sweetheart. Just wait. Blue Feather is almost finished."

"Can I do that? Can I put mud on you?"

"No. Blue Feather is Maru. God talks to her fingers."

"What is Maru?"

Blue Feather finished. Willie turned to look at her friend. Blue Feather patted Willie's sun-damaged mud-caked face. Willie patted Blue Feather's radiant scarred face.

When the young women did not respond to him, he repeated the question to Round Face Woman, "What is Maru?"

"God-talker," she answered, briefly. The boy returned to his dam.

Willie picked up her rifle and left them. "Wherever you go, carry a weapon," Pahto had ordered. She carried it, but would not let its rude reality shake her peace. She walked along the cliff wall toward the path that led up to their cave. The sun shone sharp against the cliff wall. It brought the hundreds of symbols carved there into sharp relief. She had spent hours there studying the writing, reaching for the connection. "It tells of the Old Ones," was all Long Tree would say. He could not read them either.

Willie did not look at them now, but they flickered in the corner of her eye. Heat reflected from the wall and hurried the drying of the mud on her face.

When she had climbed the rocky hillside to the cave opening, she turned to look back at the scene below her. The canoes lay just off shore. The men were doing more laughing than fishing. Except Pahto. He stared off to the south, watching. He would never relax, Willie thought. The women were busy with their handwork. Alexander ran along the water's edge collecting rocks, his blond hair brilliant in the sunlight.

Spring shimmered around her. The guardian pole with

its colors, feathers and charms seemed to Willie more hopeful than powerful. But, perhaps that is its power, she thought.

With the return of spring, Willie's hope returned.

47

It was long ago that super-heated mantle deep in the earth broke through the crust and spilled molten rock, liquid as a river, onto the land. The old ones lived on the other side of the lake then.

As its surface cooled and solidified, the lava built its own roofed channels, insulated tubes that carried the fierce flow miles across the terrain. Now, beneath the rubbled landscape of volcanic cinder was a vast labyrinth of lava tube caves and tunnels. Where their roofs collapsed or fell away, openings were formed that allowed the people access to the sanctuary of the large caverns.

Willie ducked through a rocky opening into a tube cave thirty feet wide. It was here the small band camped, in a spacious chamber with a floor smooth like a river of liquid stone. At one spot where the light from the opening barely reached, the floor gave way abruptly and spilled through to another cave below. The hole was shaped like a great burst bubble in a pot of boiling acorn mush, frozen in thick billowy stone. Willie was careful not to let Alexander play near the mush pot hole. No one knew how deep it dropped.

It was cool in the cave. Willie leaned her rifle against the smooth basalt wall and stood still for a moment while her eyes adjusted to the dim light. She found her way to where her and Alexander's moss and brush sleeping mats lay. A collection of round stones, special sticks and weather-polished bark cluttered Alexander's mat. She slung the strap of a carrying pouch over her shoulder and put the carved horse in it. She felt around and found his soft rabbit fur cloak. When the sun went down, the evening would be cool and she would need the robe for Alexander.

Her hand lingered over the bound twisted strips of soft white and gray rabbit fur. Sun Ray had made it for her son Wali. Willie had watched Sun Ray hands and tried to follow the quick movements of her fingers as she tried to make one for Alexander. Willie had not finished hers before they had to flee. Now Alex wore Wali's.

As she touched the cloak Willie felt a connection with women's hands—since time's dawn making fabric to shelter their children. This robe enveloped the love of everywoman to protect everychild. Willie thanked Sun Ray and pressed her lips to the cloak before stuffing it into her pouch. Sometimes her sorrow ached like joy.

Her reverie was disturbed by shouts from outside. She moved toward the cave opening. The shouting was shrill, not playful. Her heart raced. She picked up her rifle and ran outside. Alexander screamed. The sun blinded her. She stumbled down the rocky path.

Alexander had wandered along the shore away from the women. Now he was running back toward Blue Feather and Round Face Woman. Five horsemen were riding out of the woods. The man in the red hat was riding hard, well ahead the others. Red Hat. He rode hard toward Alexander. The sun sparked the froth of water splashing up from his horse's hooves. Alexander screamed and fell and ran again. The fishermen paddled hard for shore. The women ran toward Alexander. The man in the red hat leaned out of his saddle and reached his hand down, ready to grab the boy when he drew close enough to him.

Willie reached the edge of the water. She stood in Red Hat's path, took careful aim with her rifle and fired. A brilliance of red exploded at his throat. He fell from his horse face down into the shallow water of the lake. She turned her sights on the bearded rider at the head of the four horsemen. He raised his hand to halt his men's advance. Alexander threw himself onto Willie.

"Blue Feather!" she yelled. "Take Alex off me. I can't aim." Blue Feather pulled the boy away and ran back to Round Face Woman. Pahto's men beached their canoes and ran toward their rifles.

Willie squinted into her sights. She had him. Her breath came tight and her hand trembled, but she held her sights true. There was a stillness around her. The only sound she heard was the keening moan that came from her own throat. Nothing moved except his blue riding cloak that turned up in the breeze and flashed its edge of red silk.

He began to walk his horse slowly to where she stood. Pahto and the others stood armed and ready behind her, but no one fired. There was shouting from men on both sides. The voices were familiar to her, but she could not sort them out. They seemed from a dream, the shifting dream of a conscious dreamer, where reality evades and substance shimmers.

"Hold your fire, Pahto!" Miles called out.

How many times had she dreamed of his voice and called out to him in her sleep?

"Take your men and go from here! You are not headman here," Pahto challenged.

Marcus pulled his horse up next to Miles. "We don't

want anybody hurt, Pahto," he said calmly.

"You come with our enemy Red Hat!" Pahto shouted back.

Her moans were whimpers now and tears streaked the mud that clung to the peeling skin of her face. She still held her rifle raised, but her arms felt weak.

Miles kept his eyes on Pahto and one hand on his rifle as he drew close to Willie. Men on each side yelled.

Miles reached down with his free hand and disarmed her. "You won't need this anymore Willie."

His voice fell softly on her while the tumult of shouts flew over her head.

He yelled to Pahto, "I've only come for Willie and my boy."

"No! They are with us now," Pahto answered. His use of English had always been rough, and now anger gave his tone a jagged edge. "I feed. I protect."

"I'm taking them with me, Pahto"

She looked up to see his eyes blue against the sky. It was his beard that was strange. She wanted to touch it, to touch him. She lifted her hand, tentatively, and felt the smooth wool of his pants leg.

"You bring soldiers to our camp," Pahto accused.

"I am a soldier, Pahto, but I've never brought any trouble to you and we are not bringing any trouble to you now."

He reached his hand down and touched her fingertips.

"You brought Red Hat to kill us. He kills many of us."

"No, Pahto, Nate told us he knew where you had my wife and son. That's all we brought him for, as a guide to find my family," Miles said.

She took one step closer so that she could press her

face against his leg and smell him.

"Henry," Miles ordered, "dismount and check on Nate." Henry waded into the water. Nate lay face down. His red hat floated nearby. Henry nudged him with his foot, then looked up at Colonel Early and shook his head.

"Nate can't hurt anybody now, Pahto," Miles said. "He is dead."

Willie pulled back. Her hands flew to her stubbly hair. She clutched her head to hold back the nightmare panic. Dead? He is dead? She looked to where the downed man lay in a circle of red water. She had killed Red Hat? A crazy dream. She backed away from Miles and the guns.

"Willie, fetch Alex and come along with us now. It's time."

Could his soothing voice ease her wild blood-red images?

"Mama!" Alexander called out to her.

"Put away your guns now," Miles yelled to Pahto.

"You have guns, we have guns," Pahto replied.

"We're putting our guns down now, Pahto." Without taking his eyes off Pahto, Miles turned his head and spoke over his shoulder to his men, "Lower your guns and stand easy. Marcus, bring Willie's horse up." Then, softly again, to her, "Willie, go get Alex. Marcus has a mount for you."

She turned to look at Marcus, who led a palomino of such golden color that she though they both surely were from the dream. She stared at Marcus and scratched the poison oak at her throat. Flakes of dried mud fell away.

"Come on Willie, darlin," Marcus smiled at her. "We ain't got much time."

"Now, Willie, before there is trouble," Miles said.

Willie turned back to the remnant band of Bokaima. Alexander ran to her and buried his face into her tule skirt. Blue Feather began chanting. Willie walked to where the band stood their ground, ragged and determined.

"Willie!" Miles' voice was urgent.

She tried to approach Pahto but his jaw was set hard and he would not look at her. He watched Miles. Long Tree and Charlie and Bill kept their guns and their attention on the soldiers. Blue Feather chanted louder and her eyes rolled back in her head. Round Face Woman smiled shyly when Willie approached her but drew back self-consciously, as though she were suddenly thrust into an presence of a regal stranger.

Willie stood before them. They would not respond to her. They appeared smaller somehow, gaunt figures in tattered clothes. They all looked frightened. Except Pahto.

She spoke to him in Bokaima, "Do not shoot, Pahto."

"You will stay?"

"Pahto," she pleaded with him, her voice a whisper. "I must go. Do not shoot."

"You shot."

"I shot Red Hat."

"Our enemy."

"Yes."

"Soldiers are enemies of People."

She looked back at the soldiers, warmly clothed and robust. Their mounts were sleek and well fed. One of those horses could feed the Bokaima for many days. She saw Daniel smile sweetly at her and gesture for her to come. Miles kept his gaze fixed on Pahto and slipped his rifle into its saddle boot.

"Willie," he called once more. She went to him. She lifted Little Coyote onto the palomino. The little boy sat wide-eyed and unmoving on the big horse. He clutched the horse's mane and did not cry.

"Pahto," Miles called. "I want to get Nate and put him on his horse and take him with us."

"No," Pahto answered. Blue Feather raised her chant

still higher.

Willie sprang lightly into the saddle. She always liked palominos. They were a gentle horse. Willie held tight to Alexander with both arms as Henry remounted and took up the palomino's lead rope and led them away from the encounter. She did not hear the last words between Miles and Pahto. It was not until she and Henry reached the edge of the trees that she turned and looked back at her Bokaima family.

Miles, Marcus, and Daniel were riding hard out of the camp. They had left Nate and his horse behind. When he reached Willie, Miles took up the palomino's lead rope and quickly moved his wife and son deep into the woods until Willie and the Bokaima were no longer in each others' view.

48

When the rosy twilight yielded to a star-crazed sky, Miles and Willie lay alone and watched the moon rise. Alexander had fallen in readily with Marcus, Daniel and Henry. He was content to stay with them while his parents slept apart from the others. The men were discreet and tried to insure privacy for the reunion, but there was no need. Willie could only cry.

But her tears were sweet and his arms were grand. He could encompass her sorrow. And so he held her.

The next day Miles watched Willie bathe with scented soap in a mountain stream. He gave her clean clothes and tossed her tule skirt on the fire. She studied his every move, making sure it was truly him. When Marcus took the others off to hunt, the lovers stayed behind.

They made love until their fears dissolved and their skin merged yet again. She could be strong apart from him; it was only with him she was complete.

The hunting party returned with an elk and prepared a feast. When Willie recalled the last feast she and Alexander had, she thought her heart would break; but Miles kept his hands on her, like a shawl of safety, and in bits and pieces she began to tell her story and hear theirs.

That evening by the fire, she held gentle broken Daniel and sang to him. Marcus mothered them all. Henry took over with Alexander and invented games for them to play together. Alexander insisted Henry call him Little Coyote.

The troop traveled leisurely. They were well provisioned. The weather was kind. Now that Miles had brought them all safely back together, he removed himself as leader. Marcus could decide their goings and comings. Daniel made excellent choices for camp sites. Miles talked to Willie and let the boy get used to him.

It took days for all their friends and family to be accounted for. The deaths were told first, but eventually the stories passed from sad to interesting and amazing: Willie's trek. Sherman's march.

Miles told her of the march to the sea that she had never heard about. He told her that at the time he had left the East to come look for her, Lincoln had not yet been shot. Secretary Stanton had not yet betrayed Sherman or publicly accused him of planning to march on Washington to take over the country by force.

"Cump, of course had no such intentions. He never wanted anything to do with Washington," he told her, "It was only when I got to San Francisco that I learned what happened after I left. After Johnston and Lee surrendered, all the Union armies came to Washington to march in review down Pennsylvania Avenue, past President Johnson, his staff, and all the generals of the armies. It took two days. Cump's Western Army was the second day. The parade crowd loved them. They look rough, but they are colorful with their wild uniforms and flamboyant bummers. The people think we ended the war. Cump does too. I saw a picture of him in the paper. He was riding at the head of his army and sneaking a look back at the columns following him. He is very proud of his men. When they got to the reviewing stand he left the parade and joined the President and General Grant to watch his army, his boys, pass in review. The crowd was crazy for him. When Secretary Stanton reached out to shake Sherman's hand, Sherman refused it. Right there in front of God and everybody." Miles chuckled to himself at Cump's sense of drama. "It was the talk of the Presidio. Stanton challenged the wrong man." His thoughts drifted back to Sherman, the war, his comrades. Willie could barely comprehend what he was saying. She did not know who these people were.

"President Johnson," she said, "I can't get used to it."

"And Cletis! Poor Cletis," Miles told her. "I about took his head off when he came into my camp and told us you and Alex were missing. But he was all right with it, once he understood it was news to us. He filled us in on all he knew, which helped us get started to find you."

If it were not for the real beauty of lying next to Miles, she would think she was in a dream. She was like Daniel, drifting at the edges. She tried to find that steady unsteadiness, that equilibrium she had discovered when she was alone in the woods. Perhaps that would be the best she and Daniel could ever do.

There were many things for her to get used to. Miles told her of Cletis' new family.

"Cletis? A family?"

"But what of Elizabeth? Does she know?" Willie asked.

"Elizabeth lives in San Francisco with Rune Kalevala," Miles told her.

"Living with him? Isn't she still married to Cletis?"

"She is living with Rune. They aren't married, but she got a divorce from Cletis, finally. She and Rune live in the

Bohemian quarter. He writes poetry and she wears bright scarves in her hair. They drink Italian wine and play cards a lot. She sells bread she makes with your yeast." Miles laughed at her astonishment.

"I am happy for her. She was miserable with Cletis. It's just such an extraordinary thing."

"No more extraordinary than being held captive by a band of wild Indians," Miles teased.

"No more wild than the rest of us, are they?"

"I'm sorry for making light of it, Willie, but I want you to be prepared for the reactions of civilized people who will never understand that."

"What's the difference between civilized and wild?" she asked. "Laws? Rituals? Art? Religion? I think the Bokaima have more rules than most of the people who live in San Francisco. I was the wild one in the Bokaima camp. They tolerated my ignorant heathen ways and I tried not to be wantonly rebellious, but everything was so complicated. I never liked their rules about everything. But I do like their loyalty. Their sense of belonging," her voice trailed off. "We should have brought them back with us," she said faintly.

"There's no place to bring them to."

"Are they safe where they are?"

"No."

"No?"

"Pahto and Long Tree are wanted men, Willie," Miles said. "Besides, the army has removed all the Indians from the lava beds twice before. They're not going to let the Bokaima be out there anymore than they let the local tribes. They know they're there somewhere. I wanted to find you before an official military detachment did. I was afraid you'd all have been hurt in the fighting. Pahto should keep moving."

"Will you tell where they are?"

"When we get back to the Presidio, I'll make a

report. It should take some time for any information on their whereabouts to get that far up north. I hope they'll have moved on by then. I told that to Pahto."

"Can't your report say the Bokaima aren't dangerous?"

"That's not true. They don't want to live in peace with us any more, do they? They are armed and prepared to defend themselves."

"What if they were given a true chance."

"On a reservation? You know that didn't work. As laborers on someone's ranch? Pahto doesn't want that. To return to their old ways? Too late!"

"We could stay with them and help them find a safe place."

"And starve along with them? They'd eat your pretty horse."

"They ate Glory."

"I know, my love."

"I didn't know how I was going to get back to you."

"I found you." He kissed her puffy eyes.

"Many people searched for you," he told her. Elizabeth hounded three succeeding commanding officers at the Presidio. But no one could find you. Elizabeth and your family never gave up. Your father has been searching for you all the way to Round Valley. He said there were men there who were arrested for celebrating the killing of President Lincoln. Your father was afraid for us."

"Everything is changed."

"Not us."

"Perhaps."

"I love you."

"Even changed?"

"Yes."

"I, I killed," she began. Could she say it? Could it be

true? Is no one safe? "I killed that man."
    "I know," he replied, and kissed her temple...
    "Did you kill men?"
    "Yes,"...her forehead...
    "It's not good."
    "No,"...her eyes...
    And again they knew the inevitability of one flesh, the passion that dips beneath reason and writes its own story.

High Desert Books is a services-oriented boutique publishing company based in Reno, Nevada. High Desert Books focuses on local and regional literature and fine quality writing. Visit www.highdesertbooks.com for inquiries and further information.